When We W
Belle S

This is a work of fiction. Similarities to real people, places or events are entirely coincidental.

WHEN WE WERE YOUNG

First Edition. December 1, 2024.

Copyright © 2024 Belle Shaw.

Written by Belle Shaw

Table of Contents

When We Were Young 1
Prologue 4
Chapter 1 8
Chapter 2 14
Chapter 3 27
Chapter 4 33
Chapter 5 41
Chapter 6 46
Chapter 7 52
Chapter 8 58
Chapter 9 65
Chapter 10 72
Chapter 11 78
Chapter 12 85
Chapter 13 90
Chapter 14 97
Chapter 15 103
Chapter 16 110
Chapter 17 115
Chapter 18 120
Chapter 19 125
Chapter 20 132
Chapter 21 139
Chapter 22 145
Chapter 23 153
Chapter 24 159
Chapter 25 169
Chapter 26 174
Chapter 27 182
Chapter 28 191
Chapter 29 196

Chapter 30 202
Chapter 31 210
Chapter 32 222
Chapter 33 231
Chapter 34 239
Chapter 35 244
Chapter 36 251
Chapter 37 256
Chapter 38 266
Chapter 39 274
Chapter 40 279
Epilogue 284

To all the kids who grew up too fast.
To all the ones who work so hard to protect their heart.
I am so sorry for what I am about to do to it.

Trigger Warnings

This book includes explicit sexual content and mature themes. It also depicts sexual abuse and violence towards a minor. It also has themes that involve death and family trauma.

If you or someone you know needs help, please call the National Domestic Violence Hotline 800-799-7233

Prologue

Holly
First Day of Kindergarten

The smell of wax and old paper clung to the air in the overwhelmingly large room. Pictures hung haphazardly on the walls, and I stopped to take them all in one by one. The one that caught my eye the most was one of a knight in armor in front of an intricately drawn dragon. Rather than facing the dragon head-on, the knight stood with his back to it. He leaned on his sword in front of him as the dragon looked protectively over the knight. It was stunning and different. The knight and the dragon looked so real like they would jump off the canvas and fly around the room. I wanted to brush my fingertips over the scales of the red beast. They were all magnificent but that one was my favorite by far.

My heart raced as I stood in the doorway, torn between running in to find the best seat I could get or waiting to take in every detail of the art room. The teacher moved from one side of the room where the supplies were towards the front of the huge chalkboard. She moved with ease and so beautifully while her long blonde braid danced behind her back as she helped us get settled.

Her voice rang through the room like a beacon to my soul, calling us all to quickly pick a seat. I finally moved from my spot by the door and wandered over to an open seat. There weren't desks, but groups of large tables with four chairs, two on each side. It was loud as the clash of moving chairs across the tile echoed off the white brick walls. I found a seat and put my plastic pencil box on top of the table in front of me. I was beaming as I looked around at the other students. Art was my favorite, and I knew this class was going to be the best part of my day.

A boy stumbled into the seat next to me, a big grin across his face pointed directly at me. I looked over my shoulder expecting someone to be there, but it was just empty space. I looked back at him, confused, pointing at myself in a questioning look.

"What are you looking at?" I asked coyly, raising an eyebrow.

"You! I like your freckles." He laughed as he continued to grin at me. I felt heat in my cheeks, and I quickly looked down at my lap to hide my reddening face. I stared at my hands folded in my lap.

"Hey! Don't hide. I think they're cute. Your hair too. You remind me of a fairy." He nudged my shoulder with his and I met his smile with a sheepish one of my own. That smile was contagious and something about it felt comforting and genuine.

"Alright class! Welcome to your first day of art. I hope you like where you sat today, because that is now your spot for the year. We will all get to know each other better this year, but let's start out with some introductions to get more comfortable. My name is Miss Nelson, and I will be your teacher. Take some time and talk to the other kids at your table while I get our supplies ready for today. Sound good?"

The class rumbled to life and voices bounced around us. I looked around at our table and smiled at the other students.

"My name is Holly. I love art and am excited about this class. I want to be an artist when I grow up." I looked around, a blush creeping up my neck, and the boy next to me had the same grin on his face from earlier.

"I'm Isaac. I like art but I'm not very good at it. I'm better at building things." We all smiled at him, and the other two students introduced themselves as well. Just as they were done, Miss Nelson was back at the front of the room.

"Now that we all got to know each other a little better, let's start with a fun project. Since it is the first day back to school, let's create something that reminds us of our favorite summertime activity. I have some supplies over here for you to choose from. You can paint, sculpt, make a collage with these magazines, it is completely up to you. Come up here and form a line to get your material." Her warmth made me feel welcome and inspired all at once. I looked down at my pencil box trying to think about what to make. Isaac got up and I followed behind him, leaning in to whisper.

"Art is a lot like building something you know?" He smiled back at me and thought for a moment.

"You're right. I guess I never thought about it that way. What are you going to use?" He nods towards the supplies.

"Paints. I love to paint. They are my favorite. I think I am going to try to use watercolor. What are you going to use?" I smiled a crooked grin, waiting to know what his project would be.

"I think I am going to try to use some clay. I work with my dad on cars a lot, so I think I am going to try and make my favorite car."

"That's cool! I've never worked on a car before. Is it hard?" He thought about that for a while and shrugged his shoulders.

"I guess it depends on what's wrong with it. My dad owns the garage by the pizza place on Fredrick Street. I practically live there."

"I know where that is! I live really close to that. I think my mom has taken our car there before."

"I live close too! What street do you live on?" His eyes brighten as we inch closer to the art supplies.

"Our house is a bit out on 70th street. It's the blue and white one."

"Really? I'm only a little bit up the street closer to the skate park. I go there all the time." I smiled as he beamed at me. This must be what making friends feels like. Where better to do that than in my favorite class? Art class must be made of magic.

"I've never been to the skate park. I don't really know how to skate. It looks like fun though." I blushed, looking down at the art material on the counter, carefully choosing what I want to work with.

"It is a lot of fun. I can teach you! It's not as hard as it looks." His confidence and charm radiated off him and I soaked it up. I learned two things very soon after that day. The first being that skateboarding is in fact much harder than it looks, and second, I would need Isaac's confidence and friendship more than I could ever realize.

Chapter 1

Holly
Day Before High School Graduation

The road stretched out before me, urging my feet to keep moving despite the ache that took over. I kept my head trained forward, watching, anticipating. There was no way it was that easy. At any moment, I imagined the monster I left behind lurking in the streets to hunt me down. The darkness made my mind even more unhinged than it already was. I held the ring so tight in my hand that I was sure I was bleeding. I forced myself to take deep breaths through the pain. The idea of freedom, an escape from this place was all I needed to keep pushing ahead.

The bus stop finally came into view. Letting out a long exhale, and a sigh of relief, I made my way to the counter to buy my one-way ticket to Boulder, Colorado. It was late at night, so there wasn't a soul in sight. It made a shiver travel up my spine and goosebumps erupt on my skin. Would I ever shed this feeling of being watched? Could I truly outrun my fears? There was only one way to find out, and I wasn't about to go back.

"One ticket to Boulder, please?" I asked the woman behind the ticket counter. She looked up from her nails that she was just filing and rolled her eyes. Leaning up closer to her computer, she looked up the times and prices for the tickets.

"The next bus leaves in..." she looked at her watch. "10 minutes. Do you want that one or the one in the morning?" She smacked her gum, waiting for me to answer.

"The next one, please. I want to leave ASAP." I tapped my fingers on the counter, looking over my shoulder anxiously. She eyed me with suspicion and stifled a humorless laugh.

"Fifteen eighty-two." I handed her a twenty. Once she gave me my change, my ticket printed out next to her.

I grabbed my ticket as soon as she handed it to me and made my way to the women's bathroom. Pushing the door open, I let out another sigh. My hands trembled around my ticket, and my shoulders shook with a silent sob. Once I got into the handicapped stall, I leaned into the wall and slid down, hugging my knees to my chest. Thoughts of my life flooded my memory. The pain, the heartache, but also the parts of my childhood I would never forget. As much as I needed to escape this town, I also knew somehow, I would always be tied here.

Thinking about all the moments I shared with *him,* my heart expanded in my chest. I rubbed my hand over it, trying to ease the ache. When he walks across the graduation stage alone tomorrow, I know the damage I do will forever change the future of our friendship. Leaving him behind was the necessary evil for my own freedom. Tears fell from my eyes and my hands trembled as I pictured his expression when he realized I had left without saying goodbye. Would it break him to a point of no repair? Would he move on and grow out of our years of childhood camaraderie? I couldn't think about it. I wouldn't let myself dwell on what would happen in the wake of my decision.

I crawled up and off the bathroom floor and unlocked the stall. I peered into the mirror in front of me as I dried my eyes and did my best to tame the wild red curls that were tangled together on top of my head. With a deep breath, I willed my legs to move out towards the bus that would take me away from this nightmare for good.

"Transport to Boulder, now arriving. Please have your ticket ready before you load." The intercom filled the echoing silence in the station. My heart picked up its pace as I shouldered my small bag. I stared down at the diamond ring and the ticket in my hands. My small steps towards a better life, a real future, stared back at me. The lifeless items held so much meaning, so much power. The smell of heady exhaust filled the air as the bus pulled into its place at the depot. With one foot in front of the other, I made my way to my getaway car. I handed the driver my ticket, put the ring in my pocket, and climbed the stairs.

Halfway through the trip, I finally relaxed into the seat and let my eyes drift out of the window. I watched the silhouette of the Colorado mountains fly by. The land was beautiful, rugged, and wild. It inspired so many paintings I had done in my childhood. A lot of the time, I hoped the mountains would swallow me up and help me disappear. I suppose they were in a way. I sent up a silent "thank you" to whichever angel was looking out for me. The further I got away from home, the easier it was to breathe. The sting in my chest eased, and the grip fear held on me loosened. My eyes felt heavy as my body relaxed. Finally, I let myself fall into a decent sleep.

The sound of the brakes on the bus woke me up. A small trail of drool ran down my mouth. Wiping it away with the sleeve of my hoodie, I glanced outside. It was still dark, but we were clearly in the city now. The buildings were tall, and the streetlights lit up around me. I took in every detail I could. I noted a pawn shop where I could sell the ring in my pocket. I had a little nest egg from working at the arcade, but the extra cash I could get from the ring would help me get an apartment. I had researched shelters in Boulder before I left and knew where a few were. I needed all the resources I could find to be able to land here on my feet. A little bakery caught my eye as we stopped at an intersection. It looked quaint and cozy. It almost glowed in the midst of the city. I took note of the street signs so I could go back and ask about a job there. As excited as I was to be in the city, I knew I needed a little slice of small and cozy.

Finally, the bus depot came into view. The bright lights were harsh against the soft glow of the streetlights. There were more people than I thought there would be. Men in nice clothes and women with children bustled about, getting their tickets and luggage in order. The bus stopped, and the doors opened with a loud thud. I gathered my bag, stood up, and walked out into the crisp spring air. With a renewed sense of bravery and excitement, I walked down the sidewalk in downtown Boulder to the shelter.

The warmth I felt when I walked in melted any uneasiness left in me. The woman who greeted me gave me a wild smile and stood up from her chair behind the small reception desk.

"Hi!" She beamed. The silver streaks in her hair were the only thing that gave away her age. Her smile was bright, and her frame was small, but strong. Her energy despite the time of night was exuberant, like she had been expecting me to walk in.

"Hi," I waved.

"What can I do for you tonight?" She asked as she walked around with outstretched hands. I let her greet me with a hug and melted into her arms.

"I, um, need a place to stay until I get my own apartment."

"Oh," she let me go and took in my small backpack and tired eyes. "Did you just get in?"

"Yeah, I took a bus. I just got here."

"Perfect. Let's get you set up with a room." The shelter was small but well-maintained. I took in the common areas we passed as she walked me to an open bedroom. There were a few other women on couches and chairs in the main living space. They didn't pay much attention to us as we walked by. I couldn't help but be a little curious about their stories.

"Here we go." The woman opened a door and led me into a small room with a bed and a dresser. It was simple, but it was safe. "My name is Lynn, and I am the volunteer on duty tonight. Michelle will be here in the morning, and we can get your paperwork filled out then."

"Sounds good, thank you." I set my backpack down onto the bed and reached into my pocket for the ring. I set it down on top of the dresser. Lynn watched me with empathy and a soft smile.

"Do you have any medical concerns, or anything that needs to be addressed tonight?" I shook my head.

"Actually, I was curious about a bakery I saw on the way in. I can't remember the name of it, but it was small and right by the bus station." Lynn beamed at me with a glint in her eyes.

"Yes! That's my bakery." There was so much pride in her voice.

"Really? Are you hiring?" I asked with more excitement than I have felt in a long time. She leaned on the door frame and looked at me thoughtfully. "I could use an extra pair of hands." She winked.

"Seriously?" I perked up.

"Absolutely. Tomorrow, let's make sure you are all settled here; then, I can pick you up and show you around." I smiled at her and nodded. She gave me another hug and left the room. Hope sparkled in my chest as I laid myself down on the bed. I fell into a peaceful sleep where I dreamed of a future I didn't deserve but had always hoped for.

WHEN WE WERE YOUNG

Chapter 2

I*saac*
Summer before Freshman Year

I stood there, torn between the cherry licorice and the strawberry licorice. I already had the black licorice in my hand, that was Holly's favorite. I have no clue why because black licorice is gross, but it was. I could pick her favorites easily, but facing that decision, for me, was awful. I looked between the two, tapping my finger against the package of Holly's candy. It should not have been that hard.

"Do I even like licorice?" I mumbled to myself. I couldn't help but smile as I thought about the summer we shared together so far. It was our last summer before high school. She was a better skater than me at this point. She was fearless. I almost loved watching her skate more than skating myself. Almost.

"Cherry it is." I snagged the bag of candy, walked over to the cooler section, and grabbed one root beer and one cream soda. As I headed to the counter, the bell on the door rang and a swirl of red, wild hair and freckles bounded over to me. She was the most beautiful creature I had ever seen. She still reminded me of a fairy, even more now with her delicate features. She seemed to glow from the inside out. I was pretty sure she stole my heart the moment I saw her in art class when we were 5. We were inseparable since day one.

"Oh! What did you buy me?" She laughed, hands on her hips, eyeballing the items in my arms.

"Who said anything about buying you anything? I needed a snack." I could not for the life of me keep a straight face. Not with her, anyway.

"Right. And you just out of nowhere decided you like black licorice?" She pulled the bag out of my arms, raising an eyebrow at me.

"OK, fine. You got me. It was supposed to be a surprise, but as usual, you can't stay away from me." I winked at her, and she rolled her eyes as she always did. I didn't try very hard to keep my flirtation at a minimum. She, however, was as stubborn as ever and a tough cookie in so many ways. She may have laughed off my advances, but I never gave up trying. Besides, we were starting high school in a few weeks, and I had a good feeling about it. I was also a little nervous that some football asshole would catch her eye, but I knew Holly better than that. "Do you want anything else before I pay for this stuff?" Luckily, working for my dad had it's positives. He actually started paying me.

"Hmm, no. I think this is all good. I'll eat dinner later tonight, at home. You know how my dad is about 'spoiling my dinner.'" She, again, rolled her eyes and air quoted her dad's words. Sometimes I got a little jealous of the attention she got from her parents. She complained about it a lot, but I felt like she was lucky. Most of the time, I had to fend for myself, sign my own permission slips, and make my own dinners. I ate pizza rolls a lot. My dad was always either at the garage he owned working, or drunk, sometimes both. It had gotten worse after my mom died. My memories of her were fading as I got older, but I can still remember it being different, better, with her around. Dad was never perfect, but Mom had brought out the best in him. I was left with the worst.

"Let's trade places!" I snapped my fingers. "You pretend to be me, and I will pretend to be you. I'll get a home cooked meal, and you will get your privacy." Her head rolled back in laughter, and I put the handful of stuff on the counter.

"You could *never* be me! You're too.... you." She gestured up and down my body and giggled.

"What's that supposed to mean? All I need is a wig and some of your paint for the freckles and no one would even know." I finished paying and tossed her the gross black licorice. In my best girly voice, I impersonated her. "Oh, look at me! I'm Holly. I can kind of skateboard, I suck at arcade games, and I looooooove painting!" Unimpressed, she glared at me as she opened her cream soda.

"OK, first, I am not just *OK* at skateboarding. I could skate circles around you, any day. Second, I do not suck at arcade games! I beat you all the time. So, nice try. No one would believe you were me, not for a second." She sat down on the steps outside the corner store and tore open her licorice, flopping one in her mouth. Sitting down next to her, I did the same and we watched the cars go by. "Let's count the yellow ones first. I bet there aren't very many. Yellow seems like a rare color." She sighed and leaned back, eyes on the road ahead.

"Sounds good to me. Yellow it is." I said, following her eyes to the road. We had played this game for as long as I could remember. We spent countless hours on those steps counting the cars. I don't know how or why it became our thing, but it just did. It was as natural and normal as everything else about us. We never questioned anything we did, we just did it. It was the way it always was, and I loved it. More than anything. It was an escape we both needed.

"Are you nervous about high school?" She asked through a mouthful of candy.

"No, not really. I don't think it will be that different. I just hope we have some classes together." Holly was always the nervous one. She had grown up and come out of her shell a little bit over the years, but I could still see the shy kid I met in the art room every now and then. She is feisty and stubborn around me but became more of a wallflower in a room full of people. I hated watching her shrink into herself. I wanted nothing more than the world to see what I saw in her.

"Me too. The school seems so much bigger. I hope I don't get lost." I could tell she was thinking a lot about it, and I always did my best to help, but sometimes it was hard to get her out of her own head. We sat in silence for a few more minutes and the shadows were growing longer as the afternoon turned into evening. I reached out my hand for her trash and took it to the trash can in front of the store.

"What are you guys having for dinner tonight?" I asked, helping her up off the steps. She brushed off her baggy overalls and ran her hands through her wild curls.

"I have no idea." She elbowed me in the side, knowingly. I smiled, blushing a little. She was the only one that knew what home was like for me and I tried not to bring it up. I hated complaining. It never did any good. Nobody, not even her needed to bear my burdens.

"I don't either. Maybe I will have a huge turkey, stuffed with all kinds of vegetables and smothered in gravy." She chuckled and rolled her eyes.

"Turkey isn't even that good though! It's dry and it doesn't taste like anything." She faked a gagging noise.

"Not if you deep fry it and eat the dark meat! You know, like those huge turkey legs from the fair." My mouth watered at the thought. It had been years since I had one.

"No way. I. would rather have a fat, juicy cheeseburger from the diner. It would have to have bacon, lettuce, and tomatoes though. The lettuce must be crunchy, not soggy." She shivered and laughed as we walked up the road towards our houses.

"And a chocolate, strawberry swirl milkshake," I added.

"Duh! That's a no brainer. You *know* that."

We got to my house, and we parted ways. I watched her skate up towards her house Her house had more land and space than mine did, and I was, again, just a bit jealous. I walked into my house; the screen door crashing closed behind me. I could smell something cooking in the kitchen, but I wasn't sure what it was. I could hear the TV in the living room, and dad humming in the kitchen. It must be one of his better nights.

"Hello? Dad?" I called out into the house.

"In here, Isaac! I hope you didn't eat too much candy. I made us dinner." I leaned my skateboard against the wall by the door and kicked my shoes off. If I could have a night where I didn't have to hide out, I'd take it in a heartbeat.

"Cool. It smells good, whatever it is." I walked in and sure enough, he was leaning over the stove, a box in one hand, a spatula in the other. It wasn't a sight I saw very often, so it always took me by surprise. His good days were few and far between and I cherished them the best I could.

"It's supposed to be Hamburger Helper. I hope I didn't ruin it." He chuckled, setting the box down and replacing it with a half-drunk beer bottle. My smile faltered, but not enough for him to notice. I knew better than to let my emotions show. I sat at the table in the kitchen and watched as he stirred the cheesy, sticky meat mixture. "I sure hope it tastes better than it looks," he laughed.

"I'm sure it will. You can't really go wrong with cheeseburger anything. The arcade even has cheeseburger pizza now." I watched and my stomach rumbled loud enough to get a glance from dad. His expression was soft, and he looked more relaxed than normal. I wished I knew what went through his mind when he was like this. Did he regret the years he wasted? I tried not being too hopeful. For as good as the good days were, the bad ones were even worse. It never seemed to make a difference.

We ate in silence, and I cleaned up the stove once we were done eating. He was asleep in the living room before I was even done, so I went outside on the front porch. The summer air was warm but was starting to cool off when the sun went down. You could see the mountains in the background and the trees all around our neighborhood. The smell of the trees was one of my favorites. I watched as they swayed in the breeze and the moonlight danced around them. It was nice, quiet and at times like that, everything just felt peaceful. I smiled and let the breeze move the porch swing I was sprawled out on. It ruffled my hair and made goosebumps trail up my arms.

"Hey, are you going to take up the whole swing, or are you going to let me sit next to you?" My eyes sprang open, and my heart skipped a beat. She didn't come over here this late very often, but when she did, it usually meant home wasn't a good place to be for her.

"Holl? Isn't it past your bedtime, little girl?" I teased as I sat up and made room for her on the swing. That earned me a swift punch to the arm. "Ouch! That wasn't necessary." I rubbed the spot dramatically.

"Yes, I think it was. I feel better, at least. Besides, I brought something. So, you have to be nice." She smirked at me and stuck her tongue out. "Did you eat?" A crease formed between her eyebrows.

"Yeah. Dad actually cooked tonight. It wasn't much but I didn't have to cook it, so that's a win." I smiled at her and stretched back against the swing. She handed me something haphazardly wrapped in foil and smiled again.

"I thought you may want dessert. My mom made them. Extra fudgy brownies. They are way better with ice cream, but I didn't think ice cream would make the bike ride down here."

"Oh my God, these look perfect. Tell your mom I said, 'she is the bomb.' Thanks for bringing them." I wrapped my arms around her, breathing in her flowery smell. No matter what, she always smelled like happiness, and I chased it like a high I just couldn't get enough of. She stayed while I ate my brownies, and we talked more about school, and what classes we were going to take.

"I can't believe we are actually starting high school. I honestly thought we would just be kids forever." There was something sad lingering in her voice, and I wasn't used to that. I guess, though, that's part of growing up. I just wasn't ready for it yet.

"We can be. Just because we are a year older, doesn't mean we have to stop doing the things we like to do. I'll still count cars with you and beat you at video games." I got another punch in the shoulder for that. I probably deserved that one, though.

"I hope so. I want to grow up, but I also don't want to, you know?" She stared up at the stars and, like I often did, I tried to imagine what was swirling around in that head of hers.

"I may not know the future, Holly, but I would bet my entire life's savings on the fact that you will be amazing." She stared at me with her piercing blue eyes, full of wonder and light. They contained the whole world, and I felt like I could get lost in her. I suppose I did. I continued to fall for her over and over again. I didn't think I would ever stop.

HOLLY

The air was starting to get cool and the number of people at the skate park dwindled over the past couple of weeks. Not that I was complaining. The less people here, the more room Isaac and I had to roam free. We tended to be messy, and all over the place, it was hard to pay attention to the other people when we got lost in the curves and the corners of the concrete jungle. This park had become one of our few safe places to just enjoy each other's company and the sport. It was easy to forget about all the bad things. It hadn't taken long for me to get better skating, and I think Isaac was a little bitter at first, but he got over it pretty quick. I don't think he ever got really upset about anything. I was the emotional one. He saw life through rose-colored glasses, something I always envied.

I never had to wait long for him to show up. I still couldn't help but smile when I saw him skate up the sidewalk leading up to the park. No matter what, that messy dark hair and those emerald, green eyes made my world light up. He wore his normal ripped jeans, old band shirt and ratty converse. His tousled hair whipped around his face as he skated towards me. I couldn't help but beam, when he winked at me and shot me that smug smile he wore so proudly.

"Hey, little girl! I didn't make you wait too long, did I?" He asked, jumping up to sit next to me on the concrete bench overlooking the ramps.

"No, I've only been here a few minutes. I brought you a root beer." I passed him his drink and he took it, unscrewing the top.

"Thanks, Holl. Cheers." He tipped the bottle towards me, and I met it with my own cream soda.

"Cheers," I laughed. "These bottles don't clink. It's not the same."

"Yeah, I guess. It's the thought that counts, right?" He elbowed me in the side, making me laugh. I shoved him back, playfully rolling my eyes. "Are you ready to skate? Or are you worried I am going to put you to shame?" He crossed his arms over his chest, nodding his head towards the ramps behind us.

"Oh, I am ready. Are you?" I raised an eyebrow at him in a challenge. His shoulders shook with laughter as he took off down one of the ramps, disappearing into the concrete maze.

Graffiti covered the ramps and the tunnels, and it added such a strange beauty to this place. It was a misfit, just like those of us that felt safe within it. Really, there wasn't anywhere else like it. Isaac and I practically grew up here, and I hoped that starting high school wouldn't change that for us. I was nervous. I had no reason to believe that things would change, but there was a sense of dread that washed over me when I thought about the coming weeks, and the end of our summer.

"It'll be OK, Holly. Stop thinking too much." I told myself daily at this point. It became a sort of mantra for me during that time. I tried hard to believe it. I shook my head, willing away the thoughts that so often dragged me down and pushed off on my board. Soon, all I could think about was the sound of the wheels over the ground beneath me and Isaac's smile when he wiped out in front of me.

After hours of skating, and falling, and trying ridiculous tricks we had no business trying, we splayed out in the middle of the bowl. We watched the clouds roll by in the late afternoon sky. He could always find shapes in the clouds, but I just saw fluffy cotton candy.

"Look, if you squint your eyes, just enough when you look at that one, it totally looks like a penguin." He pointed up at the sky and I had no idea which one he was even pointing to.

"How do you even see that? And why a penguin, and not a normal bird?" I turned my head to look at him, his profile shadowed by the bowl around us.

"Because, little girl, penguins have long bodies and short stubby heads and beaks. That is *clearly* a penguin." He turned, meeting my gaze. "You know, for an artist, you really have a boring imagination."

"Hey! That's not true. I have a great imagination." I poked him, and he sat up, laughing. He leaned back on his hands next to me.

"Hey, love birds. Get out of the bowl. We want to skate too, you know." We both glanced up, and saw one of the other regulars, not a pleasant one, glaring at us. Isaac stood up, helping me up with an outstretched hand.

"You know," Isaac countered. "There are nicer ways to ask us to move. No need to be an asshole." The kid scoffed and waved Isaac off.

"Oh, I'm sorry. How about this," he thought for a moment. "Why don't you two wannabes move your ass so people who *really* skate can have the bowl?" He smirked, evil seeping from his crooked smile. I started to run at him, up the wall of the bowl, but Isaac held me back, my fists flying at nothing.

"He isn't worth it, Holl." He whispered to me, holding me tight. "Let it go. Let's get out of here." I huffed, irritated at the bully, but followed Isaac out of the bowl towards the benches. As we walked away, I could hear the stupid kid singing behind us.

"Holly and Isaac, sittin' in a tree. K-I-S-S-I-." Before I realized it, Isaac turned around and bolted towards him. I heard the crunch of knuckles slamming into flesh as Isaac punched him hard. He staggered back, shocked by the impact. Isaac didn't say anything else, just came bounding back up to me with a frown.

"What was *that*?" I asked, shocked at him. "I've never seen you hit someone like that." Isaac just stared at the ground, rubbing his hand.

"He insulted you. I'm not down with that. I don't give two shits about what he says about me, but I'm not OK with him dragging you down." He looked at me, embarrassment crossing his soft features.

"Well, thanks, I guess. I mean, he definitely deserved it. It was a good hit. Who taught you to punch like that?" I smiled, nudging him. "And so much for not worth it."

"My dad. I learned from the best." He laughed, but I felt the heaviness in his words. I wished I could make things easier for him, but I didn't even know how to do that for myself. I doubt he would even let me try.

As the sun settled down behind the trees and the daylight dwindled, my heart picked up its pace in my chest. Parting ways at the end of those summer days was getting harder and harder. I knew what my family looked like on the outside. My dad played the role of a concerned parent perfectly. The real reason for his control made my chest hurt and my skin crawl. He was the one who took me to the doctor for birth control when I started my period. No one batted an eye, and my mom was just grateful she didn't have to. It seemed like my dad watched my every move and it was infuriating.

"Can you imagine in just a few years; we won't have a curfew or rules to follow? We can just exist however we want?" I sighed and leaned back watching the puffy clouds change from pink to orange.

"Crazy, right?" He laughed. "On one hand it will be really nice to be independent. On the other, I don't feel like it would be much different than it is now. For me at least." He looked at me with a sad smile, and my heart ached. That was one part of growing up that I was OK with. I would be glad for the independence. I needed it. Isaac stopped talking much about his dad after a while. I think the lack of attention he got bothered him more than he let on.

"Do you remember much about your mom?" I hugged my knees to my chest as I watched him carefully. I caught glimpses every now and then of a hurt that ran deep, deeper than even I knew. I doubt he even realized he showed it at all. I never made it a big deal out of it, because I knew Isaac would act like he was fine. He was always fine, always there to support and help *me*. He just wasn't good at being on the receiving end of it.

"A little bit, not much." He looked up at the clouds, longing in his features. His eyes shown bright with the reflection of the sunset. "I mostly remember how Dad was with her around. He wasn't perfect then, but she always brought out the best in him." He ran his fingers through his hair, taking deep, steadying breaths. "That is what I miss the most." Silence fell over us again as the rest of the kids left the park. The shadows were long, and the air grew cooler. "Ready to head back?"

"Not really."

"The longer we put it off, the worse it will be." He hopped up and held out his hand to help me off the concrete. "Let's go, little girl."

He walked me all the way back home and then headed back to his house on his skateboard. I walked up the steps to the porch, carefully opening the door so I didn't draw too much attention to myself. I should have been home a while ago. Thankfully, I could hear my mom and dad yelling at each other in the kitchen, so I went upstairs to my room to paint, avoiding the chaos.

Chapter 3

Isaac

The bell above the door chimed as I walked in, making me curse under my breath. She was already hard enough to surprise. That bell made it even harder. I knew she would beat me here. I think she liked this store even more than I did. The matted carpet floor was stained, the movie posters were fading, and we adored it. It was another place for us to enjoy being kids. I meandered in, looking at all the aisles of movie titles. A flash of red curls danced in front of me as Holly brought a movie up to the counter. We hardly ever rented the movies; we just asked them to play it on the little TVs they had in the back of the store. I walked over to join her and watched as her smile lit up when she saw me. I swear that smile was so infectious. Sometimes, I thought I was addicted to it.

"Did you pick a movie without me?" I mocked.

"Well, if you weren't so slow you could have helped me." She winked back at me, thanking the store attendant.

"What candy do you want?" I asked, eyeing the options. She looked at me and quirked an eyebrow.

"You know what I want, Isaac. We've been friends too long for you to act like you don't know. In fact, you make fun of me for being so predictable!" I laugh and shake my head, grabbing the licorice from the stand. She grabbed two cans of soda and while I bought our candy and drinks, she made her way back to the TVs that were going to be playing her movie. Plopping down on the carpet and settling in against one of the shelves, I watched her eyes glued to the screen, excitement radiating off of her. She was nearly buzzing.

"So, what did you pick?" I asked, nudging her in the side playfully.

"You'll see!" She teased back. The sound of the opening credits started, and I looked over at the screen to try to guess what it was. I laughed, looking back at her and her devious grin.

"Poltergeist? For real? We have seen this so many times."

"I know. I love it. It's scary and kind of silly. Deal with it!" She poked my ribs, making me squirm and slosh my soda around.

"Hey! Watch it. You're going to make me spill." We both looked at the gross carpet, back to each other and erupted in laughter.

"Right," she said, wiping tears out of her eyes. "Wouldn't want to make a mess. Do you think they could even tell if we did?"

"Probably not. We should bring a blanket next time. Who knows what kinds of things are living in this floor." She scrunched up her nose at me, leaning in close to put her head on my shoulder. We ate and watched the movie in comfortable silence. I barely paid attention to the movie because the feeling of her close, her breaths against me took up all my head space. I was acutely aware of her small movements. The yank of her arm when she pulled off a bite of licorice, the little, tiny jumps when the movie scared her. Eventually she stilled, her breaths even and her fingers twitching around the plastic licorice bag. I leaned my head against the shelf, eyes glued to the credits of the movie. Even when they were over and the screen went dark, I didn't move. I never wanted these perfect times to end. Wrapping my arms around her, I held her there next to me. She smelled like licorice and every breath I took; she consumed me. She became my whole world the day I saw her for the first time, and I never looked back.

The store attendant came by and tapped me on the shoulder, signaling it was time to go so he could close the store. As I started to shuffle, Holly stirred and looked up at me with sleepy eyes.

"I missed the whole thing!" She whined. She stuck her bottom lip out and pouted at me. "Why did you let me fall asleep?" Throwing my arms up in surrender, I looked at her as innocently as possible. Feigning a yawn, I stretched out and wrapped my arms around her and tickled her. Her squeals filled the room, and she wiggled as much as she could, but she couldn't get away. I was relentless and didn't let up no matter how much she begged me to stop. She eventually got an arm free and jabbed her finger into my ribs.

"OK, OK! I'll stop. You play dirty." I gasped. She just rolled her eyes.

"Right. I'm the one that plays dirty. Of course." She giggled, gathered up the trash and jumped up. Following behind, we thanked the store attendant even though he looked less than enthused that we were taking so long to leave. Tossing our trash into the bin outside the door, we started walking home. I don't know how I got so lucky that my best friend lived down the street from me, but I would forever thank whoever is in charge upstairs that it happened that way.

It was dark out, but the streetlights lit up the whole way home. We walked quietly for a little while, and as we got closer Holly tensed up more and more. I could hear the way her steps were changing on the pavement and her breaths were getting shallower. Not wanting to make it worse, I kept my mouth shut and took her hand in mine. She looked up at me, eyes glossy. She leaned into me, squeezing my hand as we walked the rest of the way home. My house was first, but I walked right past it to finish the walk with her. Her porch light was on, and the steps creaked under our weight as we climbed up them to the front door.

"Thank you for walking me home." She smiled, but it wasn't the smile she usually flashed me, and it broke my heart into pieces. I wasn't sure what happened to cause the shift in her mood, but I knew she would tell me when she was ready. She always did. I hugged her tight, breathing her in as she wrapped her arms around my waist.

"Anytime, Holl. Goodnight." I rested my chin on the top of her head and waited for her to let go of me before I let her go. I watched her go into the house and I turned and left, leaving my heart with her.

The closer I got to my house the heavier my footsteps fell. It was late and I knew what I would be walking into. The door thudded open, and I kicked my shoes off. I was greeted with silence at first, then the sound of the fridge opening had the hairs on my neck standing at attention.

"Isaac? That you?" Dad called out.

"Yeah, dad. It's me."

"Why the hell are you home so late?" His voice was harsh and mean and I could tell he was already drunk. I walked into the kitchen to get food so I could hide in my room for the rest of the night.

"I was just at the movie store." I said, snaking my way past him as he slammed the fridge door shut. I flinched at the sound and hoped nothing broke. Cleaning up his messes was nothing new to me, but that didn't make it any easier. I managed to sneak his truck keys into my pocket while his head was buried in the fridge. As much as I wanted to live free of him, having him drive drunk and hurt someone else in the process was not the way to do it.

"Watch your tone, boy," he growled as he popped off the cap of another beer.

"Sure, you need another one?" I huffed, getting the bag of chips from the cabinet and a bottle of water from the fridge. I scanned the inside of the fridge quickly. Nothing broke. Thank God.

Chapter 4

H*olly*

The first month of school went without a hitch and a lot of my nerves about freshman year went away. Isaac and I rode the bus home, and I daydreamed about the painting I was working on. It was a painting of a house. I told Isaac about it, and how I imagined the inside would look. He listened and smiled, drumming on the bus seat in front of us.

"Why an a-frame?" He asked. I thought about it, trying to conjure the image in my head.

"I don't know, honestly. It's unique, I guess. It would be in the middle of the woods so it just kind of fits." She thought for a minute. "It's not *just* a log cabin, it's more than that." He smiled, nodded and went back to drumming. I smiled at the image and looked back out the bus window. We were one of the last kids off the bus, and we both got off at Isaac's house, but he always walked me home.

"What else are you going to do tonight?" I asked, watching the road ahead of us. He paused, considering his answer for a moment. I hated that he had to take care of himself so much, especially since he was always taking care of me in some way, too. I never knew how to return his endless sacrifices.

"I'm not sure. I'll give you a report tomorrow." He smirked, softly pushing me into the grass next to the road.

"Hey!" I squealed. "Make sure you eat, ok? I can't have you wasting away on me. You can't always survive off pizza rolls." I waved my hands over him. He frowned, looking down at himself.

"Feed me more cheeseburgers from the diner and I'll be fine" He winked as we reached my driveway. "Want me to walk you up today?" I looked over my shoulders and sighed.

"No, I'm good. I'll see you tomorrow! Let's skate after school." He pulled me closer, hugging me tight.

"Sounds good, little girl." He messed my hair, and I glared at him as he turned and walked back down the street towards his house.

I walked up my front steps, the front door wide open. Mom was gone on a work trip, so dad was in the kitchen cooking. I walked through the living room and put my backpack on one of the chairs at our dining room table.

"Hey, Holly," Dad said hovering over the stove. "How was school?"

"It was good." I quickly offered. I grabbed a glass and filled it up with water and sat down at the table, watching him work. It was always quieter when mom was gone, and it made me nervous. I was the center of dad's attention, and it made my stomach turn. I took a sip of water and reached for a book out of my backpack. "What's for dinner?" I asked.

"Spaghetti. I made the sauce from scratch." He answered proudly. I nodded, trying to focus on *Pride and Prejudice*. "It should be just about done if you want to grab plates."

"Sure." I closed the book, setting it on the table. I walked over to the counter and grabbed the plates, standing on my tiptoes. His touch grazed my lower back, and I shivered at the contact. I tried to hide my apprehension, but he tried to reassure me by rubbing his thumb along my back.

"Hey, it's OK. I was just going to help you reach them." I blushed and nodded.

"Sorry, you just snuck up on me." I got the plates, and quickly set them on the table avoiding his gaze. He filled the plates with spaghetti, and we sat at the table, eating in silence. I sat on one end and he at the other. I looked down at my food, feeling his gaze rake over me. I wanted to throw my plate of food at him, but I couldn't. I just sat there, frozen.

"How are your classes? Are you reading *Pride and Prejudice*?" I nodded, again, finishing my spaghetti. I got up and rinsed off my plate in the sink. "Don't worry about the dishes, I'll get them, baby girl." My back stiffened at the pet name and I tried to breathe through the nausea that washed over me.

"OK, thanks. I am going to go get some homework done in my room. Thanks for dinner." Not waiting for a response, I grabbed my bag and ran upstairs to my room. I shut my door, turning and leaning back on it. I let my body slide down, hoping I could melt into the floor and disappear altogether. I stared at the inside of my room. I both loved and hated this room. I loved it for the escape it provided. I painted my dreams in it. My favorite art from over the years hung on the walls. Paints and old cups of water were littered all over the place. My full-size bed sat in the corner with my dresser next to it. My easel and the stool I used sat right in the middle. The painting of the a-frame house stared at me, beckoning to be finished. I smiled as I stood. I tossed my backpack on my bed and changed my clothes into one of my favorite painting outfits. I wore an old band shirt Isaac had given me and a pair of coral overalls. The paint was splattered all over them in a gorgeous chaos of color.

I sat and painted for hours, letting my heart take over. My dream house came to life before my eyes as the shadows in my room grew darker and longer through the window. My eyes started to strain, and I yawned. I got up to stretch and change into my pajamas. I pressed my ear against my door to listen for my dad moving around the house. I could hear his snores from downstairs and the TV in the background. I let out a sigh of relief and went silently to the bathroom to brush my teeth. After, I tip-toed back to my bedroom, shutting the door as quietly as possible. I set the alarm on my dresser and curled under the covers, my eyes growing heavy. I fell asleep to the thoughts of my art hanging in a prestigious art gallery.

I think I had barely fallen asleep when I heard my bedroom door creak open. My heart jumped, but I forced myself to stay as still as possible. *Not tonight, please.* I begged in my head. I could feel his presence. His footsteps fell clumsily across my room. The smell of alcohol lingered, and my stomach turned. He fell onto my bed, catching himself. He sat next to me, my back to him, for minutes without saying a word.

"Holly? B-baby g-girl. Are y-you awake?" He stuttered. I curled myself tighter, squeezing my eyes shut. His hands snaked around my waist, rubbing my side. I flinched, giving myself away.

"Shit," I muttered under my breath.

"There s-she is. I knew you weren't sl-sleeping." He laughed. I turned my head to look at him. A sardonic smile danced across his face and lust consumed his eyes. He was worse tonight than he had been. His hand gripped my arm, tightly turning me over onto my back. I fought, trying to get out of his grip, but he just squeezed harder. I yelped in pain, but he refused to let go. His other hand tore off my covers exposing me to him.

"Please," I cried. "I don't want this." My eyes stung as tears threatened to break free.

"Shh," he cooed. "I don't like it when you c-cry, baby g-girl." Stomach bile burned my throat as his hand tightened around my arm. His other hand ran up my thigh, grabbing and rubbing me roughly. He moaned as he touched me and I fought again, trying to break free. His grip loosened on my arm, but his eyes narrowed down at me.

"Are you going to cooperate tonight?" Hunger raged in his crazed, drunken eyes. I sobbed and shook, trying to get away from him. "That's a n-no then?" He raised an eyebrow at me and stood up beside my bed. I froze, fear trembling through me. He fumbled with his belt buckle, and I took the opportunity to turn and bolt off the bed. I made it to the doorway before he had a hand in my hair. Screaming in pain, he pulled me back to the bed, lacing his fingers through my curls. He threw me down on the bed with more force than he has ever had. My eyes widened as he held his belt in front of him. Fear had me shaking in front of him, weak and at his mercy.

"Please! No." I pleaded. But it was useless. Before I could get away, the crack of the belt smacked hard against my thighs. Screams ripped through me as he hit me again, and again. Tears streamed down my face, and I curled into myself, bracing for another hit. Instead, he sat down next to me. He ran his hands roughly over my legs and my stomach.

"Now, are you going to be a good girl, Holly?" His words sliced through me, ripping me apart. Wrapping my arms around myself, I nodded, relenting. He smiled, stroking my hair and running the back of his hand against my cheek. "Good." He growled in my ear as he ripped my button up pajama shirt open. He palmed my breasts, and my stomach lurched. I fought the urge to fight him. Bruises had already started to form on my arm and my legs were welted and raw from his belt. Fighting was fruitless.

I flinched as he ran his hands over them, pulling down my shorts and panties. I laid there naked and vulnerable in front of him. I looked over at my painting of the a-frame. I closed my eyes, going to that place in my head. I disappeared. I could smell the trees and the fresh air and the rough rugged wood of the house. I felt him force himself inside me and I squeezed my eyes closed even tighter. I stayed there at my perfect house, my escape, until his forceful thrusts slowed, his grunts deepened, and he stiffened inside of me. I felt the hot liquid run down my thighs and I didn't even try to contain my sobs.

He left me there, naked and bruised, and stumbled out of my room. Slowly, I got myself up and nearly crawled to the shower. Numb and broken, I washed him off of me and carefully tended to the welts his violence left behind. There was no way I could hide these tomorrow at school. I crawled back into bed, looking back at the house that had become my escape. It would be the place I disappeared to every time he came into my room at night. It was the only peace I had.

My alarm blared through the silence of my room, and I moved to turn it off. I was sore and the welts from his belt had bled in the night. I looked at the stains in the sheets, running my fingers over the patterns they created. A tragic painting of heartache. I opened the drawer of my nightstand and stared at the pills in the little pink circle container. Like a zombie, I poked one out of the foil and threw it back into my mouth. Swallowing the birth control pill my dad was so diligent about keeping track of, I let it slide down my throat dry. I winced as I felt it all the way down my throat. Slowly, I got myself out of bed and headed to my closet. It was still warm out, but I made sure to pick out a long sleeve shirt. I grabbed a pair of jeans and sat back down on my bed to try and put them on. The marks burned and I gasped as the pain radiated through me. I swallowed back tears as I pulled them over my thighs. It was hard to breathe through the searing pain, but I managed to get them up. I put on my shirt and went to the bathroom. My eyes were bloodshot and dark circles stood out underneath them. My hair was tangled and matted from where he pulled it. I hardly recognized the girl staring back at me. I ached for relief.

The nights he came into my room were always awful, but this had been the worst night ever. He had never left a mark on me. I tried my best to cover myself up with makeup, but it was a lame attempt at best. I slowly and painfully made my way down the stairs to the kitchen to try and eat something. My stomach dropped as I turned the corner and saw him sitting at the table reading the paper. He bent the corner down, peering over it at me, assessing me. He wore a gentle, concerned smile on his face and it made me feel like I was engulfed in flames. My skin was hot, and my anger boiled beneath the surface. I swallowed the lump in my throat and limped over to the cupboard to get cereal.

"Are you able to walk normally?" He asked, folding his paper up and setting it on the table in front of him. I shook my head, staring into the cabinet. "Hmm, well I can't have my baby girl hobbling around at school, can I?" His patronizing tone made my toes curl. "I'll call the school. Will you be OK here by yourself?" I nodded, relieved for the possibility of a day alone. He got up and walked over to the phone. I barely registered the conversation as I finished getting my cereal and ate in tension filled silence.

I was able to get my jeans off and put on a tank top. I breathed a sigh of relief as I laid in my bed., wrapping myself up like a cocoon. I stared at the ceiling, numb and still. The sound of the doorbell startled me, and I bolted upright. Isaac's voice echoed through the house, and I instantly covered myself with my comforter, wanting to disappear. I heard dad tell him I was sick and that I would be home today. I held my breath as I waited for him to go away. The door closed, and I heard heavy footsteps on the stairs. Dad knocked on my door, opening it halfway.

"I'm headed to work. Do you need anything before I go?" He asked. I shook my head, still sitting up covered by my comforter. He smiled at me and backed out of the doorway. As soon as I heard the front door close and lock, my body relaxed, and I fell fast asleep.

Chapter 5

Holly

I knocked way louder than I really needed to. My knuckles hit the wood of his door, and my heart pounded in my chest. I just needed an escape. I knocked again. Isaac swung the door open, concern in his eyes. I watched them widen as he looked at me. I had covered the bruises and marks from the night before and had slept off the aches and pains for the most part.

"Holly, what the hell? Are you OK?" I nodded. I wanted to scream and cry and tell him what happened, but I couldn't bring myself to do it. Isaac was the escape I needed. He moved to the side so I could come into the house. He closed the door behind us, and I could feel his eyes on me. I won't cry. I can't cry. I'm pretty sure he sees right through my bullshit most of the time anyway. I just needed space to breathe, and no matter what, I could always count on that with him.

"Want a soda?" He asked. Again, I nodded and sat at the table in the kitchen. I often wondered how he and his dad spent their time here. Did they talk? Did they fight? I had met his dad several times, but Isaac seemed pretty closed off about their relationship, so I never really asked. It made me wonder what he was able to hide. Were we both harboring hurt that seemed impossible to share? The crack of the soda can opening zoned me back into Isaac. He was wearing basketball shorts and a shirt that was a little too big. He looked like home. I smiled at him as he handed me the soda. He winked at me and opened his own sitting down across from me.

"You wanna talk about it?" He asked me. Fear flashed through me. *He can't know. He will run away so fast. I can't lose this.* I shook my head, looking down at my hands around the can of soda.

"Not really. Just mom and dad fighting again. It gets really old. I wish they at least tried to hide it from me." I took a sip of the soda, the bubbles tickling my throat all the way down. Holding out my finger, I looked at him intently and let out a burp. Our laughter filled the room, and my heart healed just a little bit. His laugh was everything to me. I swear it was magical.

"You are something else, Holl." He laughed and shook his head. I smirked and shrugged my shoulders. I would do anything to get him to smile and laugh. It was all the distraction I needed to avoid the nightmares in my head.

"I know. But you love me anyway." I joked. For a split second, his eyes darkened and I caught a glimpse of something in his expression, but I wasn't sure what it was. Anger? No way. It went away as fast as it showed up, so I didn't linger on that thought.

"I sure do." He winked. "Want to go upstairs and play some video games? I bet I can kick your ass at Mario Kart."

"Ha! Unlikely." I scoffed. "You know I am the absolute best." I followed him upstairs, and about twenty matches later I finally won my first one.

"Want to change it up? I don't think you can take much more of a beating than you already have." He laughed. I sighed, stretched out on his bed next to him as my stomach growled. I thought at first, he didn't hear it, but he got out of bed and headed back downstairs. I took the opportunity to take in his room. I had been here so many times and it felt like it always had. His posters were the same as they always had been since we were little. His action figures still stood proud on his dresser. Laundry was strewn about the room, along with his games. Isaac had always been a constant for me, never changing, always exactly what I needed. I don't even think he tried to do it, it was always just the way we were. Easy, simple.

"I made some pizza rolls. And chocolate milk." He beamed when he came back into the room. OK, maybe he did try sometimes. I smiled back at him, taking the huge cup of chocolate milk, he made.

"Where's yours?" I asked, coyly.

"Umm, I made that to share! You can't drink all that by yourself." I watched as his eyes widened as I tipped the glass to my lips. I chugged and chugged until I couldn't anymore, his expression shocked as he watched me rise to his challenge. I almost finished the cup and handed it back to him. He stood above me next to the bed speechless. I smirked up at him and let out another burp. I pat my chest with a devilsh smile on my face.

"You are absolutely ridiculous." He sat down next to me on the bed with the plate of pizza rolls, popping one in his mouth. He instantly coughed and I watched as his eyes watered while he tried to breathe.

"Hot?" I asked, raising a brow. He nodded, swallowing loudly and panting. Glaring at the nearly empty cup, he pouted.

"Ok, ok. I'll go get more." I hopped off the bed around him, grabbed the cup, and raced down the stairs to make another cup. I worked fast stirring the chocolate powder into the milk as I took the stairs two at a time. When I got back to his room, he was chewing on another pizza roll. I handed the cup to him, and he took it, gulping it down.

"Happy now?" I asked. He nodded and I took my place next to him again, grabbing the plate from him as I did. "What do you want to play next?" I asked through a mouthful of pizza roll.

"How about Street Fighter?"

"Oh good! One I can actually beat you in." I laughed as he hopped up to get it ready. Oh, and beat him I did. Badly. Several hours later, it was starting to get dark, and my heart sank. I never wanted these times to end. The rest of the world, my dad, and everything else just evaporated into nothing when I was with Isaac. It was pure bliss, and I hated leaving. Sometimes I wondered if my parents would have ever noticed if I just didn't come back. My heart cracked in two when I realized my dad would always find me, no matter where I ran. It was a force I couldn't escape, and I knew it would never end.

"Do you have to leave?" Isaac asked. I didn't realize he was watching me so closely. His eyes were heavy and his concern for me was ever so evident.

"Yeah, I probably should." I stretched again, grabbed the plates and the cup and stood up from the bed. He watched me carefully and got up after me. We headed down the stairs and I gasped when I saw his dad in the kitchen. He was sitting in the dark at the table with a bottle in his hand. He glared at me over the table and his eyes followed me as I put the dishes in the sink.

"Dad?" Isaac called from behind me. "I didn't realize you were home." His dad scoffed and stood up.

"Too busy to make dinner too, huh?" He grunted as he pulled another bottle out of the fridge. The tension in the air was so thick I could hardly breathe. I finished rinsing off the dishes we used and placed them in the sink.

"Don't worry about the dishes, Holl. I'll wash them later." He leaned against the wall, arms crossed over his chest as he glared daggers at his dad. I nodded, gave Isaac a quick hug and let myself out.

Chapter 6

Isaac

The halls in our elementary school felt, smelled and looked exactly the same as I remembered. The halls were littered with kid's drawings and projects. It was like walking into a time machine. I don't think either Holly or I had a simple childhood. She seemed to be as tight lipped about what she had to deal with as I was. I think we inherently understood that we needed each other in a way we didn't truly understand yet. Between trying to keep my dad alive, and myself and Holly trying to survive her parent's constant fighting, we relied on each other to savor the simple moments we did have. Being back in elementary school was the reminder we both needed to stick together. It was a flashback to where it all began. I couldn't help but smile when I remembered the shy girl I sat by in art class. Now, she was turning into an amazing person who had come out of her shell little by little. At least, with me she was.

When Holly was asked to come help the art teacher with a big brother, and big sister program, she jumped at the opportunity. She had been talking about this for weeks. Her painting had become a form of therapy for her. She knew how helpful it was to her and couldn't wait to see it help someone else too. It was a perfect opportunity for her. It was the end of the first day of the two-week-long program they set up. I couldn't wait to hear about it all, not that she would give me a choice, anyway. I smirked at the thought of her rambling on and on and it made my heart swell in my chest. She needed this just as much as that little girl did.

I rounded the corner into the hallway that led to the art room. This place was so special. It was where Holly and I interacted for the first time. I don't think I could ever forget that day. Lingering in the doorway, I crossed my arms and leaned on the jamb. She looked at home here. The little girl she was working with looked at Holly like she hung the moon. The laughter echoed through the room, and I listened to them banter back and forth.

"I like my purple penguin!" The little girl said, biting the end of her paintbrush.

"I *really* like your purple penguin." She crouched next to the little girl, laughing after they dotted each other's noses with paint. Holly kept her art to herself a lot, so I felt like I was getting an inside view of her in her element. She was truly incredible. The art teacher got up from her desk and smiled warmly at Holly and her student.

"You did great work, Angela! I can't wait to see what else you two come up with. Pickup is in about five minutes, though, so let's get supplies cleaned up, ok? I'll make sure to keep your painting safe while it dries. You can get it tomorrow." The girls nodded and giggled as they put their supplies away. Holly caught me in the doorway and the blush that crept across her cheeks was adorable.

"Hey," I called out to them. "Your purple penguin is pretty cool." The girl beamed up at me, proud of her work.

"Thank you!" Before I knew it, the little girl's arms were wrapped around my waist in a tight hug. With my arms out to my sides, I gave Holly a look that hopefully conveyed a cry for help. All I got was stifled laughter. Awesome. I patted Angela on the back and thanked her for the hug. She took off to grab her backpack and headed to the office to get picked up.

"Thanks for that!" I said, throwing my thumb over my shoulder. She rolled her eyes as she finished cleaning up the last little bits of materials.

"Angela is a sweetheart." Her smile lingered as she leaned against a shelf. "Want to see a project I have been working on?"

"Always!" I loved seeing these parts of her. She leaned off the shelf and wandered through the tables set up throughout the room. I followed behind, memories flicking through my head. She grabbed a canvas that was leaning on an easel in the back corner and hugged it to her chest

"Promise not to laugh?" She bit her lip, nervously, avoiding my eye contact.

"Promise." I held out my pinkie, interlocking it with hers. "Pinkie promise." I declared. She slowly turned the canvas around and I took in every detail. I knew this picture.

"It's th-"

"Movie store." I finished, looking at the two painted figures. Her hair was unmistakable. My arm was draped around her shoulders. Soda cans and licorice wrappers littered the stained carpet. "This is amazing, Holly!"

"You really think so?" She asked sheepishly, looking at her own work again.

"Umm, yes. Are you going to hang it up?" I moved so I was behind her and looked again at the painting. "It really is incredible. You even got the stains in there." Her shoulders shook with laughter against me.

"I want you to have it." She turns and holds the canvas out in front of her, an offering of sorts. My breath hitched, and my eyes widened. I couldn't take this from her. Could I?

"You're sure? I am going to hang this up on my wall, you know that right?" She smiled, winked, and nodded her head slowly. Whenever she gave me pieces of herself like this so freely, I cherished every moment. I knew what her art meant to her and her future. The idea of getting a piece of it to keep, made me feel so whole. She was the missing puzzle piece to my life.

"I was hoping you would." I looked at it again, pride washing over me.

"I hope one day you see yourself as the talented, beautiful person you really are. Inside and out."

"Me too." She sighed with an unmistakable heaviness in her voice.

"That's how that little girl sees you. She loves you, Holl." I nudged her with my hip.

"I love her too. She's amazing. I'm glad I get to spend some time here with her. It seems like we both need it."

"Everything ok?" I questioned.

"Yeah, she just has a hard time at home and struggles to make friends in her class. We were hoping this program would help her."

"Is it?" She smiled and looked past me, out of the window where Angela climbed in the backseat of a car, apparently jabbering away.

"Yeah. I think it is." I hugged the canvas under my arm and wrapped my other arm around her shoulders.

"How about this," I whispered into her ear. "We drop this bad boy off at my house, then we grab a movie at the drive-in tonight?"

"Can we get snacks?"

"Duh."

"Popcorn?"

"Of course."

"Licorice?" I paused, her face deviant and hopeful.

"For you, my little artiste', anything." I hugged her closer, taking note of every freckle, every strand of hair, and every sparkle in her eyes, committing them all to memory.

We walked out of the hall, taking our time through the school remembering and laughing at our kid antics. She stopped when we reached the doors to leave and turned around looking at the foyer.

"Do you think we will come here when we are old and gross and still remember all this?" I stared at her, taking it all in.

"I don't think I could ever forget. I just don't want to get old and gross." I laughed. She shook her head at me and walked towards the doors.

"Come on, old man. Let's go."

Chapter 7

H*olly*

The drive in wasn't very crowded. It was almost like an underground secret place. We loved it though. The people here were always fun, and the vibe was perfect. We took his dad's truck loaded with blankets and snacks and a radio. The air was just the right amount of crisp and the sun was setting behind big, pink, puffy clouds. I made a mental note to paint that image later. I had changed out of my painting clothes into my favorite pair of black jeans, dusty pink sweater and white chucks. My hair fell loose around my shoulders.

"Ready?" Isaac asked, pulling the keys out of the ignition.

"Yep." I opened the door and slid out, taking in the area. There were maybe a dozen cars. It was a double feature tonight and people were getting settled in their cars or, like us, the bed of a truck. I grabbed the radio and walked back to the tailgate.

"Why don't you go get the snacks and I can get everything ready?" He handed me some cash and lowered the tailgate.

"Ok." I pocketed the cash and headed over to the concession stand.

"Hey, Holly!" The older man greeted me. I waved and smiled at him. "Let me guess." He pressed his finger to his chin pretending to think really hard. "One large popcorn, one package of black licorice, and two root beers?" He looked at me, waiting with pursed lips.

"You had me at black licorice. Am I really that predictable?" We both grinned at each other. I handed him the cash and he got to work gathering the food.

"I'm old, Holly. I like predictable." He laughed, handing me the change which I dropped in the tip jar. "Enjoy your movie!"

"We will, thank you." I piled all the stuff in my arms and headed back to the truck. Isaac was sitting on the tailgate, waiting. The blankets were spread out and pillows he somehow snuck by me were stacked up against the back. He looked perfect, in his ripped jeans, faded black shirt and worn-down checkered vans. The messy mop of hair on his head was wild. He hopped down and grabbed the food from me and put it in the bed. He helped me up, and then got in next to me. We moved the blankets around, settling in. The weight of his arm around my shoulders was a comfort. I leaned into it and took the package of licorice. Opening it, I wafted it under his nose.

"Gross. Why would you do that to me?" He coughed and gagged, always such a drama king.

"One day you'll like it." I sunk back into my spot against him and took a bite.

"Not a chance." He threw a handful of popcorn in his mouth.

The sun continued to set behind us making the screen start to glow. Excitement ran through me. I loved watching movies. Especially like this. The drive in made it so much better. The smell of the trees in the air, the coziness of the truck, it was all perfect. These were the moments that I clung to when I needed them most. They kept me alive and hopeful. Closing my eyes, I inhaled Isaac's scent and felt the weight of him next to me, around me. He was everything I ever needed.

"What movies are playing?" I asked, watching the screen in anticipation.

"I have no idea." He laughed.

"What? What if they suck?" I gasped dramatically. He gave me a side eye, silently but effectively, calling my bluff. My eyes widened when the opening credits for the Poltergeist started. "You did know!" I punched his thigh and angrily took a bite of licorice. He laughed, not denying it.

"I saw it was playing tonight with *Sleepy Hollow,* and I knew it wouldn't take much convincing for you to come out tonight." He threw a piece of popcorn in the air, leaning forward to catch it on the way down.

"Let me try." I snatched the popcorn from him, throwing a piece into the air, but missing terribly when it tumbled down. It ended up, lost in my hair. Isaac chuckled, pulling it out and throwing it in his mouth.

"Let me throw it and you can try to catch it. It's easier than trying to throw it yourself." He grabbed a piece from the bucket on my lap and leaned away, tossing the popcorn towards me. I watched it and moved a second too late. It landed in my lap. I sat back with a thud, throwing the rogue piece in my mouth.

"Here, try it again." Isaac took the bucket from me and leaned away again tossing a piece towards me. I moved forward sooner this time, catching the popcorn on my tongue.

"Yes!" I shouted, throwing my hands up. "Throw me another." I caught almost every single one he threw, until I got too distracted by the movie. We settled back in together and watched in silence until the end credits. Isaac stretched beside me and got up from under the blanket.

"I need to pee. Do you need anything?" He asked, edging towards the end of the tailgate.

"No, I think I'm good." I handed him the empty popcorn bucket to throw away.

"Cool, I'll be right back." I leaned back onto the pillows, hugging my knees to my chest. More cars had shown up, but it was still pretty quiet. I looked at all the cars, the people and relaxed into the bed of the truck.

"Holly, is that you?" I startled, looking around the truck to see who asked me that. I inched my way towards the tailgate, scooting down the bed. I spotted a couple of guys I recognized from a few of my classes. I'm pretty sure they were on the football team. "It is you!" One of the guys, tall and built, smiled at me. I waved, not sure what their names were. They got closer and leaned against the side of the truck. Goosebumps erupted over my skin watching them cross their arms over the side of the bed.

"Can I help you?" I asked, trying not to sound too cold or bitchy.

"That depends. Are you here with your skater boyfriend?" The two looked at each other and laughed.

"Isaac?" My brows cinched together trying to figure out what they needed. "He just went to the bathroom."

"Well, want to come watch the second movie with us in our truck? We are probably better company for you." The other guy who had been quiet so far winked at me.

"No, I think I'm ok here. Thanks for the invite though." I attempted a smile, and tried to wave them off but they didn't budge.

"Come on, don't be like that." Mr. Winky whined. Like, actually whined. I rolled my eyes and didn't respond. "We can give you a way better time than he can."

"What is that supposed to mean?" I squished up my nose at the thought of going near either one of them. They just laughed at me as their eyes roamed over my body. It felt intrusive and gross. The guy that talked to me first walked around the tailgate and put an arm on either side of me, boxing me in.

"Don't play coy, Holl. Everyone in our high school is fucking around. Might as well show you how good it can be." Bile rose in my stomach and a flash of fear paralyzed me.

"No." I whispered.

"No?" He cupped my chin, pulling my face towards him forcefully. I closed my eyes tightly, the sound of bone hitting flesh erupting in front of me. I squeezed my eyes tighter, cupping my hands over my ears.

"Cool it bro! We were just messing around." Mr. Winky.

"Sure, you were. Pretty sure I heard her tell you guys to fuck off." Isaac nearly growled. "Don't bother her again." Their heavy footsteps faded, and I opened my eyes, searching for Isaac.

"Hey, it's ok." He brushed my hair out of my face gently. "Those guys are jerks. I'm sorry I left you alone." His eyes looked pained, guilty almost.

"It's ok. I'm ok." I nodded, breathing in and out.

"Do you want to stay for the next movie, or do you want me to take you home?" He asked, searching me for any unspoken answer I may give.

"No, we can't let them ruin it for us. Come on." I waved him back into the truck as I slid back, pulling the blankets over us. He wrapped me in his arms, where I fit perfectly. I let his steady breaths lull me to sleep before the movie was even half over. It was the best sleep I could get, especially when I had another monster waiting for me at home.

Chapter 8

Isaac
Sophomore Year

Excitement flooded through me as I shoved the last few items into my backpack. I was shocked to get the invite from Holly to go with her family camping. For the first time since we met, her parents gave her the ok to ask me to tag along. Her parents had always let me hang around and didn't really interfere with our friendship, but I always got the impression they tolerated me for Holly's sake. I glanced over at the clock on my nightstand and hurried to put my socks and shoes on. I had never been away for a weekend, and I jumped at the opportunity. I didn't ask my dad, I just told him where I'd be. Somehow, he didn't fight me on it. I figured I'd take the win.

Bolting out the door and down the street, Holly's house came into view and all three of them were bustling about trying to get everything together. When Holly saw me jogging towards them, she dropped her bag and closed the distance between us. I wrapped my arms around her waist as she hugged me tight. I never got enough of her. She gave me a quick peck on the cheek and pulled me towards the car that was already looking pretty overloaded.

"Are we all going to fit in the car?" I asked. Her mom, Jenn chuckled, and Holly shrugged her shoulders.

"I guess we will find out." She grunted as she threw her bag and mine into the trunk of the car, struggling to close it. I reached up and grabbed the trunk and leaned into it to shut it. I looked up to meet Holly's glare.

"I had it!" She crossed her arms and popped her hip, sass pouring from her. I just shook my head and laughed.

"Sure, you did, baby." Her dad said as he came around to shake my hand. I took it and thanked him for letting me tag along. "Of course. Holly wouldn't give it up. We had to give in." He laughed and reached for the driver door.

"Everyone ready?" Jenn asked. Holly and I nodded, climbing in the back seat.

The drive wasn't too long but long enough for Holly to pass out leaning on the window. I glanced at her and smiled when she let out a snore. Her parents talked quietly in the front seats, and I watched the Colorado aspens fly by me. I felt a sense of freedom for the first time in as long as I could remember. I had a tie to my father that wouldn't ever let me go far. My fear of him hurting himself or getting in the car after he had been drinking consumed me most of the time. I was letting myself have this weekend, though. I needed it. It seemed like Holly did too.

When we got there, the campground was littered with other groups throughout the park. It wasn't busy and the site they had picked was tucked away by the tree line. I helped put up the tents while Holly and Jenn unloaded the rest of the bags and set everything up. About an hour later, the sun was high in the sky and the crisp air blew through the park. I brought a hammock and tied it up between two trees. It was one of the only gifts my dad had gotten me years ago. Holly watched me with excitement in her eyes.

"A hammock?" She gasped.

"I believe that's what these are called, yes." I winked at her over my shoulder.

"Will you share it with me?" Her eyes wide and her bottom lip between her teeth, my pulse quickened.

"Absolutely." I offered my hand to help her get in and she was nearly buzzing with excitement. Once she was in and settled, I leaned on the tree by her feet and watched her close her eyes as I swung her gently back and forth. I'm not sure how long we stayed like that. Holly's eyes popped open when Jenn yelled for us to come eat lunch. I helped her out, my hand lingering on her lower back as she looked over her shoulder at me with wide, hopeful eyes. Our gazes locked and heat filled my lungs. Her hair, her eyes, her smile, I was completely mesmerized by her.

"What are you looking at me like that for?" She asked, nudging my shoulder. I struggled to find the words to say, because words didn't do her justice. Swallowing, I answered her the best I could.

"You are so beautiful, Holly. You always have been." Her eyes dropped from mine and her cheeks flushed. Her tilted smile took my fucking breath away.

"You're not so bad, yourself, Isaac." And just like that, she took off to go eat leaving me stunned. Was she flirting? Had we been flirting all this time and I never picked up on it? It has always been so easy between us, I never really thought too hard about changing anything about the relationship we have had since we were six. Does she want that? My head was reeling, and I had no idea what to do now. I decided acting like everything was normal was the best option, so that is exactly what I did.

We ate lunch all together. Everything tasted so good out here. We spent more time around the hammock, her with a book and me with a knife and a stick. I made the perfect fire poking stick. As the sun was setting, we headed back to where the tents were set up and I started a fire to roast brats on. As the fire came to life, Holly and Jenn prepared the buns, and all the condiments. My mouth started watering just thinking about it. They put on quite a spread. I was once again reminded of how lucky I was to have Holly in my life.

"Isaac, how much longer until we can roast these dogs?" Her dad asked coming up behind the picnic table with all the food on it.

"It's ready!" I beamed back at them.

"Great, I am so hungry." Holly sighed. We all got our forks and brats and surrounded the fire. We cooked, and laughed, and every chance I got, I stole a glance from Holly. Her eyes finding mine and lighting up an inferno in my chest. When everyone was done eating and several s'mores were inhaled, her parents said they were going to turn in. They had one tent for them and one for each of us.

"Don't stay out here too late." Jenn warned us. She eyed Holly and smiled an easy smile. Her dad followed behind her and soon the light was out in their tent.

"Want to play a game?" Holly whispered, scooting her chair closer to me.

"Depends. Will I win?" I smirked, as she punched my shoulder.

"Guess we will need to find out."

"What's the game?" I asked, raising an eyebrow down at her. She smiled a truly evil genius smile and I'm pretty sure I died right there.

"Hide and seek." She said, not dropping her gaze from mine. "I am going to go hide," she pointed to the trees behind me, "and you are going to come find me." I ran my hands down my face and let out a long, dramatic exhale. Sitting up and leaning my elbows on my knees, I turn my face to meet hers.

"Holly?" I asked.

"What?" She pouted.

"Run." I smiled a wicked smile at her as her eyes widened and a thrill shuddered through her. She took off into the treeline and I waited a few seconds for her to find her spot. I took off after her in a jog, slightly nervous to be running through the trees at night. It was dark, but my eyes adjusted quickly. Before long, I could hear her shallow breaths and her footsteps ahead of me. I trailed after her as quietly as I could until that perfect flash of red curls flew around a tree a few yards ahead of me. I snuck around the other side which put me at her back. Perfect. I reached out, wrapped my arms around her waist and cupped her mouth to stifle her scream. Turning her around, I smiled. The air danced around us. The coolness nipped at our skin. The smell of the clear forest air made everything seem alive and beautiful. Her fair skin glowed in the moonlight making her eyes a pale gray. She was ethereal out there. I could have stood there and stared at her for the rest of my life.

"Found ya." With a playful wink I let go of her and let her catch her breath. Her eyes shone in the moonlight through the trees and the freckles that covered her nose danced across my vision. She was breathless and laughing and truly carefree in this moment.

"Yes. Yes, you did. Did you even count at all?"

"I counted." I shrugged.

"Ugh, to like two maybe."

"No! It was three." She elbowed me in the ribs as she walked by to head back to the campsite. "Holl," I ask, grabbing her hand to turn her back to me. "Can I ask you something?"

"Sure?" She eyed my warily.

"Will you be mine?" I wasn't even sure what I was asking but I knew I needed to hear the words.

"Your what?" She shifted her weight back and forth nervously, like she wasn't sure of herself or me, for that matter.

"Just...mine. My Holly?" I looked at her and watched every muscle twitch in her face as she thought about what I was asking. Finally, she beamed at me and stepped closer. She closed the space between us and looked up at me.

"Haven't I always been?" Before I could answer, she tiptoed up to me and gave me a peck on the lips, then once again walked away leaving me breathless. I watched her disappear and had to tell my lungs to take in the night air and for my feet to follow her out of the trees. The cool air seemed to shift and have a bite to it. Her words If she believed she'd always been mine, would it stay that way forever? How would this conversation change the dynamic of whatever relationship we would have? My mind reeled and I eventually got my feet to work and headed back towards the tents.

Chapter 9

Isaac

I made my way slowly through the trees, back to the campsite. Sticks and leaves crunched under my boots, echoing through the woods. I zig zagged through the trees but slowed when I caught a glimpse of Holly talking to her very angry looking father. His arms were crossed tight across his body and the veins in his neck pulsed as he spoke to her. Her head hung low, and her fists were clenched at her sides. I edged closer to try and get an idea of what was being said, but the sight of his hand raised over his head like he was going to slap her had my feet moving and my vision red. I sprinted out of the trees towards them.

"Holly!" I shouted. "Looks like you won. I must have gotten turned around in there." She spun around, eyes softening with relief. Her dad's eyes shot daggers into me, his hand lowering and his stance shifting. "Think you could give me a hand with covering the wood?" I threw my thumb over my shoulder, not taking my eyes off Holly's father. His jaw clenched, he nodded, moving past us. I started to follow, but Holly gripped my elbow.

"Don't say anything." She pleaded, fear covering her soft features. With a silent apology, I followed the piece of shit to the pile of wood. He already grabbed the tarp, and we got to work covering the firewood. As he stood back up, I gripped his arm, gaining the attention I needed from him.

"If I ever see or hear about you touching her, I will personally make sure it is the last thing you do." I growled, spitting on his boot. When he looked up at me, a wicked Cheshire-like smile took over his face. He tore his arm out of my hold and moved closer to me, our noses nearly brushing. I could feel his breath on my face, and it made everything inside me coil tight. Adrenaline burned through me.

"Noted." He sneered, and then walked away. Anger, fear, and confusion washed over me all at once, paralyzing me. I watched him leave me there, completely at a loss of what to do or what was happening. There was more to it, and no one was saying anything. I never questioned Holly's safety until that night. It would be something I would regret for a long time.

"What the fuck?" I muttered to the trees around me, running my hands through my hair. Holly had already gotten into her tent and the light was off. I couldn't risk going in to talk to her, so I headed to my tent, thoughts spiraling out of control. The zipper echoed through the night, and the stale smell of the tent wafted over me. My sleeping bag was laid out with my bag on it. I kicked my shoes off, pulled my shirt over my head, and tried to settle into the sleeping bag.

I tossed and turned, sleep evading me. Was Holly in a worse situation than I thought? I would know, wouldn't I? I know her better than I know myself most days. The vision of Holly's fear in front of her own father haunted me. I couldn't get it out of my head. It played on repeat, the intensity increasing every time it flashed across my consciousness. My chest tightened and my breaths came shallow and ragged. Sweat gathered across the back of my neck as my body flushed with heat. My stomach rolled, saliva pooling over my tongue.

I ripped the sleeping bag open and bolted for the zipper of the tent. As soon as the hole was big enough to crawl through, I shoved myself out into the night air. Standing, I ran to the backside of the campsite. I rubbed my fist into my chest trying to ease the burn, but I lurched forward on a dry heave, and then another, and then everything I ate spewed out in violent chunks.

"Isaac?" Jenn called from behind me. "Are you ok?" She tiptoed closer, placing her cool hand on the back of my neck. I nodded, the best I could. Lifting my head, I saw Holly come over as well, concern in her eyes.

"Did you get sick?" She asked, joining her mom by my side. My body flushed with embarrassment. I managed to nod and tried to calm my breaths. "I'll get you a water bottle." She said as she disappeared. I hung my head, my hands on my knees. Looking back up to see where Holly was with the water, my eyes met cold, evil ones that smirked at my vulnerability. I kept my eyes locked with his in a silent battle of wills. My skin crawled and my body itched to chase him down and beat his face in.

"Deep breaths." Jenn said next to me, running her hands over the back of my neck. Holly came back with the water and her face fell when she followed my gaze to her father outside of his tent. I looked at her, took the bottle and unscrewed the cap.

"Thank you," I looked at Holly in between taking small sips of water.

"Do you need anything else?" Jenn asked.

"No, thank you." I smiled gently at her. "I'm not sure what that was." I stood up, capped the bottle and headed back to the front of my tent.

"If you need anything, come get me." Jenn said over her shoulder as she headed back to the tent. They both went in, leaving Holly and I outside.

"Isaac-" She started, but I put my finger over her mouth. I nodded over to her parent's tent and shook my head. I didn't trust them to not listen to us. I took her hand in mine and helped her back into her tent.

"Goodnight, Holl." I smiled a soft smile and carefully zipped up the tent.

I WOKE UP TO THE SOUND of birds chirping in the morning sun. The tent was warm and wet droplets of dew gathered on the canvas. My throat burned from spewing brats everywhere and my head throbbed. I grabbed the lukewarm water bottle from last night and chugged, coughing as I swallowed it down. Stretching and trying to get my bearings, I yawned and slipped on my shoes. I unzipped the tent and made my way outside. It was quiet, the grass damp and the morning breeze rustling through the trees. Jenn sat in a chair by the fire ring with a cup of coffee and a book. I grabbed a chair and settled in next to her, laying my head back.

"Hey, how are you feeling this morning?" She asked.

"Like death." I groaned. She laughed and went back to her book. We sat in comfortable silence for a while, which I was glad for. I was not ready to function yet. "Can I have some coffee?"

"Of course." She bookmarked her page, got up and headed over to the food. I followed behind her.

"I can get it, if you want. I just wasn't sure where it was." I offered.

"Nonsense. Go sit down. I only have instant coffee, is that ok?"

"Is it caffeinated?"

"Absolutely." She laughed.

"Then yeah, it's just fine." She laughed again and I headed back to the camp chair and settled into it. My eyes were heavy, and the warm morning sun felt like heaven on my skin.

"Here you go, Isaac." I took the foam cup and let the hot coffee thaw my aching body. The sound of a zipper rolled through the campsite, and I smiled at the wild ball of red hair that crawled out of the tent.

"Is that coffee I smell?" Holly groaned as she stumbled out.

"It is, indeed." I taunted, sipping loudly on my cup of coffee. She glared at me, nearly making me spill it as I shook with a quiet laugh.

"Don't worry, honey. I'll make you a cup." Jenn winked at me and got to work. Holly grabbed a chair and moved in next to me, sighing as she relaxed under the sun.

"Your dad went to town this morning to go get more ice. He should be back soon." I stiffened in my seat, flashes of last night invading my mind. Holly and I exchanged glances. She knew she owed me a conversation.

"Holly, after coffee would you want to go for a quick hike?" I asked, raising an eyebrow at her. She sunk further into her chair and nodded.

We finished our coffee, I started a small fire to burn our trash, and we got dressed for our hike. We waved to Jenn behind us and smiled. We walked in silence for what seemed like hours.

"Holly." I nudged her. She looked at me, eyes distant. "What happened last night?" She sighed, stopping by a fallen log. She slumped down and patted the space next to her. I moved and sat next to her, letting her take her time.

"It was nothing." She offered.

"Try again." I demanded. She huffed and crossed her arms.

"He is just…protective. He got mad that we went off in the dark." Her nose scrunched up with the lie and I had to stop my eyes from rolling out of my head.

"He was going to hit you!" I grabbed her by the shoulders, making her eyes meet mine. "*Has* he hit you?" She looked away, moving out of my hold and just shook her head.

"No. Please, just drop it." I watched her walk away, yet again, shutting me out. There was no way in hell I would be dropping anything. She had just taken over the last little bit of my heart I had left. She didn't realize it, probably never would, but she held my heart and soul, and I knew it would be the end of me. We never talked about that night again, and she became more closed off about her life at home than ever. I was a kid, and had no idea how to handle her, the situation or myself for that matter.

Chapter 10

H*olly*
Junior Year

The rain trickled down the window of the booth we were in. I hadn't heard a single word Isaac said since we sat down. My head was foggy, and my body ached. I cried myself to sleep again last night and had to wear makeup to cover my puffy eyes and the marks left behind by my own personal nightmare. We were starting the second half of our junior year in a few days and I was counting down the days to graduation. Would I even make it?

"Holly?" Isaac nudged my foot under the table. "Do you want to share a shake like usual?" The concern in his eyes swallowed me whole as I nodded my head. "Cool. We will have a large chocolate and strawberry swirl shake and a plate of fries, please." He told the waitress. The diner was a fifties style vintage diner. It was actually built in the fifties, and they maintained it pretty well. It was one of our regular spots, and it felt like a version of home I had in my dreams. The booths were full of couples, kids and other locals. They ate and laughed and smiled around me. I smiled at the older couple in a booth behind us, also sharing a shake. Would that be us? Could Isaac and I be that couple one day? *Not if you leave him behind.* Shaking the thoughts away, I re-engaged with Isaac who I realized had been staring at me for who knows how long.

"What?" I lean on the table meeting his stare with my own.

"You seem distant. Everything ok?" I sighed, leaning back against the booth and looking back out the window.

"Yeah, just stuff at home. It's heavy, you know?" He nodded, watching me. "How's your dad?"

"Frustrating as hell, per usual." He runs his hands down his face and crosses his arms across his body. "Every time I think he is getting a little better, he just gets worse. Plus, he dropped a pretty big bomb on me the other day."

"What did he say?" I raised my eyebrows.

"After graduation, he is retiring and giving me the shop to run."

"That's pretty cool! Aren't you excited?"

"Not really." We both leaned back as the waitress dropped our shake and fries off. "Thanks," he smiled up at her.

"Isn't that what you were kind of planning to do anyway?" I shoved a delicious, crispy fry into my mouth, chasing it with the shake.

"I suppose, but he just took the option away from me instead of asking me. I just feel trapped in it."

"I understand that." I muttered as I sank into the booth. Isaac pushed the plate of fries closer to me inch by inch, wiggling his eyebrows at me. I laughed and threw a handful in my mouth. Even when he was dealing with his own shit, he still made my happiness a priority. It made me feel selfish at times. Did I do the same thing for him? I don't even know if he realizes he does it. I looked at him and pushed the plate closer to him, attempting to do the same eyebrow dance. He looked at me and laughed so hard some of the shake he just sipped came out of his nose. That of course set off another round of uncontrollable laughter from our booth. We clutched our stomachs and wiped the tears from our cheeks, trying to breathe. Isaac shook his head and chuckled as he wiped his shake filled nose.

"Oh my God, people probably think we are delusional." I choke out.

"Let 'em! They're just jealous anyway." He smiled at me and liked it always did, it warmed me up from the inside out. His smile was magical, and I wanted it imprinted in my brain for all of eternity. "What about you?" He asked.

"What about me?"

"What are you going to do after graduation?"

"I think I want to head to Boulder. There is an art gallery there that I would kill to have my art in someday." I sighed. It seemed so far off, just out of reach of my own reality.

"You'll make it happen." He smiled and nudged me. There was a sadness in his eyes, though. It hurt to think about leaving, but I didn't have the heart to try and make it work here.

"I have an idea!" I shout, startling Isaac across from me.

"Ok?" He questioned.

"Let's go get a Polaroid camera and take pictures. Let's document our final years in school. It'll be a fun way to look back on all this!" I was so giddy at the idea that I felt like I was buzzing. He shrugged his shoulders.

"OK. Let's go. But-" he hesitated. "If you think I will ever forget anything we've done together, you are very wrong." I punched his shoulder and laughed. "I'm serious." My wide eyes met his. "I can't go anywhere without being reminded of you." He smiled as I let his words wash over me.

I rushed out of the booth, Isaac put his cash down on the table and followed behind me to his truck. He followed me around to the passenger side, opening the door for me and helping me in. My gaze followed him as he jogged around the hood and jumped in the driver's seat. The engine purred to life, and he pulled out of the parking lot onto the main road. The radio played Metallica, and I watched as Isaac sang and drummed his fingers on the steering wheel to the beat. Reaching forward, I spun the volume dial to nearly max volume and I watched as Isaac's smile took over his face. His eyes lit up watching me sing along. We drove like that the whole way to the store, our voices sore from singing at the top of our lungs. Sometimes you just need to belt out metal songs at the top of your lungs to feel better. It was cathartic, really. It was probably healthier than screaming into my pillow.

Isaac and I hopped out of the truck, the doors slamming behind us. We walked up the store, the bell dinging as we walked in.

"Do you want to ask if they have any?" I asked Isaac as I scanned the store.

"No, it'll be like a game. Whoever finds it first doesn't have to pay for it." He winked at me as he took off in one direction in pursuit of our camera. I ran the other way, my eyes peeled for any kind of electronic that would clue me in. I passed books, toys, food, but no cameras. I huffed a stray hair out of my eyes as I turned in circles. I didn't even see Isaac. I walked back towards the main aisle and headed in the other direction. I passed the pharmacy and cosmetics and turned when the aisle came to a tee. I squinted ahead of me to see what was at the end of the aisle and my heart raced at the display of cameras and computers.

"Yes!" I shouted, getting the attention of an older lady in front of me. "Sorry," I mouthed. I took off towards the display but slowed when Isaac came into view holding a Polaroid camera in his hands. His devilish smile made goosebumps erupt all over me. I shivered and crossed my arms, giving him my best pout.

"I win, Holl. Pay up!" He handed me the box. I took it, glared at him and walked back towards the front of the store. He put his arm around me as we walked together. I was still pretending to be mad, so I gave him the best cold shoulder I could. We got up to the counter and I put the camera on the belt. I went to get money out of my pocket, but my wallet wasn't in my back pocket where I had put it when we left. Frantically, I patted the rest of my pockets only to come up empty. My heart sank and I looked at Isaac, who was trying to stifle a laugh.

"What's so funny?" I asked him, still frazzled.

"Are you looking for this?" He pulled out my wallet and dangled it in front of me. I tried to reach for it, but he snagged it away too quickly. He laughed, took out his own wallet and handed the cashier the money for the camera.

"I was supposed to pay for that!" I pulled on his arm, and he just turned and smiled.

"Did you really think I would have let you pay? You've known me long enough to know that taking care of you is the best thing ever. Just let me do it." He gave me a knowing grin and handed me my wallet back.

"How did you even get my wallet?" I stared at it in my hands and then back up to him.

"It was on the seat in the truck. Probably fell out of your pocket." He nodded towards the door, taking the receipt from the cashier. "Thank you." He waved. He handed me the camera and I was already ripping the box open. I tossed the trash in the bin outside the store and jogged back to the truck. He helped me get in and as I turned around in the seat, I snapped a photo of him leaning on the truck door. The photo printed out and I waited for his megawatt smile to show up on the film. The photo was perfect. I smiled at it as he started the truck. Volume still at full blast, Isaac immediately started singing along to the Iron Maiden song. I snapped another photo. We spent the rest of the night taking pictures. When we had to part ways, we sorted the pictures, and I hung them up all over my walls in my space. His warm presence was such a welcome change in my room. Now when my dad paid his visits, I would have Isaac there to help me through it.

Chapter 11

Holly
Senior Year

I could smell the teenage spirit from outside the doors of the arcade. It was a place that was crawling with angst, competition, and mindless fun. The owner was a huge nerd and could tell you about every single game in the place. He also kept a stock of comic books that I loved to sort through and read. I loved the art in the comic books and some of my own paintings came from their inspiration. Ben, the owner, had picked up on that and shared his collection with me. When I walked in, I spotted the group of familiar faces and smiled, waving. Isaac was playing with one of the kids we knew from the skate park. He was definitely winning, his smile a telltale sign of victory. Before I headed over to them, I stopped at the counter.

"Hey, Ben!" I called.

"Hey, Holly. How's it going?" He smiled, his messy salt and pepper hair tied loosely in a low ponytail. It was the only sign of his age. He acted like one of us most of the time, and I adored it.

"Pretty good. Do you have any new comics to show off?" I wiggled my eyebrows, hoping he had something good to share.

"You know what, I actually do! Since you have read pretty much my whole collection, I figured I needed to up my game." He winked at me, disappearing into the small office behind the counter. I glanced behind me, catching Isaac high fiving his opponent. "Here it is! Still in the plastic and everything." Ben waved the comic in his hand proudly. I leaned on the counter, handling the book with care.

"Teenage Mutant Ninja Turtles?" I asked, taking in all the details of the cover.

"Issue one! It was released in 1984." His wide smile showed off his pride and I couldn't help but share in that.

"This is amazing!" I carefully took it out of the plastic, examining every page.

"Want anything to drink?" He asked.

"Sure, I'll take a cream soda." I smiled at him and disappeared back into the world of the Ninja Turtles. He came back with the soda and opened the bottle, handing it to me. Finishing up my look into Ben's latest prized possession, I placed it carefully back into the plastic and laid it on the counter.

"Thanks, Ben! I'll have to draw you some Ninja Turtles." I grinned at him and made my way over to the group that was now gathered around a Pac Man game. Isaac caught me walking over and smiled at me.

"Make way, guys! Make way! The queen has entered." I blushed, pinching Isaac. "What?! Everyone knows you are the Pac Man champion, Holl." He rubbed the spot on his arm I just pinched with a grimace.

"I suppose you aren't wrong." I rolled my eyes. "I'll play next." No one had yet to beat my score, and I was hoping it would stay that way for a while. It was a weird thing to be good at, but I was sure proud of it.

"Alright, Holly. You're up." One of the guys said, moving out from in front of the game. I reached into the pocket on the chest of my overalls and grabbed quarters, loading them into the machine. Once it started, the whole world disappeared and it was just me and the ghosts, battling it out. I weaved through the maze, dashing out of the way of the monsters. The music played, and the dots disappeared one by one as my little companion ate them up. I passed levels on levels, but eventually I wasn't fast enough, and GAME OVER flashed across the screen. Cheers erupted around me as my name stood strong at the top of the list of players.

"Tell me your secrets, oh wise one!" Isaac laughed, bowing in front of me dramatically.

"Oh please, this is the only game I am good at. It's not like I can do that with any game." I rolled my eyes, silently gloating in the attention. "I've got quarters." I jiggled my pocket, making the coins clink together. "What are we playing next?"

Laughter and playful competition filled the arcade and Ben sat behind the counter, watching with a sparkle in his eye. I wondered what it would be like to live your dream. He did exactly what he wanted to and got what he wanted out of life. It had to be so freeing. I wanted that freedom more than anything. I wanted to be able to take what I wanted out of life and watch my dreams unfold before me. It had to be possible, right? I thought of painting and Boulder more and more. It always seemed just out of reach. Close enough to imagine, but too far to see it clearly. Could I even survive until I was able to leave? I looked around at my friends, at Isaac and decided then and there that I had to survive. One day at a time, I would make it, and I would make my own dream come true, no matter the cost.

Ben made his way over to our group huddled around the skee ball. We all took turns tossing the balls into the caged targets, whooping and hollering whenever we made it.

"Hey, Holly?" Ben tapped my shoulder.

"Hey!" I smiled.

"Can I borrow you for a second? I have something I want to show you." His shy smile danced across his face. I nodded, following him back over to the counter. "Wait here, just a second." He went back into the office and came back a few minutes later. "I got another new comic to show you. He laid the book on the counter, sliding it over to me. I picked it up and looked it over.

"Susan Storm?" I asked.

"Yeah, she's from the Fantastic Four. She's the Invisible Woman."

"Nice! Can I look through it?"

"Actually, I want you to have that one. It reminds me of you, and I think you'll like it, especially the artwork in it." He smiled, sheepish, but genuine. I leaned over and hugged him as best I could.

"Thank you, Ben! This means a lot. I can't wait to read it." I started to head back over to the games. "Hey, Ben?" I called. "Are there any extra shifts I can pick up?" He thought for a minute.

"Yeah, I think there are. Before you leave, come let me know which ones you want." I smiled and shot him a thumbs up, turning to head back over to Isaac. This place had become more than just a place to work. Ben was more of a father figure to me than I had ever had. He taught me responsibility and made me feel welcome. This arcade was his baby, and I was so lucky to have been included in that. It was more than just games. It was a home away from home, just like the park. My own home was a nightmare, and Ben gave me a place to call home.

"Hey, Holl!" Isaac called over. "You're up, girly." He waved me over, and I thanked Ben again, hugging the book close to me.

WHEN I GOT HOME, I plopped on my bed. I laid on my stomach and held out the book in front of me. Susan Storm, the Invisible Woman, was beautiful. She looked strong and every bit the heroine I was sure she would be. I flipped through and stopped when an image caught my eye. The words above it echoed in my head as I read them over and over again.

"I know that darling. But... But I know a lot of other things now. Things I think I've been trying to put aside, to postpone... Something a lot like growing up, perhaps. The Psycho-Man did more than twist my emotions. He forced me to look into the deepest corners of my soul, forced me to confront who I am, what have I become. When we rocketed into the cosmic ray belt, when we gained our powers, we lost something. An innocence. A child-like naivety. For a long time, I've tried to go on as if we're still the same people we used to be, As if I was still the same. But I'm not. Not after all that's happened to us. Not after what the Psycho-Man did to me. There is no Invisible-Girl anymore, Reed. She died when the Psycho-Man twisted her soul. From now on, I am the Invisible Woman!"

TEARS WELLED IN MY eyes, as I stared at the powerful woman on the page. Her story resonated deep in my bones, and I knew Ben sensed it too. I never talked about my home life much, and maybe that was all he needed to know to figure out it wasn't good. Somehow, he saw right through the mask I put on display for the world. It comforting to know I had someone like that in my corner. I needed it more than he probably even knew. I felt this connection to her that I knew was silly, but I needed to read more and know her better. I read that comic a dozen times that night and every time I did, I felt less and less alone. I felt another part of my soul start to heal. I got up and went to my easel, getting a new canvas. I pulled out the colors I wanted and got to work creating my own version of the Invisible Woman.

Chapter 12

Isaac
Spring Senior Year

 The spring air made everything feel alive again. It was like a weight had lifted and the world was breathing for the first time in months. With graduation coming up, there was a giddiness and excitement that lingered. I couldn't help but smile thinking about all the places, and all the things the years had brought. Childhood didn't seem so far behind, but adulthood lingered over us. Most people in our school were going to college, some were staying and attending community college. My fate was sealed in the garage, and I tried my best to think about it as positively as possible. I never could shake the trapped feeling despite that.

 I pulled into Holly's driveway, the truck packed with blankets and a radio for the movie. Honking a couple times, I leaned over and unlocked the passenger door. When she walked out of the house, I pulled the latch on the door, opening it wide for her. She hopped in, smiling at me warmly.

 "Hey," I smiled.

 "Hey, yourself." She winked back. "What movies are showing tonight?"

 "I think it's *Scream* and *Halloween*."

 "Perfection." She raised her fingertips to her mouth, making a chef's kiss and laughed, propping her feet up on the dash. Her worn out white converse weren't so white anymore and her jeans had more holes in them from the skate park. She wore a black tank top underneath one of my zips up hoodies that hung off her shoulder. The cuffs had holes in them where her thumbs poked out. I turned the volume up on the radio and we spent the entire drive singing along, terribly.

We had our pick of places, so we went front and center. I put the truck in park and bounced out, helping Holly out the passenger side. I handed her some cash, and she bounced away towards the concession stand. While she was gone, I got to work setting up the blankets in the bed of the truck, propping up our pillows, and I even got some lights to hang around the inside of the bed. They twinkled in the twilight, and I stepped down, admiring my handiwork.

"Isaac, it's beautiful!" I heard her squeal behind me. "The lights are a nice touch." She put the snacks down, grabbed onto my shoulder and hurled herself up. I watched as she settled in, wiggling until she found that perfect spot.

"Perfection." I winked, giving her the same chef's kiss. A blush crossed her cheeks as I settled in next to her. The cartoon advertisements danced across the screen and Holly laughed at them like she did every time we came here. I watched her raptly, taking in every feature. The fear of the future our friendship had was overwhelming. Rather than fretting about the ending of it, I tried my absolute best to savor every minute I had with her. I think deep down I always knew what we had was finite.

"Hey," she elbowed me.

"What?" I looked down at her.

"Remember that one time you punched that asshole that wouldn't leave me alone?"

"Which time?"

"Huh?" Her brows knit together.

"There was the kid at the skate park and then the dumbass here."

"Oh yeah!" She beamed. "I forgot all about the skate park kid."

"I don't think I could forget about anyone that did anything to you." She turned, looked at me with a heaviness in her eyes.

"You're like my own knight in shining armor." Her lips quirked up.

"I know. I think it's my life purpose, princess." She stiffened next to me, turning away.

"Please don't call me that." I raised my hands in surrender.

"Yes, ma'am." I saluted and she laughed, relaxing back into me as the opening credits started. The crinkle of the plastic licorice bag and gasp from Holly when she jumped were the only sounds on top of the movie playing in front of us. It was a comfortable quiet, but it felt heavy, like it was the start of a goodbye I wasn't ready to say. Halfway through the movie, Holly twitched by my side. Looking down, her eyes were closed, and the licorice abandoned by her side.

"Hey," I nudged. She stirred, rubbing the back of her neck.

"Sorry," she smiled, cheeks flushed.

"Do you want to stay? I can take you home if you want to sleep." She shook her head, stuffing a string of black licorice in her mouth.

"Question?" I asked.

"Answer," she responded, eyes still on the movie.

"What are you doing after graduation?" She stilled, slowly turning to me. "I know you've been talking about Boulder, but are you really leaving?" She sighed, putting the bag next to her and pulling her knees into her chest.

"Yeah, I need to. I want to get my art out there, you know?" I nodded. "There isn't much for me here after graduation. Not really."

"Right." The pain of her words cut through me like a razor. Trying to hide my hurt, I leaned my head back on the cab of the truck, everything I wanted to say dying somewhere between my head and my heart. I couldn't make her stay. And I couldn't make it harder for her to leave, either. So, I swallowed my pride and wrapped my arms around her. The soft, clean scent of her hair had a hint of sweetness, and I let it overwhelm me. The freckles that danced across her face etched their way into my memory. I latched onto it like it was my lifeline.

"Will I see you again?" I had to know. I couldn't live with the unknown of the coming days. Was it really the end?

"I don't know." She whispered. "I wish I did." I brushed away the lone tear that escaped down her cheek with my thumb.

"Promise you won't forget me when you make it big?"

"I don't think that's possible." She laughed. "You have been my whole world since we were six. Promise you won't forget about me?"

"Holly," I straightened, pulling her closer to me. "I won't forget a single second. You're everywhere for me. I can't even go to the store without thinking about how gross you are for liking black licorice." She gasped, slapping my chest playfully.

"Not fair!" She squealed as I tickled her ribs.

By the end of the second movie, I don't think there was any space between us. She was piled on my lap as I held her through the credits. The cars started to leave one after another, but she stayed still. Her eyes were open, but distant and I could feel her heart pounding.

"You, OK?" I brushed the hair out of her face. She nodded, turning to sit back next to me. We packed up the blankets and pillows and I rolled the lights back up. As I opened the passenger door for her, she turned and looked at me. Before I could say anything, her arms were around my neck, her head buried into me. I wrapped my arms around her waist, holding her tight. We stayed there, in each other's arms until she broke away, tears in her eyes.

"Holly." I wiped my fingers over her cheeks. Cupping my face in her hands, her lips gently met mine in a chaste kiss. The small touch left me breathless and heartbroken. Even though we still had time before graduation, I knew this was it. She was going to vanish from my life and leave me to pick up the pieces of my heart she would inevitably leave behind.

Chapter 13

Holly

I set the silverware on the table, lost in my dreams about Boulder and leaving this town for good. Mom brought in three glasses of water and set them down on the table. The air was thick with tension. It had been consistently for months now. She gave me a sad look, squeezed my shoulder gently and went back into the kitchen. Dad's footsteps thudded down the stairs, elevating my heart rate with every step. Would he always have this power over me? No. I was leaving. As soon as I walked across that stage. Classes were done, and I was free, but I wanted to walk with Isaac. I owed him that much. Three more days. I made it this far already, I could do it.

"Dinner smells great." Dad said as he sat in his seat at the table. Mom came in and put his plate in front of him, and I went in to plate our food. I would miss Mom's cooking, but I knew enough to get by on my own. Plus, the job I had lined up in Boulder was at a bakery, and I was excited to learn even more. I smiled, the taste of freedom making my mouth water. I took our plates to the table, setting Mom's down first and sitting down in front of mine.

"Thanks, princess." Dad said, smiling down at me. "Let's say grace." I watched as he took Mom's hand as she reached for mine. I held hers gently but swallowed as my dad's calloused touch sent spikes of adrenaline through me. His wicked grin, aimed at me, made my head spin. He gripped my hand in his, and closed his eyes, hanging his head. Mom followed suit, blind to the monster that lurked beneath the surface. I never knew if she was willingly ignorant, or he was really good at hiding what he did. She was away for work so much, and I never had the courage to tell her. They fought, a lot, but he never hit her that I saw.

"Father, thank you for this meal and the hands that prepared it. Thank you for family, for love and for your many blessings. Watch over us as we prepare Holly for her adult life. Keep her safe and close, always. Amen." Mom squeezed my hand before she let it go, but Dad lingered, and his eyes raked over my body. I smiled, pulled my hand free and tried my best to eat the food on my plate. The table was quiet as dinner went on, and I helped clear the dishes from the table once we were done eating.

Mom and I worked in the kitchen, cleaning up dishes and putting away leftovers. Her forced smiles and empty conversations filled the silence between us. Once the last plate was dry, I wiped my hands on the towel and headed upstairs to my room. I needed to escape the heaviness of being around my parents. With Mom's apathy and Dad's monstrosity, it was too much. I felt a little guilty for not telling them about my plans after graduation, but I knew if I told my mom my plans, my dad would easily coax it out of her. I couldn't risk him me. I needed to end the cycle of horror that surrounded him. The verbal abuse towards mom and the sickening trauma he inflicted on me was enough for several lifetimes. The promise of freedom didn't completely take away from the heaviness of leaving. Saying goodbye to Isaac was something I was not prepared for. He had been my rock for most of my life so far and leaving him behind was going to shatter me. I changed into my painting clothes and got the supplies I wanted out.

I sat in front of my canvas, hoping some inspiration would come to me. My mind replayed all the scenes of my life up to this point, the good and the bad. When I finally got a picture in my head, I got to work. Colors blended together perfectly as my brush glided over the canvas. The image in my head came to life before my eyes. I worked the brush over the canvas until my eyes grew heavy and my body started to ache. I set the brush in the water cup on my easel and stretched my arms over my head, twisting to get the ache out of my back. Grabbing my robe, I headed to the bathroom to shower. I turned the water on as hot as it would go and let the steam fill the room. I watched my reflection, I hardly recognized myself anymore. I had dark circles under my eyes, and my face didn't have the summer color I was used to. My freckles still peppered my nose and my cheeks. I traced the patterns delicately before I slipped out of my clothes and into the shower. I washed the day off of me and let the hot water run over my skin. I melted into it and breathed deeply, in and out.

Once the water lost its intensity, I turned it off and reached for my towel. I dried off and wrapped it tightly around me. I toweled off my hair and pulled on my fluffy robe. Hanging the towel back up to dry, I pulled the door open and stepped back out into the hallway. The house was quiet, but I could hear the noise of the TV in the background as well as Mom and Dad talking softly. I tiptoed back to my room, put on my sleepy pants and hoodie then crawled into bed. My eyelids were heavy, and my body was tired. I let sleep wrap me in its warm embrace.

My door creaked open, waking me, and those familiar footsteps fell into my room one sure step at a time. He was sober tonight. I squeezed my eyes shut, bracing for whatever he wanted with me. The sound of his breathing filled the space, his metal belt buckle echoing in my head. Cold bombarded me as he ripped the covers off and straddled me, pinning me down. One hand cupped my mouth, the other held my wrists above my head. He lowered himself onto me, his scent inescapable.

"Shhh." He stroked my hand with his thumb. "Can you be a quiet little princess tonight, Holly?" I nodded. "Mmm. That's my good little princess." His hand moved from my mouth and to his belt, whipping it from his pants. I stayed still, hoping to keep his violence at bay. He carefully wrapped his belt around my wrists, fastening it to the headboard. I tried to keep my breathing still and my eyes closed, leaving my body limp. His calloused hands teased the hem of my hoodie and slid up my rib cage. He reached my breasts, squeezing hard. I whimpered and tried to move from under him, but his weight was too much.

He sat up, his hand flying across my face. The sting made my eyes water and my stomach turn. I turned my head away from him, towards the painting I was working on. I felt him move off of me, stripping my pants off as he did. The sound of ripping of fabric mixed with his heavy breath made my skin itch. I laid there in front of him in my hoodie and panties, desperate to cover myself. I willed myself to look anywhere but at him. His hands slid up my hips, pulling the fabric of my panties to the side. He growled and moved over me, forcing my legs apart with his knees. I pulled my wrists, trying to loosen the belt, but it was too tight. My fingers tingled and my shoulders ached. I bucked my hips trying to throw him off, but he just laughed.

"You needy little princess." He backhanded my cheek again, making stars erupt in my vision. I wished he would hit me hard enough to knock me out. At least then I wouldn't remember the feel of his dick inside of me. His hands gripped my hips, hard over the bruises that were still there from the last time he raped me. My chest shook with tears that started to run freely down my face. His hand ran through my hair, pulling it tight. Without warning, he slammed into me, and it took everything I had in me to suppress my scream. He slammed in and out of me without any restraint. He was a feral monster taking every last bit of me he could. I felt like I was being ripped in half and my silent cries shook my entire body. His hand moved from my hip to my throat and squeezed. My body trembled and my vision blurred. The creaking of my door sounded over his heavy breaths and skin slapping skin. I opened my eyes just enough to catch a glimpse of my stunned mom outside the door.

Her eyes were wide, and her hand covered her mouth. Then she was gone, and my vision was filled with my dad's face, drenched in the pleasure he was robbing from me. His hand tightened around my throat painfully, and his pace quickened. His gaze met mine as his cock twitched as he came hard, panting. As he released my throat, I glared up at him, anger and hurt consuming me. I leaned forward, him still inside me, and spit all the moisture I could muster on his devilish face. My fear for him was overcome by an overwhelming desire to prove to myself that he didn't take everything from me.

His eyes darkened as he wiped the spit off of his cheek. He pulled out of me, dragging his finger through his come and pushed it into me. I squirmed and flailed to get away from him, but he gripped my cheek and shoved his finger into my mouth. I gagged as his taste invaded me, his finger swirling around my mouth. Without a second thought, I met his eyes, glaring, and bit down as hard as I could until I tasted copper. He screamed, jumping off of me and clutching his bleeding finger.

"You bitch." He muttered. I laid there, still tied to the headboard, blood and come running from my mouth. He hitched up his pants and stumbled out of the room. Without him on top of me, I was able to move and use my teeth to undo the belt around my wrists. They were raw and sore. I needed to get to the bathroom, so I crawled down the bed and pulled my robe on, cinching it closed. The hall was clear, so I ran to the bathroom, locking the door behind me. I stared at the mess I saw in the mirror, a feral smile taking over my pale face. My eyes were wet and the ghosts of the tears I shed stained my face. Blood soaked my lips. I ran my finger through it, feeling the stickiness and tasting it. Staring at my reflection, I drew my finger through the blood on my mouth drawing a sadistic looking smile on my face. A maniacal laugh shook its way through me as I spit into the sink. I had to take control of my life. I had to leave. Not in a few days, tonight. I washed myself up, determination coursing through my blood. I busted out of the bathroom and into my bedroom, grabbing anything I could and stuffing it into my backpack. I leaned down onto the floor, reaching under my bed for the locked box I had my money in. I folded up the cash, ditching the box on my bed, and putting a clean pair of sweatpants on.

    I shouldered my backpack, opened my window, and threw one leg over. A cold hand wrapped around my wrist, and I jolted, jerking my arm back, nearly losing my balance. My mom's face was twisted in pain and maybe guilt. I relaxed just enough to give her a nod.

    "Holly." She whispered. "I'm sorry." She shook her head, as if that would erase what she witnessed earlier. I shook my head and looked her in the eye.

    "It's too late for that, Mom." I watched a lone tear escape and trail down her flushed cheek. She let go of my hand, only to look down at her own left hand. She tugged off the diamond ring that was supposed to represent love and commitment and handed it to me.

    "Take it. Please. Use it to help you get on your feet." I glanced down at the ring and back up at her. Her silent pleas tugged at my heartstrings, and I quickly took it from her. She nodded, helped me the rest of the way out of the window, and watched as I leaped down. Landing on the cool spring grass, I looked ahead at the road and took off in a sprint, not sparing the house of horrors behind me a second glance.

Chapter 14

Isaac

Graduation was supposed to be an exciting day. It was the day we got to be free, be adults, and figure out life for ourselves. It wasn't supposed to feel like a goodbye I wasn't ready for. I knew this day was going to come. She had told me as much. As soon as we graduated, she was moving to Boulder. She said it was for her art, but I knew there was something else to it. There had to be. It was eating me alive not knowing what would happen to us. We'd grown up together, saved each other, and been through hell and back. And for what? If I could follow her around the world I would, but with the garage becoming mine to manage and my dad to babysit I couldn't bring myself to do it. I was sitting in a prison of my own making, and I hated it. I guess we all need to grow up at some point.

Name after name was called across the stage and we all went up, shook hands and grabbed a piece of paper. When Holly's name was called, no one went up on the stage. People clapped, because that's what they do. But an emptiness flooded my mind, and my heart shattered in my chest. She was already gone, and she took my soul with her. When I looked back at the empty stage, I decided then and there that if I wasn't good enough for her to stay, I would move on with my life. If she couldn't look me in the eye and say goodbye, I knew she wrote this town off and everyone in it. Every moment with her from the years flashed before my eyes. Over the years, the life and spark in her eyes had faded for everyone else, except for me. I was the lucky one who got to see those moments. To see her laugh, and cry and create a life in her dreams. Those moments would have to be enough for me because I wasn't for her to want to stay.

We all walked across the graduation stage without her. I came here today as a kid and am leaving it a broken shell of a man. I met my dad outside the auditorium, and he shook my hand and actually hugged me. I returned the sentiment, and we walked out the door to his truck. Pulling off my cap and gown, I threw it in the backseat and climbed in the passenger side. We drive in a tense silence for miles.

"Are you ready to start learning more about the garage?" He asked, shifting gears. His hand rested on the gearshift and trembled. His drinking had made his body betray him. He was a broken, shell of the man he once was. I looked at his hand, then at him and shrugged. My prison bars felt like they were closing in on me. I was trapped in this life, with no simple was out. He chuckled humorlessly and shook his head.

"I thought we were past this teenage angst bullshit."

"Sorry." I caved, wanting this conversation to end before my mouth got carried away.

"Where was your girlfriend today, by the way?" I scrunched up my nose, his mediocre attempt at caring was too little too late.

"She has a name. It's Holly. You should know that. We've been friends since we were six." I looked over at him and a wave of sadness washed over him for a split second. Resolve took its place, and he cleared his throat, shifting in his seat. "She left for Boulder already."

"She skipped graduation. Sorry, kid. I knew you were close." Anger swept over me like a swift summer wind. It took everything I had to not yell and scream everything flooding my head. I gave in, needing to release the tension in my body and the ache in my chest.

"Do you though?" I spit.

"Do I what?"

"Know that we were close. You didn't even remember her name a fucking second ago, you useless alcoholic." My fists clenched in my lap as I stared at him. My chest rose and fell with angry breaths. His eyes were wide, and his knuckles white across the steering wheel. We sat in silence for what felt like hours. Locked into each other, years of resentment spilling over the threshold of what my head could handle. I would always be a kid in his eyes, with immature and silly problems. All he cared about was my two good hands to use a wrench for his own profit. He didn't deny anything I just said to him. That fact alone was the proof I needed that he knew. He knew he wasted his life and our relationship. He didn't need to say the words

He pulled in the driveway and barely put it in park before I bolted out and into the house. I needed to get away from him as fast as possible. He didn't chase me and didn't try to stop me. I am not sure if I wanted him to. I just wanted to go to sleep. Plopping down on my bed, I rolled over and pulled out the joint that was hidden in my headboard. I got it from a friend at the skate park and was saving it for after graduation. It was going to be our way to celebrate, but I had to celebrate alone. So, I did.

I woke up to my mattress dipping under someone's weight. Still reeling from the joint, I shot up expecting messy red curls. The sight of my dad's face was peering into mine instead. Mad at myself, I flopped back down looking at the ceiling.

"Isaac, did you smoke in here?" There wasn't accusation in his tone, only concern which was odd. I figured he would kick me out, and maybe I was even hoping for a fight.

"Yes." I waited for the fireworks, but they never came.

"Do you know why I started drinking?" The question made me sit up, look at him and try to figure out his motive. My brain was still foggy. He wasn't giving anything away easily. His face was stone cold.

"I always assumed it was because Mom died," I answered, swallowing the lump in my throat. He looked up at the ceiling and back at me slowly like the words would be written somewhere in the space between us.

"Partly, yes, I suppose it was that. Her death was hard on me, sure." His face fell and he looked so stricken with loss and sadness. I don't think he had ever brought her up before. "But I think it was mostly because I didn't know how to be a parent without her. She loved you so much. I didn't have a clue what to do after she died." His honesty was a punch to the gut. "I wasn't prepared to live on my own with a kid to raise, and I was too proud to ever admit it."

"So, you blame me for the mess you made with your life?"

"No. I blame myself for the mess I made with both of our lives. She always wanted more for you and for me too, in a way. She was proud of the garage and poured her heart and soul into it. Probably even more than I ever did. It's why I want you to be a part of it. I never asked you what you wanted because I never imagined anything different than you by my side. Somewhere along the way, I royally fucked it all up." Stunned, I stared at him as he got up.

"What am I supposed to do with that?" Defeated, I looked at him for answers. Why was he talking to me about this now?

"I don't know, Isaac. Honesty is not my strong suit, and emotions sure the hell aren't either. I guess, just try to understand."

"Understand what? How you neglected me my whole life, never showed any interest in me, drank my childhood away, and gave up? I think I understand that perfectly." Anger coated the words I spewed at him. Fuck his feelings.

"I suppose you probably do understand all that. Saying sorry isn't something that will fix it, either. All I'm asking is for you to not give up on me." He turned towards the door and walked away. "Next time you get high, at least burn some incense or something. It stinks in here." Then, he was gone. He left me with that giant bomb to stew.

"Why does everyone do that to me?!" I grabbed my pillow, brought it to my mouth, and screamed as loud as I could until my throat burned, and tears streamed down my cheeks. Would I recover from this? Could I live with myself knowing I wasn't good enough for Holly or my dad? I had to. Because somewhere deep inside my head and my heart I hoped she would come back.

Chapter 15

H*olly*
10 years Later

My high heels clicked loudly on the linoleum floor in the foyer of the funeral home. I forced myself to breathe as I looked at all the people coming in and talking to each other. Everyone looked at each other with sympathy and sadness. The heavy atmosphere was suffocating. I wiped the sweat off my clammy palms onto my dress. Forcing myself to move forward, I took another step into the building. People hugged me and told me they were sorry and honestly, I barely even knew those people. Their faces were a blur in the chaos of my mind.

Walking into the main area where the casket was, I locked eyes with my mother. She smiled flatly at the woman talking to her and excused herself from the conversation they were having. She walked over to me, wrapping her arms around me. I stood there, motionless. I didn't know what to feel or how to react. Her husband was dead. People were mourning, sharing stories with each other. All I could think about was the monster that came into my room at night and stripped me of my innocence. All I could feel was his hands wrapped around me in ways no father's should ever be. Bile rose up into my throat and threatened every one of my senses. I gently hugged my mom back.

"I'm so sorry." I said softly into her hair. She let go of me and cupped my face in her hands.

"Me too, Holly." She wiped her tears and took my hand, walking up to the casket. I trailed behind her, and as we got closer, my heart raced. It felt like the walk was miles long. My throat closed up as I tried to force myself to breathe. I didn't want to make a scene, but my body was betraying me like it always had when it came to him. The room spun around me and the only thing tethering me to the moment was my mom's hand in mine, guiding me forward.

When we got to the casket, I let go of her, gripping the side of the frame. He looked nothing like I remembered. His skin looked like plastic, and his clothes were pressed and perfect. I stared at the shell of the man that was my father. Anger rolled through me in waves and my body heated. I couldn't move. I just stood there, the only words that I could think to say was "fuck you" but the words died in my throat. They wouldn't mean anything to him now anyway. It wouldn't hurt him as badly as I wanted it to. I just hoped his soul was rotting somewhere miserable.

Mom gently stroked my back bringing my attention back to where I was and how many eyes were on me. I turned away from him and stood next to my mom staring blankly ahead of me. Anger turned into relief, and then turned into numbness. My mind went to the safe place inside my head, the place where no one could reach me. I lingered there as people walked in, paid their respects and found their seats in the room. I smiled and thanked everyone the best I could as they came through. His corpse behind us burned holes into me like he was watching me, waiting in the shadows. My skin was flushed, and I desperately fought my desire to run as far away as possible. I came for closure, but the old wounds still festered.

"I'm so sorry for your loss, Holly." An older woman stood in front of me. I smiled at her, trying to hold it together.

"Thank you," I answered softly, reaching around her to return her hug. My eyes caught a pair of emerald ones in the doorway. My breath caught as his gaze burned into me. I let go of the woman, breaking eye contact with Isaac. My heart beat heavy in my chest. I wasn't prepared to face him. I left him high and dry after graduation. My need to get away hurt him, and I don't know if we could ever come back from that. I gave him wounds of his own. As if today wasn't overwhelming enough. He walked slowly down the aisle towards us, stopping to talk to a few people on the way. His eyes were the same shade of emerald, green I always got lost in. Soft lines formed around them, showing just how much time had passed between us. When he smiled, they crinkled and made him look carefree and happy. His work in the garage had paid off. He was lean, with broad shoulders and sun-kissed skin. His hair was longer on top but cropped close on the sides. He was the perfect mix of the kid I knew and the kind of man I imagined he would be. I watched with bated breath, trying to find an escape from this.

"Jenn, Holly," he greeted us. He hugged my mom tightly. He let go of her, his jaw tensing. "I'm so sorry."

"Thanks for coming, Isaac. It means a lot." She patted his arm and glanced my way. He followed her eyes, and his gaze fell to me again. He was stunning. He wasn't the eighteen-year-old I left behind. He was tall and strong. He filled out his button-down shirt perfectly, unlike the lanky kid he had been. I was an idiot for leaving him behind. I swallowed hard as his arms wrapped around me. The spicy scent of his cologne filled the air, and I breathed it in, basking in it. He stroked the back of my hair gently and I closed my eyes, embracing his touch. It was electrifying. Too soon, he let go and stood up in front of me, a heaviness in his eyes that was never there before. Did I cause it? I don't think I would ever forgive myself for being the reason behind his pain.

"Thanks for being here." I managed to choke out.

"Of course," he smiled softly. "I wouldn't miss it." At that, he walked away and found a seat towards the back, his eyes never leaving me. The funeral home manager came up to us and let us know it was time to start the service. My mom nodded and we found our seats in the front.

I barely heard anything that was said about my dad. It was all a lie anyway. No one knew what he was like, what he did behind closed doors. As much as I wanted to stand up and tell everyone what a monster he was, I couldn't. It was my pain to bear and my shit to work through. I'd let the people believe the lies. I silently let these people mourn a man that ruined me. I stared blankly ahead while the service ran its course. At one point my mom took my hand in hers, squeezing gently. It was supposed to be a comfort, but it wasn't. She was just as guilty as he was.

One by one, people came up and shared stories about my father. Some people cried, others smiled, and some even laughed. Anger started to roll through me again. Hearing those happy memories and stories of how amazing he was made my skin crawl. Nausea was brimming under the surface of my carefully crafted mask. I was the only one who was traumatized by this monster. Bitter tears streamed down my face, and I had to bite my lip to keep from screaming. I was alone in my misery, again. I felt like I was sixteen being torn apart by the man who was supposed to protect me all over again. Even in death he still tormented me. There was no escape from the damage he inflicted on me, no matter how fast or how far I ran.

The preacher dismissed us, and the pallbearers came up to carry his casket outside. Mom and I were the last ones to leave and as we walked out towards the doors, I brushed past Isaac in the foyer before heading outside. His simple touch made my body feel like it was on fire. His eyes on me were soft and gentle. My heart longed for his comfort. I turned and stopped in front of him.

"I'll meet you outside, mom," I said over my shoulder. She nodded and disappeared through the doors. "Isaac," I choked. He cupped my face in his hand and brushed my tear-streaked cheek gently.

"Shh, little girl." He smiled. "It's OK." My heart melted and new tears burned my eyes. I fell into his strong arms, and let the tears fall. My whole body shook as I sobbed into him. He held me tight, letting me let go of everything I was holding back. All the regret, the anger, the hurt cascaded out of me in a waterfall of emotions. He was there like he always had been, as if nothing had changed. As I started to calm down, I leaned away from him gazing into his captivating green eyes.

"Let me drive you." He said. I nodded, grateful that he always knew exactly what I needed even after years apart. He took my hand and led me out to the parking lot. He opened the passenger door for me and helped me inside. The cabin smelled like him, spicy and strong. I breathed him in slowly, trying to calm myself down more. My head was starting to pound, and my body ached. He walked around and climbed in next to me after he put the orange flag on the top of the truck. It roared to life, and we slowly rolled into the procession. We sat in silence for the ten minutes it took to get to the cemetery. The tension between us pulled at my heart. There were so many things left unsaid between us. I swallowed the lump in my throat as we parked in the long line of cars.

"Are you going to be OK?" He asked, looking over at me hesitantly. I wanted to scream the truth at him. I wanted him to know how relieved I was that my father was dead, and how angry I was that he died without knowing how much I hated him. Instead, I just nodded my head and opened the door, hopping out. My heels sunk into the grass as I walked around the hood and followed the rest of the crowd to the canopy over the open grave.

The smell of dirt and flowers filled the air. My mom sat in the chairs by the casket, and I sat next to her. The pastor talked about death not being the end of the story and how we would be reunited with our loved ones again one day. The words of comfort for the rest were torture for me. I shifted uncomfortably in my chair as the service ended. People slowly trickled out, and eventually, it was just my mom and me, Isaac, waiting behind us. Her face was blank as she stared at the casket being lowered into the ground. Slowly, she stood and walked towards the gaping hole in the ground, grabbed a handful of dirt, and tossed it in. I stood up after her, watching her leave to go to her car without a word. I glanced over at Isaac, who was still waiting, watching me. Nausea curled in my stomach. Resolved to end this, I tore my eyes away from Isaac and back at the casket in the ground. Leaning over, I gather all the moisture in my mouth and spit it directly in the middle of the casket. I took a rose from one of the flower arrangements littering the area, tucked it into my hair, and walked away.

Chapter 16

Isaac

Sitting at my desk, my thoughts wandered to the woman that showed back up into my life after ten long years. I was shocked to see her, and even more shocked at how much she had changed. Watching her at the funeral raised so many more questions than answers about what happened years ago. After she vanished, her family went dark on me. They weren't at graduation, and I never heard from them again. I tried to talk to them, but they always shut me out. Her dad got sick and then the rest was history. I had heard that Jenn had moved out shortly after Holly left, but I didn't know where and took the hint to stop looking. It was hard to not take any of it personally, because I was left in the dark. Which is why I was shocked to see Jenn standing in the doorway of my office.

"Hey," she waved awkwardly.

"Hey, Jenn. Come in." I stood up and gestured to the seat across from my desk. She walked in, setting her bag down and sinking into the chair. She took a deep breath, looking at anything but me. "How are you doing?"

"If I told you, you wouldn't believe me." She sighed. I leaned back in my chair, crossing my arms over my chest.

"Try me."

"I'm glad, Isaac. I'm glad he is gone." Her confession wasn't a surprise to me, based on how she and Holly acted at the funeral. "I'm glad Holly came." She looked down at her hands in her lap.

"Me too. It was good to see her."

"Isaac," she looked up with tired eyes. "I have a favor to ask."

"OK?"

"Will you come and attend the reading of his will? It is going to be hard on Holly."

"And me being there will make it easier?"

"No, probably not." She laughed. "But you have always been a safe place for her. Something I wasn't. She is going to need the support." A deep sadness radiated off of her. She had the same freckles and curls that Holly did, but the glow was gone. Weariness and regret had taken its place. Wrinkles had formed over her clear blue eyes. They were watery and unfocused like it took everything she had to come to me today. Her helplessness tugged at my heart. How could I say no?

"When is it?"

"It will be tomorrow morning at the law office in town. Ten am."

"I'm not sure she is going to want me there. She hasn't spoken to me in ten years. Apart from the funeral yesterday, anyway. She seems pretty closed off to everyone."

"I know." Her eyes wandered again as she shifted uncomfortably in the chair. "There are things that happened to her that drove her away. It isn't my place to tell you what happened, but I think she may come around to you. She has a lot of healing to do, and the fact that she even showed up to the funeral means a lot. It isn't going to be pretty, and I know she will fight it with everything she is."

"And you won't tell me what happened?" I racked my brain, trying to think of anything that would make sense.

"No, I can't. I need to rebuild my trust with her, too. Going behind her isn't going to help that. It's her story to tell." She reached into her bag and pulled out an envelope. "Here," she set it down on the desk. "I found these in her room, and I think you should have them." I picked it up and opened it. Memories flooded my head like a violent waterfall. All the pictures from the Polaroid smiled at me like ghosts of another life. I set the envelope back down on the desk, clearing my throat.

"Thank you, Jenn. I didn't realize you still had these."

"I took them when I moved out." Her smile twitched behind her haunted expression.

"Tomorrow, at ten, then?" I asked.

"Yes. Here is my cell phone number if you need it, along with directions to the office." She put a post it down on my desk, stood up and grabbed her bag. "Isaac?" She asked as she turned to leave. "Be patient with her, OK?" I nodded and smiled a gentle smile as she walked out.

I let out an exhale, running my fingers through my hair. "What the hell is happening?"

I definitely couldn't focus on work after that, so I grabbed some of the paperwork I needed to look over and my laptop and headed out to the lobby of the garage. "Hey, Leah, I am going to take an early day. I'll have my phone on me if you need anything, OK?" She gave me a thumbs up and I walked out the main doors. I felt like Jenn had dropped a major bomb on me, but I still didn't know anything or how to help Holly. If she even wanted my help.

I drove home, picking up Chinese food on the way. I set the food in the kitchen and then dumped the rest of my stuff onto the table. Food first, processing all of the pieces to the puzzle I was just dropped into would need to wait. I couldn't stop the onslaught of questions I had running through my head. Why did Holly's mom wait a decade to talk to me? What was behind Holly's reaction at the graveside? What am I missing from the years I knew her? What was I in for letting Jenn rope me into this?

I continued to stuff the Chinese food in my mouth while my thoughts ran through me like a freight train. I couldn't get Holly out of my head. I worked so hard to get over her leaving, all for her to invade all of me all over again. She wasn't the girl that left me at that drive-in that had me questioning our future together. She was a woman with more baggage than I ever realized, and I wasn't sure if I was ready to take all that on. Was I ready for her to break my heart again? Would I be able to survive history repeating itself? I already knew I wouldn't be able to stay away, especially now that Jenn asked me to be there for her at the lawyer's office. I hung my head and rubbed my eyes, willing myself to be prepared for what this was going to do to me. Holly was always worth it, and I wouldn't trade our time together for the world. My world was a little bigger now that I wasn't a kid anymore, though. I couldn't help but wonder what I would end up trading in this time around.

Chapter 17

H*olly*

The lawyer's office was stale and intimidating. I walked in, dreading the process of dealing with whatever my father left behind. I wanted nothing to do with it and to leave as soon as possible. I just needed to tie up the loose ends here, and I would go back to my own version of reality. I ditched the heels for a pair of flats, left my hair down, and dressed as comfortably as possible without looking like a complete bum. Not that he deserved any of that, but I had to keep my own self-respect together for the sake of my own sanity. I was already on the verge of losing it just by being there.

My mom was waiting on one of the chairs in the hallway, so I made my way over to her, nodding my head to acknowledge her. I knew that she wasn't the true villain, but she wasn't innocent either and I couldn't bring myself to forget that. Her lack of action despite knowing the monster she married will always come between us. She nodded back, a half-smile dancing across her features. my eyes stayed glued to the door ahead, and I did my best to calm my racing heart. My knee bounced slightly, nerves racking my body. Closing my eyes, I focused on breathing. In, and out. In, and out.

A warm, strong hand squeezed my knee, my eyes flashing open. They were met with soft, familiar ones in front of me and my heart slowed its rhythm just enough.

"Hey, Holl. It's OK. Breathe with me?" He tucked a loose curl behind my ear, his eyes never leaving mine. We took breaths together, and my nerves calmed. Isaac smiled at my mom, got up and moved to the seat next to me.

"Valles family?" The lawyer called. We stood up and followed her into the room. She gestured for us to sit in the plush chairs in front of the desk. Mom and I sat, while Isaac stood back a little bit. "My name is Ana, and I am honored to be the one to handle the affairs of your loved one." She shook our hands one by one and smiled softly. It took so much effort to not simply walk out, leaving this whole mess behind me. Like he could read my mind, Isaac's hand brushed my shoulder, the pad of his thumb moving up and down.

"His will is pretty straightforward. His financial assets, other than the house, go to Jennifer Valles." She nodded to my mom. "And the house, including everything in it, goes to his only daughter, Holly Valles." The words echoed through my head, the room spinning. No. That was not the plan. I didn't want anything tying me back here. This was supposed to be the end, not a fucked-up twist that leaves me tied to this place. My escape plan was falling apart in front of me, my grip on reality running through my hands like grains of sand.

"What if I don't want it?" I asked, interrupting whatever Ana was going over. She blinked at me and glanced at mom, unsure of how to handle the outburst.

"Well," she cleared her throat. "You can always do an estate auction for the belongings inside and then sell the house."

"How long does that take?" I asked, trying to hide the desperation in my voice.

"It could take months, honestly. I am not super well versed in the real estate market, but I could try and find you some-"

"Months?" Tears welled in my eyes. "I don't want to be here for months!" Panic started bubbling, and stars danced in my vision.

"Hey, Holly!" Isaac's hands were on my shoulders, shaking me gently. "Breathe, it's OK. We're here with you."

"What else do you need from us?" I heard mom ask Ana. My eyes stayed glued to my hands folded in my lap. Isaac stayed in front of me, keeping me centered.

"Just some signatures, but I can send them with you today, then you can mail them back to me when they're signed. They just need to be sent in within sixty days." A shuffle of paperwork and a couple handshakes whirred around me as I was guided back out to the hallway. I collapsed into a chair, my face in my hands. A mix of hurt, anger, embarrassment washed over me. Mom sat next to me, gently rubbing circles on my back. I could feel Isaac next to me, giving me space but still there. Just like he always had been.

"I'm sorry." I muttered through my hands.

"Nothing to be sorry for, Holly." Mom answered. "I didn't know he was going to leave the house to you. It was a shock for me too."

"Don't you still live there? Can I give it back to you, somehow?" Isaac and Mom shared a look, making me realize just how out of touch I had been for so long.

"I don't live there, honey. I haven't for almost eight years."

"Eight years?" Her eyes were filled with unspoken apologies and heartache. My eyes fell to the empty space on her left hand. She may have been just as guilty for being so blind to the monster she married, but she did what she thought she could to help in the end.

"Yes." She sighed. "I moved out soon after you left that night. I couldn't be there anymore. Here is all the paperwork. Sign it when you are ready, OK? I don't know if you want this, but I am going to give it to you anyway." Mom handed me the envelope of papers and got up to leave, squeezing Isaac's shoulder as she did.

"Holly, I can't pretend to know what this is doing to you, but I know what it is doing to me. I had no idea this was going to happen. If you need help sorting things out or anything at all while you are here, please let me know." She sighed, looking down at her feet. "I wasn't there for you when you needed it. I don't know how to fix it, but I want to try." At that, she smiled a sad smile, turned and walked out the door.

Isaac took her place next to me, and we sat in silence. I brushed my fingers over the sticky note. As much as I wanted to ignore her and get the hell out of town, I felt a pull towards her I never had before. Once a gentle numbness replaced all the panic and anger, I leaned my head on Isaac's shoulder. His steady breaths were soothing. He laid his head down on mine, and I let his presence soothe my bleeding heart.

He shifted after a little while, bringing my attention to Ana who crouched down in front of me. Her eyes were soft, and caring. Not what I would expect out of a lawyer.

"I'm so sorry, Holly. I can't imagine having to go through this." She looked from me to Isaac. "You can stay here as long as you need to. If you need anything, you can ask my assistant at the desk. I need to step out though. Here's my card if you have any questions about the paperwork." I nodded, took the glossy, chic card and watched her leave out of the front doors.

"You wanna get out of here?" Isaac nudged with his shoulder.

"You wanna house?" I sighed.

Chapter 18

Isaac

The regular smell of coffee and fried foods was a comfort. My nerves were going haywire, and I wasn't sure how to handle the delicate woman standing next to me. We weren't kids anymore, and she seemed more closed off than ever. The waitress behind the bar waved us in and we found a booth tucked away towards the back. Sitting across from her in the same diner felt so normal, and yet so foreign at the same time. I had convinced myself that I would never be here with her again, and had accepted that, albeit reluctantly. I watched her fidget across the table and couldn't help but smile.

"What is that look for?" She asked, looking around at the diner. It had hardly changed since she left.

"Nothing," I waved off. She frowned at me and pouted. The Holly I knew was still in there, buried beneath whatever was battling it out in her head. The waitress came over and greeted us, pulling me back to reality. I wasn't even sure if I could eat.

"What can I get you two to drink?" She smiled, her pink uniform was faded and stained with coffee, but her smile was warm and inviting. "Isaac, want your usual?"

Holly raised her eyebrow at me, but I nodded and thanked the waitress. "For you, darlin'?" Hands on her hips, she waited for Holly to respond.

"I'll have whatever he's having."

"You got it. I'll have those out. Let me know when you're ready to order food."

"Thanks, Donna." I smiled, looking back down at the menu.

"Should I be worried?" Holly asked, looking over the top of her menu at me.

"About what?"

"What did I just order?"

"Guess you'll have to wait and see." I shrugged, mindlessly looking through the menu. After a few minutes of silence, Donna brought our drinks out. Holly watched, her face unreadable. Two chocolate and strawberry swirl shakes, with two straws each sat in front of us. I watched Holly's face redden while she looked down at the shake, and back up at me. I smiled and sipped my shake.

"Why two straws?" She asked. Her hands were folded in her lap, and she looked like the shake could have been poisoned.

"I'm a creature of habit." I stretched out across the booth, eyes easy and a crooked grin painted on my face. I knew at that moment, with this broken shell of a woman across from me, that I would do everything to crack the code that is Holly Valles.

Donna came back over, ready to take our food orders.

"I'll just take a large plate of fries, I think." I winked at Donna, who smiled and turned to Holly.

"Oh, um, I think I'm good with the shake." Holly answered. Donna tucked away her pad, smiled and walked back behind the counter. Holly shifted uncomfortably in the red vinyl booth. It squeaked beneath her. I watched her carefully as I continued to sip on my shake.

"This is probably a very stupid question, but are you OK, Holl?" She sighed, looked at me and took her first drink of her shake. She visibly relaxed and nearly moaned as she did.

"I forgot how good these were." She sighed. "Honestly, I don't know. I was planning on coming to the funeral, wrapping up whatever I needed to here, and then heading back. I wasn't expecting to get the house. I have no idea what to do with it."

"You could rent it out." I offered.

"I don't even know what it looks like, or what shape it's in. I don't think I want to know."

"Where are you staying?"

"At the hotel downtown. I will probably have to see about extending my reservation."

"Can't you stay with your mom?" She stiffened and looked away.

"I don't think that is a great idea." Donna placed the fries down between us, and an extra plate to share. She winked at Holly and left us again. "We don't have the deepest relationship. I'm not sure I want to spend any more time with her than what is absolutely necessary. She was gone a lot when I was young and we never really had that mother-daughter bond." I nodded, grabbing some fries and tossing them in my mouth.

"Are you going to want anything else to eat?" I put some fries on the extra plate and slid it to her. She grinned, and leaned on the table, shoving a fry in her mouth.

"No, I haven't had much of an appetite since I've been here. This is perfect, though." We sat and ate, making some small talk. She told me bits and pieces of her life in Boulder, the bakery she worked at and the gallery she enjoyed visiting.

"Lynn has pretty much taken me under her wing since I showed up at the shelter the night I left."

"Shelter?" I asked, frowning enough to catch her attention.

"Yeah, I didn't have an apartment set up, but I knew where there was a decent shelter to go to until I got settled." She took a deep breath. "Lynn was the volunteer that night and she owns a bakery that caught my way on the bus. I asked her about it, and it turned out she was the owner. She hired me on the spot." She smiled wide. She looked proud of herself and what she did to claim her life.

"Are you still painting?"

"When I can, yeah. I work a lot, and it makes it hard sometimes, but nothing in a gallery yet."

"Relatable," I muttered.

"Did you end up taking over the garage?"

"I did. Dad is semi-retired and trying to keep his life together. I manage the garage and will own it once he decides to let go of it completely."

"Do you like it?" She asked hesitantly. Thoughts of the same conversation we had when we were young crept up. I sighed, leaning back in the booth. I stretched my arm across the back and watched Holly's eyes follow my movements and shift in her seat. Interesting.

"It's honest work. It isn't as bad as I thought it would be. The team is great, and the customers are happy with the way I've been running it." Did I like it? Sure. Was it fulfilling? Not really. I never really had a chance to explore what I would actually want to do, and I never thought about it, because I didn't want to get my hopes up. I was good at it, and that's all that mattered.

"But it isn't what you want?" She raised an eyebrow at me, stuffing more fries in her mouth, unashamedly.

"Is working at a bakery what you want?" I countered.

"I honestly have no idea." She huffed a laugh and sipped her shake. We finished our food, paid, and headed back out to my truck. I opened the passenger door for her and helped her in. Jogging around the front I hopped in and started the engine. The radio played, and music filled the cab, Holly humming along with it out of instinct. The afternoon sun shone in the windshield rendering my sunglasses useless. I popped the visor down, blocking most of it. My eyes fell to the picture clipped there and I smiled, glancing over to Holly. She turned to me and her eyes widened when she saw the picture.

"You still have this?" She reached over and unclipped it, running her fingers over our teenage faces.

"I have most of the ones we took." I couldn't help but grin at her, as little bits and pieces of those walls she worked so hard to build around her heart started to crack ever so slightly.

"I should still have some in my old room."

"All the more reason to go." Her face fell and she put the picture back up on my visor. Those walls came right back up as quickly as they started to weaken. The rest of the drive to the hotel was silent and my heart squeezed in my chest. Jenn's words rattled around in my brain. I couldn't force her to open up, or to talk to me. I had to chip away at her little by little. I was determined to, no matter the cost. Holly was in my grasp, and I wouldn't let go of her no matter the cost. She wasn't going to disappear again, not without answers.

"Thanks for the ride." She slid out of the truck as I shifted into park.

"Anytime. Hey, wait!" I called. I pulled one of my business cards out of my pocket with my cell phone number on it. "Here. This is my cell phone number. Call me if you need anything." She took it, smiled and walked into the hotel doors.

Chapter 19

Holly

H I stared at the blank ceiling for long enough. Between the house situation, and the interaction with Isaac over the last few days, my mind was tired. I was overwhelmed and I wasn't sure what to do about it. I let out a groan.

"One step at a time." I muttered to myself. I rubbed my hands over my eyes and flipped the covers of the hotel bed. I felt like a stranger there, like someone from the outside looking into the small town I once called home. Everything felt different, but the only thing that had really changed was me, and the war in my mind. With the threat of my dad being gone, this town felt empty. Wasn't it supposed to make me feel better? Was the trauma he inflicted so ingrained in me that I wasn't sure how to live without it? Looking back, I think that was one of the biggest reasons I never risked telling anyone about his abuse. In this small town, it would become my identity, and I refused to let him have that power, even in death. I don't want Isaac to see me differently if I told him what happened.

Speaking of Isaac, when did his forearms get so sexy? He wasn't the lanky kid I knew anymore. He filled out and became a man, a gorgeous one at that. His smile was the same and the skin around his eyes crinkled when he let it shine. Seeing him at the funeral was comforting, but being around him in the diner made me itch to touch him. I never allowed myself to see Isaac like that as a kid, because I feared my own body and the damage, I endured would hold me hostage. I held on to the innocence in our relationship like a lifeline. After a decade of denying myself, seeing him made my body come alive. Frustrated with myself and the betrayal of my body, I took myself into the shower and thanked the heavens that the shower had a detachable shower head.

After my shower, I slipped my clothes on and dug through my bag for my white chucks. I wasn't sure how they were still intact, but they were still holding on. I pulled them on, grabbed my wallet and phone and headed out of my hotel room. Downtown was quaint and everything was within walking distance of the hotel. I headed towards a coffee shop to get a caffeine fix and to figure out what I needed to do in order to get this old life packed away for good so I could leave.

"Good morning!" The barista welcomed me from behind the counter. The shop was cute. It had opened after I left, so I took it all in. It had a perfect mix of modern and small-town feel. The espresso machine sparkled behind the counter. The baked goods looked like they were fresh behind the glass. They had everything from muffins to traditional French macarons. My mouth watered. I had gotten spoiled working at the bakery in Boulder. Nothing was better than fresh baked goods.

"Good morning," I waved, walking up towards the counter.

"What can I get started for you?" Her smile was warm, and her brown hair was swept back in a loose braid. Her black apron had flour all over it and her cat-eyeglasses slid down her nose as she looked at her register.

"Can I get a caramel latte?" My eyes moved back to the display case. "Do you make your bakery items in house?"

"We do. I make them fresh daily." She beamed at me.

"Oh man, then I definitely need one of those Madeleines." She nodded, ringing my order up.

"The Madelines are my favorite. You'll have to let me know what you think." She took my card and got to work on my order. I found a seat in the window while I waited and pulled out my phone. What was I supposed to do now? The paperwork loomed over me. Maybe if I just ignored it, it would all go away. That was my go-to after all, right? Pretend it never happened and go to the happy place inside my head. The barista brought over my coffee and pastry, setting it down gently on the table.

"Thank you," I smiled.

"Of course. Let me know how you like it. I'm Audrey, by the way."

"Will do, thank Audrey. I'm Holly."

"Nice to meet you, Holly. Are you new in town?"

"No, I grew up here. I moved when I graduated a decade ago." I laughed.

"Well, thanks again for stopping by. Let me know if you need anything else, OK?" I nodded and she made her way back to the kitchen. I sipped my coffee, made it to perfection and let my eyes roam out to the road. It was all so familiar, but I still felt so far removed. It was like a dream or like I time traveled. It was surreal. A wave of brown hair caught my eye right before the bell chimed over the door.

"Welco-Oh! Hi Isaac. Want your usual?" My heart stuttered. I told myself not to look, to ignore him and focus on the pastry in front of me. Since when did he have the effect on me?

"Sounds good, Aud. Thanks." I kept my eyes glued to the window, but I could still see them in the reflection. Why was I responding like this? I felt like I was intruding on their personal exchange. I set my mug down, leaning back in my chair. Isaac's eyes met mine in the window and it felt like my soul erupted. He took his coffee from Audrey, thanked her and made his way over to me.

My heart beat faster with every step. What the hell was happening to me?

"Hey, Holl." He took the seat across the little round table. His knees brushed mine as he sat, and my stomach decided to do somersaults. I smiled at him and sipped my coffee. Deciding that having my mouth full was easier than making conversation, I picked up my pastry and bit into it. *Oh, sweet Jesus.* It was heaven on my tongue. My eyes rolled shut and a stifled moan escaped my lips. His eyes widened as they traveled from my eyes to my lips around the pastry and back up. *Please, God, strike me dead right here.*

"So, umm what do you have going on today?" He asked, clearing his throat. I carefully chewed my Madeline and attempted to swallow.

"I need to get some things for my hotel room. I don't want to eat out the whole time I'm here." He nodded. "I should probably sign and return those papers to the lawyer's office too." I didn't want to drag my time out there any longer than I had to. I wanted to get in, get out, and go back to Boulder, where my life was. Throwing a house to deal with and old childhood memories made things complicated. Complicated was scary, and I wanted to avoid it at all costs.

"Want me to drive you?"

"That's not necessary. The fresh air will probably do me some good." I crossed my arms across my chest, trying to be confident in my answer. "Plus, I don't want to keep you from the garage."

"Nah, they don't need me. The team basically runs itself anyway." He watched me finish my pastry and grabbed me another latte in a to-go cup. "Ready?" He asked, holding his hand out.

"What are you doing?" I didn't move.

"Not giving you an option. I can tell you aren't ready to deal with a lot of this, so let me help you. We can go get some groceries for your room." His bright smile showed off his dimples and sparkly eyes and I immediately caved. I took his hand held out to me and got up, moving towards the door. His laughter trailed behind me as I huffed out the door. Was I that easy to read? Or did he just still know me that well? I decided not to linger on those thoughts.

"See ya, Audrey!" He called over his shoulder. He tried to open the truck door for me, but I beat him to it. Smirking, I hauled myself up into the truck and slammed the door shut.

"Where to?" He asked, starting the engine.

"The grocery store." I looked intently out the window.

"Yes ma'am." He laughed. We drove the familiar streets, and I watched as the town and all the people went about their day. What would it have been like if I had a normal life here? Would I have my own place, a career, a family? It hurt to think about. I never considered having any of those things for myself. Seeing the grocery store come and go as we drove by snapped me out of my daydream.

"We just passed the store." I pointed out the window.

"Yep. Sure did."

"Did we get a new one since I left?"

"Nope." He grinned and continued to drum his fingers on the steering wheel.

"So, where are you taking me, then?"

"A different store."

"I swear to God, Isaac. I am not in the mood for-" He pulled into the tiny parking lot outside of a corner store, one I knew well. He got out of the truck, and I watched him circle around, opening my door.

"Come on," He waved. My breath was heavy in my lungs. Memories of us as kids flooded my head. I couldn't pass out. Nope, not here. *Just one foot in front of the other, Holly.* Isaac's patience was unnatural. He pulled the corner store door open, and the bell rang above us. My hands covered my mouth as I gasped. The checkered floor was the same as I remembered. The aisles were stuffed, and posters and ads lined the walls. It was exactly the same. It looked the same, smelled the same, and -

"Holly? Isaac?" An old man's voice boomed.

"Tom?" My eyes widened as he came around the counter and scooped me up in a hug. "Good to see you, kid!" His smile was infectious. His bushy mustache still made me laugh.

"Good to see you, too."

"I'm sorry to hear about your dad, kiddo." His eyes softened, but I waved him off. I didn't want thoughts of him to ruin this. Isaac had already started meandering through the aisles and stopped at the candy. He had a package of black licorice in his hand. He grabbed a package of cherry as well and headed up to the counter. I leaned against it, watching him. He had a devilish grin on his face, and I couldn't take my eyes off of him no matter how hard I tried.

"Ready?" He asked.

"For what?" I raised an eyebrow.

"I thought we could hang out and see what color cars people drive these days." My mouth dropped as he plopped down on the step outside the store, opening his bag of candy. I slowly made my way over and sat next to him. He handed me my black licorice and we sat and counted cars. Just like that, I was a kid again and he was my safe space. If I let him, Isaac could break through the defenses I set up around my heart. The question was though, did I want him to see how broken and bruised I really was?

Chapter 20

Isaac

Holly stopped trying to find excuses to not see me, eventually. I thought I had scared her off after our corner store adventure. She spent the next few days finding reasons to avoid me. I was relieved to wake up to a text this morning asking to meet for coffee. I wanted to handle her delicately, but I wasn't sure how long that would last. I wanted to be everything she needed to move on, even if that meant I had to let her go again at some point. Some part of me has always and will always love her. I will take any piece of her I can get. My entire life has been centered around taking care of the people around me. Holly being here, right in front of me, made me want to claim her and keep her here forever. I was so torn between doing what I thought was best for her and what I truly wanted to do for myself. I spent every waking moment trying to think of ways to get her to snap out of whatever daze she was living in. Something happened to her, and I needed to know what it was so I could figure out how to help her move on. Jenn wouldn't tell me, and Holly was tight-lipped about it. I didn't want to make her even more closed off. More than anything, I wanted her to open to me. I realized after watching her moan over that damn pastry, maybe I wanted her open to me in more ways than one. I had to shove those feelings out of my head, though. I was on a mission and letting my dick do the thinking was the last thing I needed.

I walked into the coffee shop, greeting Audrey while she prepared my order. Holly was sitting at the same table, with an eclair. I scrubbed my face with my hands, trying to get myself to focus on the task at hand. Operation Holly was in full effect. I couldn't stray from the task.

"Here you go, Isaac." I grabbed my wallet, but she waved me off. "Holly already paid for it." I put my wallet away, grabbed my coffee and headed over to the woman who had fully implanted herself into my brain. Again.

"Thanks for the coffee." I said as I sat down across from her.

"No problem. Want to split this eclair with me?"

"I don't think I can say no to fresh baked goods." She laughed as she carefully cut the eclair in half, judging the sizes of the two halves. She gave me the slightly bigger one.

"I'll have to bake something for you, sometime. I've learned a lot at work. I really enjoy it." She talked through a mouthful, and I couldn't keep my eyes off of her.

"I'd like that." I bit into the eclair and stifled my own moan. We locked eyes and laughed, chewing through the delicious pastry.

"You know, I bet Audrey could use some help if you were looking for something to do while you were here."

"Is the store hiring?" Her brows pinched together in thought, and my chest tightened at the idea of her considering getting a job here.

"I'm not sure. Audrey owns the place, and I have only seen her and one other girl in here." I nodded over to where Audrey was carefully arranging cookies in the case.

"What's the story there?" She asked.

"What do you mean?" She rolled her eyes over the rim of her mug.

"You two obviously have a history." I glanced at her pout, reveling in the hint of jealousy in her voice. Was she jealous? If she was, I could work with that. That gave me a crack in her walls to loosen up.

"Audrey? Nah, I just come in here all the time. The garage is about a block that way." I pointed out the window. "I come in here to do paperwork when I need to get out of the office." If I wasn't looking, I would have missed the way her shoulders relaxed at my explanation. A hint of a smile danced behind her coffee mug. I chuckled and stuffed the rest of the eclair in my mouth. "My wife is overseas teaching kids how to basketweave." The way her eyes widened into saucers made her look cartoonish. It took everything I had not to spit out the éclair I was chewing.

"Wife?" She choked, setting her mug down slowly.

"I'm kidding," I laughed. "No wife or girlfriend to speak of. And no kids, either." She looked relieved and I laughed again, letting her stew in those emotions for a little bit. "Have you signed the paperwork for the lawyer yet?"

"No, I haven't. I don't know why it is so hard to just scribble my name on a piece of paper." Her face fell, and all the humor of the previous moment faltered. A crease between her eyes formed as she looked at the contents of her mostly empty mug. "I just don't want to deal with it." She shrugged off her statement and downed the rest of her latte.

"Its closure, I guess. The last step of this process." She hummed, thinking it over. "Want me to look it all over with you? You could bring it by my office in the garage."

"Maybe." She looked up at me as she wiped her mouth with a napkin. "What do you have going on today?"

"I need to make the schedule and go over some maintenance stuff for the equipment. I should be done by three. What about you?"

"Is the skate park still there?" She smiled a wicked smile that made my heart feel like it was going to explode. I haven't seen that smile in a decade.

"Sure is. I still have our boards."

"Well, want to go and see how bad we can eat shit?"

"I can't think of a better way to spend the day. I'll text you when I leave the garage this afternoon."

"Perfect."

"DOES NO ONE LIKE TO skate anymore? This place is a ghost town." I heard Holly call while I pulled the boards out of the back of my truck.

"Some kids still do, but not like we used to. Now they all have phones." I rolled my eyes and handed her the board.

"I brought sodas." She said, a blush creeping across her cheeks. "These bottles clink." She handed me the bottle and I twisted off the cap.

"Cheers!" I held up my soda as she clinked her against mine. "You ready to get your ass handed to you?" Her eyes sparkled with mischief as she looked at me. Before I knew it, she took off in a sprint towards the bowl.

"Last one in is a rotten egg!" She shouted behind her. I took off running, but she disappeared into the bowl before I got there. I got to the edge, balanced my board and placed my feet perfectly. I dropped in, bending my knees as I flew through the concrete jungle.

"Just like riding a bike, huh?" I asked Holly as we laid down in the bowl watching the sky as the sun set behind the clouds.

"It really is. I'm sure I will be sore tomorrow though." Holly laughed, twisting a strand of her hair between her fingers. I rolled over on my side and watched her watch the sun set. The light bounced off her eyes and made them shine like diamonds. My hands ached to touch her, to trace the freckles across her nose. I wanted to breathe in her hair and memorize the feel of it through my fingers.

"Why are you looking at me like that?" She turned and smiled at me. I laughed and turned my eyes back to the sunset.

"It's hard not to look at you."

"What do you mean?"

"When we were young, I couldn't stop looking at you, Holly. Now, it's impossible."

"No, we aren't young anymore. Definitely not the kids we were. But being back here makes me feel like it." She sat up and hugged her knees to her chest, a numbness covering her expression.

"Why does that sound like a bad thing?" I asked, watching her carefully. She looked torn between two lifetimes, like she wanted to relive our favorite times together, but it cost too much of her heart. "Do you want to talk about it?"

"Talk about what?" She asked me, looking over her shoulder at me.

"Any of it." I sat up so I was next to her and brushed a stray curl behind her ear. She breathed heavily and turned her head up towards the clouds, watching them glide by.

"I'm not sad my dad is dead." I let the confession hang in the air. This was her space and her time to talk, and I didn't want to shut her down. "He was awful and fucked up and I hated him." She looked at me, eyes watery, a hint of relief in her expression. "That feels good to say out loud."

"You can say anything you need to. You know I'll listen."

"I know." She smiled, leaning her head down on my shoulder. "Can I tell you a secret?"

"Always."

"I thought you were dating Audrey." She laughed.

"That was not what I was expecting." I laughed and leaned back on my hands. I stretched my legs out in front of me. "I never really got into the dating scene." I admitted.

"Really?" She looked genuinely surprised.

"Really. With the shop and trying to figure everything out for my dad, I just never had the energy for it."

"Hmm. Interesting."

"Is it?" I watched the blush creep up her neck and cheeks.

"I just figured you'd have the wife and kids, white picket fence. Or at least a girlfriend. Wait. You're not gay, are you?"

"Definitely not." I laughed. "I have had a few casual friends with benefits, but nothing serious. What about you? Any romance in Boulder?"

"No, I'm not good at relationships." She sighed. "Although, I have a really good one with the vibrator in my sock drawer."

"What the hell, Holly?" I choked on God knows what as she cackled maniacally beside me. "Jesus Christ, woman. You can't do that to me."

"What? You said you would listen."

"Yeah, I guess I did." I shook my head, trying to get the image of Holly sprawled out, legs spread, getting herself off out of my head.

"You ready to head out?" She asked.

"Yeah. Do you want me to drop you off at the hotel or do you want to grab dinner?"

"We can grab dinner." We walked back to the truck, and I swear I didn't look at her ass the whole way. OK, maybe a little. It was going to be a long night.

Chapter 21

Isaa

I was wrapping up there when my phone rang. I dug it out of my pocket and answered it.

"Hey, Holly."

"Hey. Umm. I have a question."

"OK, hit me."

"Is the movie store we used to watch movies in still there?" I laughed and shook my head. We had been traveling full speed ahead on memory lane.

"Yes, it is actually. I think they even got new carpet recently." Silence echoed on the other end. "Holly?" I pulled the phone away from my ear, but her picture still smiled up at me.

"Yeah, sorry. I'm still here. Would you want to go there with me tonight?"

"I thought you'd never ask." She laughed and we agreed on a time to meet there. I hung up, checking the time. I had a few hours until we were going to meet. I grabbed my laptop and headed out to my truck.

When I got home, I took in the state of my house. I kept it pretty clean, but I decided to straighten things up a little bit. I worked on the dishes in the sink and made sure the bathrooms were decent and at least a little welcoming. We hadn't made plans for her to come over, but I decided I was going to ask her to. I was tired of guessing and trying to read between the lines of our conversations. I never really came out and told her how I felt when we were teenagers, and I wasn't going to make the same mistake. I wasn't going to let her leave again without knowing how I felt about her. What could possibly go wrong?

THE LITTLE STORE SAT off the main road and it lit up like a beacon in the night. I don't think I ever saw anyone there who was younger than me. I stopped in every now and then and picked up the movies we used to watch, though it had been almost six months since I'd been in. The attendant waved as I walked in and started looking for Holly. It didn't take long to find her in the horror section. She ran her fingers over the titles, a distant smile on her face.

"Do you think there are any that we haven't watched?" I asked, startling her out of her daydream.

"Probably not," she sighed. "Do you think they will let us pick one out to play on the TV?" The TV in the back of the store wasn't the same as it was when we were young, but it would do.

"Definitely. What are you thinking?" I leaned against the shelf and crossed my arms, watching her look over the titles. She looked at my arms, and then backed up to meet my eyes.

"You can't do that." She waved her arms in front of me frantically.

"Do what?" I looked over myself, trying to figure out what the hell she was upset about.

"Do the whole leaning, arms crossed, thing." Her eyes narrowed on me as I stifled a laugh.

"Well, excuse me for offending you while I was just over here existing." She huffed her hair out of her face, red and flushed and looked back to the movies. I took the opportunity to push my luck and moved behind her. I put one arm on each side of her, caging her in against the shelf. She turned, her blue eyes dark, and her chest rising and falling against me with every breath.

"Is this better?" I teased. I could hear her swallow, and her eyes moved from my face and moved down until she gasped and turned around. She pretended to look at the titles again, but I found the one we both knew she was going to pick. I leaned in, grabbed her hand and led her to the Poltergeist.

"I think we both know what you want to watch." I whispered against her hair. She shuddered and took the movie. I moved back, giving her room so she could take it to the counter.

"Can we watch this on the TV back there?" I heard her ask. "I also want to get these." I heard the plastic crinkle as she put her gross licorice on the counter. She met me in the back, and we watched the TV come to life. I sat down and leaned against the end of the shelf. Gripping her hips, I pulled her down next to me. She let out a giggle and settled in next to me. The opening credits started as she struggled to open the package of candy.

"Let me help you." I leaned over and tore open the bag.

"Thanks," she smiled, eyes lingering over my mouth. We watched the first ten minutes of the movie before she started squirming. Her leg brushed against mine and it was hard for me to focus. I gripped her knee, and she looked up at me.

"You need to stop squirming, or I am going to have to leave you here to watch this on your own."

"What?" She asked, eyes wide. "Why?"

"Because Holly. We aren't kids anymore and you have no idea what you do to me." Her eyes bounced from my eyes to my lips, to my lap and back up again. I watched as her throat bobbed and her pupils dilated in front of me.

"I'm not-" she sighed, put her licorice down and looked at me. "I'm not good at this."

"Good at what?" I watched her expression go from fear to confusion and then to lust.

"Flirty, sexy stuff." She leaned her head against the shelf, a flush of embarrassment floating across her skin.

"Holly, we don't have to do anything you don't want to do. I will never pressure you into anything, but I need you to know that I have always had feelings for you. You were my whole world when we were young, and I don't think you ever stopped. Seeing you now, after all this time, it only makes me want you more."

"Isaac?" She whispered. "Would you kiss me?" Her eyes darted to my lips and where our thighs brushed together.

"Thank, fuck Holl. I thought you'd never ask." I slid my hand up the back of her neck, closing the space between us. Our lips barely touched, and my body felt like it had been set on fire. Heat enveloped me as I traced her lips with my tongue. Her lips parted and her hand squeezed my leg. We pulled apart, panting even after a simple kiss. She looked at me with hooded eyes and I knew then that she was going to ruin me. Holly had always had my heart, and now I was going to give her my body and soul to own and use. I let her take control as she leaned into me, kissing me again. It was quick and it was chaste, but it left me breathless, nonetheless.

"Thank you." She muttered. I looked down at her. Her eyes shone and her cheeks were flushed.

"For what?"

"For being patient with me." She wiped her eyes and turned back towards the movie. "Like I said, I'm not good with this stuff and I don't want to be a tease. I want you too, Isaac. But I need to go at my own pace, OK?" I cupped her head in my hands, looking into her diamond eyes.

"I promise you, I'm not going anywhere. I will be here every step of the way, for whatever you need. You are worth the wait, Holly." I swiped the lone tear away with the pad of my thumb, pulled her into me and held her like that through the rest of the movie. Once the end credits ended, I squeezed Holly just enough to wake her. I don't know when she fell asleep, but I clung to every second I had with her there in my arms.

"Did I fall asleep?" She asked with dried drool on her mouth.

"Yeah, you did." I laughed.

"I don't want to go back to the hotel." She sighed.

"Where do you want to go?" She looked at me, twisting a curl between her fingers.

"Can I stay at your place?"

"Yeah, of course." She looked sheepish, almost embarrassed. "I have a guest room, you can stay as long as you want." She smiled, nodded and wrapped her hand in mine as we walked out to the truck.

Chapter 22

Holly

Isaac and I set up his old game system in his bedroom. He had kept all of his old games, and we decided it was time to enjoy a little more nostalgia. I swear it felt like I had time traveled these past few days. It was like we were kids again, and our world was perfect. It was a welcome distraction, and I loved every minute of it. We played Mario Kart for hours on end, only stopping to order pizza. We stayed in our sweats all day and curled up in his bed to eat.

It was perfect. He was perfect. I know the way I left him after graduation was cruel. I thought for sure I had ruined any chance we had of picking up where we left off. I hadn't even considered it as an option. He proved me wrong though. We had not only picked up where we left off, but our chemistry had changed, evolved into something so much more intense. I was too jaded when I first got back to see it, but his gaze lingered longer than normal, and his soft touches marked me. It was like he was awakening my body to endless possibilities, one long look at a time. The burn was slowly consuming me, and I had no idea what to do with it or how to act.

Isaac got up and went over to the pizza box on his dresser. He nudged a piece towards me, and I nodded, even though I had already eaten enough pizza to make me feel like I was going to bust. He plopped back down next to me, handing me my piece. He stared at me over his pizza, watching me. I blushed and focused on my pizza trying not to give my thoughts away too easily. We ate in silence, watching each other. When we got up and went to the bathroom to wash the pizza grease off our hands. I laughed as we fought over the water, and I jammed my hip into his. He laughed, a low deep laugh that made my thighs clench together and my heart rate speed up. Isaac was still *my* Isaac, but he had grown to be so much more. Isaac wasn't a kid anymore. He was all hard muscles and strong features. His eyes were the same smoldering green though. I couldn't get enough. I followed him out of the bathroom, and he stood, suddenly towering over me in the doorway.

He looked at me differently, or maybe I just had never really recognized it before. He looked at me with an insatiable desire that took over every feature. It scared me. The thought of being touched made me want to puke. I couldn't handle this with Isaac. What we had was perfect, and I didn't want my fear to ruin it. We weren't kids anymore and his childhood crush on me had grown into something different, stronger. I shook my head, trembling in front of him. I stared at the floor unable to face his disappointment in me.

"Hey?" He whispered, tilting my chin up with his finger. "I know this is different, and I know it's weird. We aren't kids anymore, Holly." He chuckled darkly. This side of Isaac was new to me. Where he was all sunshine and smiles, he was also raw and fierce. I wanted to see it. Feel it.

"I know. I just." I let out a hefty breath, tears stinging my eyes. *Come on, Holly. This is Isaac. My Isaac. He's safe.*

"Just what?" His lips curled in a sweet smile. "How about this?" He thought for a moment, stepping back from me. "I want to kiss you, to touch you. I'll be slow, patient. You stop me whenever you need to, OK? We've got all the time in the world." He stood in front of me, taking my hands in his and interlocking our fingers.

"OK." I whispered. He smiled, taking a step closer to me. Glancing down to my lips and then back up to my eyes, he smiled. And then, his lips were on mine. At first, I froze, trying to catch up with what was happening. He pushed to deepen the kiss, and I finally let him, earning a deep groan. I closed my eyes, and fought hard to stay in the moment, and not disappear in my head. I wanted to be fully with him at that moment.

I'm OK. I'm safe. I want this. His hands left mine and he cupped my face. His tongue danced around my lips, deeper and needier. A small moan escaped me as my body tingled and I let him in. Warmth spread over me and settled low in my belly. He gripped the back of my neck, opening me up even more. His other hand splayed across my stomach, sliding underneath my t-shirt. I opened my eyes, pulling away from him.

"Are you OK?" He whispered into my hair. He didn't move but waited for me.

"Yes," I answered. Eyes wide, I looked at him. Desire flashed across his face as he looked at me. He closed the space between us again, kissing me softly behind my ear, down my neck, while his other hand palmed my breast over my bra. My head rolled back as I let him move around me. He kept his promise and moved slowly. He was patient with me while emotions flooded over me. I was terrified, but I trusted him. I was also more turned on than I ever had been before. I didn't want to admit it, but the way he knew my body made me ache for more.

He walked us backwards, my legs hitting the bed. Gently, he put his hand on my back and guided me down. I laid there, panting and waiting. He stood above me, taking me in. He was breathing heavily, and I could see his cock hard in his sweats. He followed my eyes down and smirked.

"See what you do to me, little girl?" He groaned. "I won't make you do anything you don't want to do, Holly. But I do want you." He leaned over me, placing one hand on either side of my head. He bent down and kissed my forehead softly. "It's all about you tonight though. It's all for you. I want to worship you. I want you to feel so much pleasure that you forget your own name." I shuddered under him.

"What are you going to do?" I panted. He stood up and I propped myself up on my elbows. He let out a heavy breath and his jaw ticked.

"Holly, I am going to run my mouth over every inch of you. I am going to eat your pussy and make you come hard. And then I am going to do it again." I blushed at his words. I had been his best friend forever and I have never heard him talk like that. It was uncharted territory. New, feral and enticing. He played with the hem of my shirt, gently riding it up to expose my stomach.

"And again." He kissed my navel, sending shivers down my spine. "And again." He looked up at me, his eyes heavy and his smile wicked. He pulled up my shirt even more, kissing along my stomach. "And again. Take your shirt off." He commanded. Again, I shuttered at his command but obeyed eagerly. He palmed my breast, my nipples hardening at his touch. He pulled my bra down, taking the aching peak into his mouth. I elicited a deep moan as he sucked me in. I arched my back as he reached around me to unclasp my bra. With one swoop, he flung it to the floor. He took my other nipple in his mouth and nipped the bud. I squirmed underneath him, but he eased the pain, licking me.

He did exactly what he said he would. He kissed every part of me. He was slow, methodical, like he wanted to savor every inch of my desperate body. He made me feel adored, cherished even. He wasn't using me to get off or get his fix. He wanted me to feel pleasure. Bliss washed over me as I laid underneath him. I allowed myself to feel every sensation, every movement. His hands traced the elastic of my sweatpants. My skin tingled at his touch. I leaned up on my elbows to watch him. He gripped my pants and tugged at them hungrily. I lifted my ass off the bed and the pants were quickly tossed aside. He looked at me, like I was his last meal. I shivered under his heady gaze and that wicked smile danced across his face. His fingers ran along the crease of my thigh, sliding under the side of my panties.

"Take them off." He groaned. I obeyed, shaking as I leaned down to slide them off. "Fuck, Holly. You're perfect. Are you wet for me, baby?" I nodded, breathless, waiting. "Do you want me to stop?" His eyes met mine and I felt weightless. I needed him, I needed a release from the pent-up tension.

"No, Isaac." I moaned. "Don't stop." Before I even got the words all the way out, he was kissing the inside of my thigh. I squirmed beneath him, desire setting sparks off inside my head. It started out as a smolder, building up inside me, but it burned hotter as he kissed everywhere else but where I needed him to the most. I groaned and whimpered at the ache. He laughed a deep laugh as his finger ran along my soaking lips. My hands gripped the sheets as I bucked against him.

"Tell me what you want, Holly." He growled, watching me.

"I need more, Isaac. I need - Ugh!" I groaned in frustration. I didn't know what I needed, and I definitely didn't know how to ask for it.

"Use your words, Holly. Tell me what you need." His fingers ran gently over me, waiting.

"I need your mouth. I need your mouth on me." I whimpered. He stroked my throbbing clit with his finger.

"Here? You want me to suck your pretty little clit?" I nodded and he did exactly what he said. I cried out as bursts of pleasure exploded all over me. I never knew I could feel this good. My hips bucked against him as he buried his face in me. His tongue lapped up my weeping cunt like he needed it to survive. I buried my hands in his hair.

"Isaac, I'm gonna-" I exploded around him. His finger curled inside me, and I could feel myself clenching onto him. He didn't let up, either. He kept going, moving frantically, as wave after wave crashed through me. Once I started to come down, he slowed his movements. He kissed my inner thigh, trailing up towards my stomach. He leaned over me smiling. I could see my arousal all over his face and it only made me ache for more. It was the most incredible thing I'd ever seen.

"You alright, baby?" He asked. I nodded, running my fingers through his messy hair. He looked like a kid who just got his favorite toy on Christmas morning. I laughed at the thought. "Do you know how long I have been waiting for that?" I punched him in the shoulder, blushing.

"Isaac! What the hell?" I shook my head and watched as he rolled over, so he was next to me on the bed. He pulled me into him, and I nestled into his chest. We laid there quietly, content to be in each other's arms. After a few minutes, he stirred and rolled over on his side. He ran his fingers over my naked body, leaving me shivering under his touch.

"You are so fucking beautiful, Holly. Always have been. Getting to see you like this is a dream, baby." He looked me up and down, soaking it all in. I closed my eyes and let myself be admired. Pleasure and love and adoration were all new to me and I never wanted this to end. He laid back down on his back, pulling me on top of him. I straddled him and my hair hung over us in curtains. He ran his fingers through it, pulling me into him.

"Holly?" He breathed into me.

"Hmm?" I turned to look at him, that evil smile back on his face. My eyes widened.

"I want you to sit on my face." I squealed as he moved down the bed at the same time he gripped my hips. I hovered over him, timid and unsure. He wrapped his arms under my legs pulling me down onto his face. My head rolled back as his tongue ravished me. Finally, I relaxed and settled over him. He unashamedly sucked and licked, and tongue fucked me into oblivion. Stars danced across my vision. My second orgasm exploded through me, but he kept on going, ignoring my pleas and cries for him to stop. My toes curled and I hung onto the headboard for dear life. I rode the waves until I eventually became a pile of goo on top of him. He slowed, and finally stilled underneath me. I rolled to the side, collapsing next to him. We both sighed and stared up at the ceiling.

"Want to take a shower?" He asked me. I turned and looked at him nodding, lost for words. He got up and helped me off the bed and into the bathroom. He started the water and stripped out of his sweats. I tried not to look at his erection, hard and leaking precum. It was mouthwatering. He helped me into the shower and followed behind me. I let the hot water run over me as he reached for my shampoo. He lathered it in his hands and gently washed my hair. I closed my eyes, embracing the warmth of the shower and his touches. There was nothing sexual about what he was doing, but it made my heart feel like it would explode out of my chest.

He rinsed out my hair and did the same with the conditioner. Then, he lathered up the soap on my loofah and started washing me. I turned around, so my back was to him, and he washed my back. I could feel his erection against me, so I turned around, rubbing my hand over it. Heat flashed across his face, but he grabbed my wrist, stopping me from touching him.

"Isaac?" I looked up at him, trying to read the emotion on his face. He just shook his head.

"Tonight was for you. I don't want you to do anything because you feel obligated to. I want you to touch me because you *really* want to." I blinked up at him, feeling rejected, but also grateful he wasn't expecting anything from me. That was my Isaac. Selfless. I loved him even more for it. He continued to wash me, and I washed him in return. It was sensual, romantic and so very Isaac. He was slowly peeling away the layers of my heart despite my best effort. I owed him the truth of why I left, I just didn't know how to open up to him without losing him completely.

I slipped on one of his shirts and some clean underwear and slipped under the covers in his bed. I had slept next to him before, but this felt different, more intimate. My cheeks flushed at the sight of my clothing strewn across the room. Isaac came out of the bathroom in a pair of boxers and curled up next to me. Wrapping me up in his arms, he kissed my cheek gently. We laid there in silence for a few minutes.

"Hey, Holl?" He whispered.

"Yeah?" He hesitated, and I tensed, turning to look at him.

"We need to go to the house. It's your inheritance. We need to go through it and figure out what you want to do." I stilled, frozen in fear. I couldn't face that house. When I left, I swore I would never go back. I intended to keep that promise to myself.

"I can't," I whispered.

"I'll be right there with you, baby. Whatever happened, whatever is keeping you from that house, you need to face it. You won't be alone, I promise. I'll face it with you." I didn't say anything, and he didn't push the subject anymore. I knew he was right, but I just couldn't stomach the idea. I'll have to tell him the truth, which means he will know just how used and broken I really was. My fear of losing him gripped me tighter than ever. It was either having Isaac's love or telling him the truth of my past and my father. The universe wouldn't let me have both.

Chapter 23

H*olly*

I stared at the coffee in my cup, blankly. I was dreading this. I knew what was coming, and I had no way to prepare my heart and soul for it. I haven't stepped foot in my childhood home for a decade and I was hoping to make it forever. But now that house was mine and I needed to do something with it. My father is finding ways to torture me still, even in death. What would it take to get past this and actually move on? Would I lose Isaac in the process once he learned how damaged I was? These questions plagued my mind, consuming me from the inside out.

"If you wanted an iced coffee, all you had to do was ask." Isaac walked into the kitchen, a sarcastic glint in his eye. He stopped in his tracks once he took a better look at me. "Hey, I'll be there the whole time. We will get through this, I promise." He came around behind me, hugging me close. I took a deep, steadying breath.

"I just want it to be over with," I whispered. He squeezed me tighter and took my coffee from me. Spinning me around, he brushed my hair out of my face.

"It will be, this is just the first step. It's always the hardest. I will be with you every step of the way, no matter what."

"Thank you," I kissed his cheek, and headed to the bedroom to get dressed. I pulled a loose t-shirt out of my suitcase and some leggings and laid them out on the bed. Pulling my pajamas off, I watched myself in the mirror. I wished I could see myself the way

Isaac did. I wish I could forget the abuse, and the trauma and everything that came with it. For the first time, when I looked at my reflection, I saw a woman. The traces my father left behind were slowly disappearing. The pleasure that Isaac was able to draw from me changed everything. No man has ever touched me, except my abusive dad. Isaac would never be my first, but it was starting to feel like it. Even though we haven't actually had sex, he felt safe, like I could give that part of myself to him. He is so patient and understanding. I slipped the rest of the clothes on, brushed my teeth, and walked back out to the kitchen.

"I had made breakfast burritos for the week. Do you want one?" He asked, pulling his head out of the fridge when I came back in.

"Sure. That sounds good." I leaned against the counter and watched him work.

"I also made you a fresh cup of coffee." He stood and turned around. "Unless you really did want iced coffee?"

"I like iced coffee, but I'll take the fresh cup." I held the mug up to my face, letting the steam and the aroma melt my nerves. He finished warming up the burritos, we ate, and he hauled me into the truck.

Every minute of the drive seemed like hours. My hands were sweaty, and no matter how many times I wiped them on my leggings, they didn't stop. I bounced my leg and looked out the window. Eventually, Isaac grabbed my hand and ran his fingers through mine. I looked over at him, tried to smile, but I can't imagine it was much of one. We didn't say anything, he didn't ask questions, and I slowly crawled into a shell of myself.

"Holl?" I felt Isaac's hand on my shoulder. I didn't realize I had closed my eyes and fallen asleep. "You ready?" I blinked, getting my bearings and trying to center my thoughts. The house sat in front of me, looming and threatening. My stomach turned and my eyes burned. I couldn't put this off any longer. I heard the driver door shut as Isaac got out and came around to help me out. My hands and legs were shaking, like my body was going to give out if I got any closer. I swung my legs around, reached for Isaac's outstretched hand and slid out of the truck. One wobbly step at a time, we walked up to the door. The key shook in my hand, and I couldn't get it to unlock. His warm, calm hand wrapped around mine and guided the key into the lock, turning until we heard it click. He turned our hands around the knob and pushed the door open.

The stale air hit me like a tidal wave. My lungs were tight, and my feet stayed glued to the porch. I was ushered into the foyer, and the surroundings swirled in my vision. I couldn't focus on any one thing. It was a blur, and my body revolted against the memories bombarding my consciousness.

"Breathe, baby." Isaac wrapped his arms around me, walking us to the living room. "Is it the same as you remember?"

"Yes." I whimpered. He leaned down to look at me, his unanswered questions swimming in his expression. All I could do was shake my head. If I tried to talk, the breakfast burrito would be making a reappearance. He let me go, taking my hand in his and walked me through the main floor. Dust was everywhere, but underneath everything was exactly how I remembered it. We cleared the floor and when he headed towards the stairs, I froze, staring up at the looming mountain before me.

"I can't." I cried.

"Come on, Holly. I'm right here. Let's do this together, yeah?" He waved me forward.

"No. You don't understand. I can't go up there." The room began to spin again, and my throat constricted. My breathing turned labored, and my eyes welled with tears. Collapsing onto the floor, I grasped at my throat trying desperately to breathe. I heard him come back down the stairs and felt him wrap his arms around me.

"Shhh. It's OK. I'm here. You're alright." He brushed my hair out of my face and kissed the top of my head. Snot and tears ran down my face like rivers. My cries turned guttural, almost animalistic. My entire body shook, sweat pouring from me. I gasped for air and clawed at Isaac's arms around me.

"No!" I screamed. "Get off me!" I pushed, and flailed, and kicked, but he wouldn't let me go. "Stop! Pl-please!" I felt the arms around me loosen, but he didn't let me go.

"Holly, it's me. You're OK." I took advantage of the little freedom I had in his grip and pushed away from him with all the strength I had. Bolting up the stairs, I ran into my room and slammed the door shut. Falling to my knees, I slowly realized where I was. I wrapped my arms around my knees and scooted to the wall. Eventually, I looked up. My half painted Invisible Woman canvas stared back at me like a ghost. I heard the door creak open, and my vision went black.

ISAAC

Holly was unconscious on her childhood bedroom floor. My heart raced, and questions flooded my mind. I had no idea being back here would have caused such a reaction from her. I wouldn't have pushed her to come back if I'd have known this would be the outcome. I rushed to her, checking her eyes, any signs of life. I just got her. I can't lose her again. Her breaths were steady, which was an improvement to what they were. Her skin was clammy and sweaty. I looked around the room, and I noticed a painting that she must have started before she left. It was left exactly how it was. It looked like her, but I wasn't sure.

"OK, Holly. Let's get out of here, yeah?" I scooped her up in my arms, and carried her down the stairs, then out the front door. I got her settled into the passenger seat and buckled the seat belt. Making sure she was in order, I closed the door gently. I dashed around to the driver's side and put my key in the ignition, the engine roaring to life. Before I shifted into reverse, that painting flashed into my head. I didn't know why, but I knew I couldn't leave it behind. I threw the door open, ran up the porch and took the stairs to the second story two at a time. I grabbed the painting and the few Polaroid pictures that remained. Holly was still passed out when I got back to the truck. I slid the painting in the back seat, got buckled, and put the truck in gear.

The bumps from the road must have made Holly come to, because when I looked at her, her eyes were wide and full of emotion. She looked terrified. She didn't say anything, and I didn't want to press her. I just put my hand on her knee and drove us away from the horrors she just relived.

Chapter 24

H*olly*

The drive back from the house was quiet. I never wanted Isaac to see me come apart like that. There was no denying the truth now. I owed it to him to explain why my childhood home held so much power over me. I couldn't form the words, no matter how many ways I ran through it in my head. I stared out the passenger window, avoiding Isaac's concerned glances. I felt sick keeping him in the dark for all those years, but at the time, my dad had such a choke hold on me. I tried telling my mom so many times, but I couldn't face her either. I couldn't stand being seen as weak, used, vulnerable. So, I powered through it with a well cultivated mask.

We pulled into his driveway, and he silently got out of the truck, walking around to open my door. He helped me out and into the house. I sat on the couch as he walked past me into the kitchen. He came back with a bottle of water, set it in front of me and sat across the room in the overstuffed chair. I could feel him looking at me and my stomach turned. What if he was disgusted by me? What if he saw me as nothing more than the damaged girl, I always saw myself as? There was no way I'd survive that.

"Holly." He said, breaking the silence. "Talk to me. What happened in that house?"

"I. I can't." I sniffed. The memories, the nightmares all came back to me like a hurricane. I felt everything, all that he did to me, the way he manipulated me. Everything I fought so hard to hold back, to keep a secret was clawing its way to the surface. This was the moment I knew I had to give it all up. I needed to tell him, and the words were right there. But where do I start? Would I survive the aftermath of this revelation?

"Not an option anymore. I am here to help you pick up the pieces, but I need to know. I need to hear it from you." His voice was calm but commanding, and confident. It eased my nerves just enough. I took a deep breath, grabbed the water bottle, and opened it. My whole body shook as I took a drink.

"I don't know where to start," I muttered.

"From the beginning." I looked up, his eyes piercing through me and my walls I worked so hard to build for so many years.

"I was 11." I winced, memories flashing through my mind. He didn't move, didn't say anything, just listened.

"Dad started coming in my room at night while mom was gone for her work trips." My head spun and my mouth dried. I took another drink, shaking even more. Isaac sat in front of me, patient and waiting.

"He did things to me, things no father should ever do." Tears stung and I scrunched my nose trying to keep them at bay. "Freshman year was when it started getting...violent." I squeezed my eyes shut, trying to block out the visions threatening to invade my mind.

"Is that why you were sick and missed school so much?" Isaac asked. I nodded. I wrapped my arms around myself, trying to breathe through the nausea that always wreaked havoc on me.

"He would hit me, sometimes with his belt." I couldn't stop the tears from falling at his point. I covered my mouth as a deep, guttural sob shook my entire body. Isaac got up, wrapping his arms around me. He stroked my hair and rocked me, back and forth, like a child. I gripped his arms so tight I probably left bruises, but he didn't flinch or move away. He stayed there with me.

"Isaac," I muttered, quickly covering my mouth again. I pushed away from him, bolting for the bathroom. I kicked open the door and fell to the floor in front of the toilet. He was right behind me, helping me up and holding my hair as I gripped the toilet. I puked so much, I think everything I ever ate came up. I leaned over shaking, for what felt like hours. Once I calmed down enough to move, he left and brought me the bottle of water and a cold rag. He handed me the water and wrapped the cold cloth around my neck. I sat against the tub, knees pulled in towards my chest, head resting on my arms. I couldn't look at him, but I could feel him next to me. We sat there, in silence until he gently pulled me up. He helped me change into a t-shirt and I kicked off my jeans.

"Are you OK?" He asked. I shook my head, shame and disgust washing over me.

"I just want to lay down." He was quiet. It looked like he wanted to press the issue, to keep talking. He didn't say anything, and his eyes danced over me like he was assessing me for any damage or clues on what to do. Rather than pushing me, he stood up in front of me and held his hand out. He helped me into bed, kissing my forehead softly. My eyes were heavy, and I gladly let sleep wash over me.

I'm not sure what woke me up, but I instantly felt uneasy. I stretched out my hand only to find a cold, empty bed. I sat up, my eyes adjusting to the dark room. I looked around for Isaac, and it took me a few minutes to realize he was sitting in the chair across from the bed. He was watching me with so much intensity. The only signs of life he gave were his darkened eyes on me and the heavy rise and fall of his chest. The moonlight danced across his perfect body. He didn't move when I met his gaze. There was a fire in his eyes that wasn't ever there before. It was burning, violent and terrifying.

"Isaac?" I whispered nervously. His mouth twitched and his jaw tightened. He turned his head to look out the window and my heart sank. I knew it. He couldn't even look at me. A lump formed in my throat as I dropped my gaze to my hands in my lap. My worst nightmare wasn't my dad. It was losing Isaac in the aftermath of the storm my dad made of my life.

"I wish he was still alive." He mumbled, still looking out the window.

"What?" I snapped. He turned to look at me, his stare just as intense. I've never seen him angry or upset, not like this. A nervous energy coursed through me.

"I wish he was still alive so I could kill him myself, Holly. I'd kill him over and over again until there was nothing left of his miserable existence." He leaned forward in the chair, resting his forearms on his legs. He looked powerful, dangerous. I didn't know what to do with this version of Isaac. His words held so much power over me though. Watching him in this light, seeing how affected he was by my pain, it made my all senses come alive. I wanted him, needed him in every way possible. His emerald eyes I loved so much burned a hole in my very soul. He imprinted himself so strongly into my life that the rest of the world simply faded away when he looked at me.

"Isaac," I nearly moaned. He was laser focused on me, watching my every tiny move. My breaths were heavy, and my fingers twitched, aching to reach out and touch him however he'd let me.

"Why, Holly? Why didn't you tell me?" He was leaning back again, his legs spread, and his shoulders relaxed against the chair. Hurt flashed across his face, and it stabbed my already fractured heart. My breath hitched and a single tear ran down my cheek.

"No one would have believed me." I whispered, ashamed.

"That's bullshit and you know it." His tone was harsh, and it sliced through me, leaving me breathless and desperately empty "Holly. I love you, I always have. If you would have told me -"

"Stop, Isaac. It doesn't matter now. He's dead. It's over, it's been over since I left. Please, jus-"

"Just what? Pretend like nothing ever happened? How?" His eyes smoldered and fists clenched on his knees.

"Just help me move on. Please." I begged. I looked up at him with hooded eyes. My body hummed and I needed him. My heart was raw, beaten and used and he was my antidote. He always had been.

"How?" His eyes flared.

"I need you, Isaac." I cried. He sat there, looking at me, assessing me.

"Prove it, Holly. Show me you're ready to stop living in the past."

His words sent a surge of energy through me. I got up off the bed, shaking, and onto my hands and knees beside it. His eyes stayed glued to me as I crawled to him, slowly, deliberately. It felt like miles and the closer I got the faster my heart pounded in my chest. Adrenaline flooded my body and my ears rang. The world around me fell away and all I could see was Isaac, devouring me with his eyes.

When I was in front of him, I placed my hands on his clenched fists, interlocking our fingers. His chest heaved as he watched me. My body sparked, came alive with desire. An ache settled into my core as I knelt before him. He looked down at me, a dangerous smile flashing across his face.

"Take what you want, little girl. I'm yours to use and to destroy. I won't touch you unless you tell me to, but I will willingly give you all of me." I looked at him, my body aching, my eyes flooding with tears. "All of that pent up anger, hurt, and pain, unleash it, baby. Fuck me until you forget what he did to you." Emotions that had been simmering beneath the surface boiled over and I frantically worked through what I needed in my head. I looked at him, scared, angry, excited, and so intensely turned on I thought I would explode right there on my knees in front of him.

"Take them off." I ordered, pulling at his boxers. His stomach rippled at my touch, and he shifted so I could rip them off his body. He sat in front of me, naked, waiting. His cock was hard in front of me, and I was nearly drooling at the sight of it. On my knees, I leaned over him, taking his length in my mouth. It was velvety, and delicious against my tongue. His groan vibrated through him as I sucked and licked and devoured all of him in a sloppy mess. I gagged, tears running down my cheeks. I was coming apart in front of him and using him just like he demanded of me. I held all the power, and I basked in it. His head rolled back, and I watched him in awe as he groaned. He kept his promise. He didn't touch me, and he didn't move against me. I can only imagine how much this was torturing him, but I didn't care. We moved at *my* pace.

I snaked one hand down my stomach, feeling my own curves and appreciating my body for the first time ever. I ran my fingertips around my hips and slowly down to my soaked pussy. I touched myself in ways I never could before while I kept sucking his perfect cock. My whole body came alive as I thumbed my clit in small circles. My cunt was weeping, and I knew I was going to explode any minute. I put one finger inside myself, bringing myself so close to the edge. I looked up at him, watching him eat me alive with his eyes. His fists clenched on either side of him, fighting his urge to fuck my mouth.

I slowed my pace so neither of us could come yet. I let him go with a pop and slowly moved my fingers from inside me. Not taking my gaze off of him, I licked my arousal off my own fingers, slow and sensual, taking in the way he watched me. So much desire. So much need. All for me.

"Fuck, Holly." He growled. I stood, placing my wet fingers to his mouth.

"Shh." I teased, smiling up at him. I slowly climbed up, straddling him on the chair. He didn't move, but his eyes watched me like I was torturing him. In a way, I was. I needed this power. I needed to reclaim my own sexuality that was robbed from me years ago. I gripped his dripping length and rubbed it against my swollen clit. I moaned, letting my head roll back. My wild curls fell around me enveloping us in the moment.

"Take my shirt off, Isaac." He moved so fast I barely even realized what was happening. I lifted my arms up so he could pull my shirt over my head. "Touch me." I pleaded.

"Where, baby? Tell me what you need." His voice was molten liquid and scorched every inch of me. I leaned in close, gripping him again. He stiffened in my hold, and I reveled at the connection between us.

"I want you to suck my tits while I use your cock to get off." His eyes widened, and he froze. He stared at me with adoration, and pure primal energy. He squeezed one breast with one hand and took another in his mouth and I moaned in ecstasy. I shifted over him and slid myself over his length. I couldn't bring myself to fuck him, not yet. But I would still use him to find my pleasure. We both groaned in desperation as I slowly moved against him. When I slid over him like this, he hit my clit perfectly. I grabbed his free hand guiding it to my ass and he squeezed, undoubtedly leaving marks behind, and rubbed me. I rode him like that until my whole body shook with need. His own pleasure radiated off of him as he let me explore his body. He was made for me, and I for him. There was no doubt in my mind.

"Tell me what you need, little girl." He purred. I gripped the back of his neck, moving my hips faster against him. His erection slid through me and across his abdomen. "Fuck, baby. You're perfect."

"Touch my clit." I muttered, chasing the orgasm that was just out of reach. As soon as he touched me, stars exploded in my eyes and my skin rippled with goosebumps. "Faster," I cried. He worked me over as I grinded against him furiously, my hips digging into him. I could feel myself clench around nothing, but I still screamed as I came crashing over the edge. He gripped my ass, my cunt trembling around him. Sweat ran down both of us in waves of pleasure. My body turned to mush, and I slowed, but his hips bucked off the chair, as he chased his own orgasm. He groaned and stiffened, hot liquid coating both of us. I moaned at the feeling, coming down from my own high. I thought for sure the anxiety would kick in, but it never did. He never gave me the chance to spiral.

His hands roamed over me gently. The only sound in the room was our heavy breaths. He brushed my hair out of my face and scooped me up in his arms. I wrapped my legs around him as he carried me to the bed. With a flop, we both went down. He hovered over me, kissing my neck softly. I could feel him stiffen again against me and I groaned, my eyes rolling back. My entire body was sensitive, a ticking time bomb ready to explode.

"How's It feel to hold all the power, little girl?" He said, running his hands over my shivering body coated in our mixed arousals. I stared up at him, his eyes soft and filled with emotion.

"Like I'm alive again." I answered, letting every insecurity go.

"Good." He smiled. "Because now, I am going to make you come so hard you think you died." My eyes widened and he sat up, kneeling on the bed. He gripped my hips and pulled me towards him, lining himself up between my lips. His patience was perfect. Before I could even protest, he was grinding over me, hard and unrelenting, hitting my clit every time. I cried and screamed as I came, over and over again shattering around him. He didn't stop until he was spilling all over me again. It was messy, and feral, and beautiful. I never knew so much pleasure could happen without even fucking each other. I laid underneath him, my body and soul a pile of lifeless putty waiting to be remodeled into the woman I deserved to be.

"Do you want to know what my purpose in life is, Holly?" He asked, splaying his hands across my stomach.

"Hmm?" Was all I could manage to mutter. He leaned down, picked me up in his arms, and carried me to the shower. He stepped over the edge of the tub with me wrapped around him like a koala.

"It's to make you realize that your future is worth living." He brushed the hair out of my eyes, staring deep into my being. He set me down on my wobbly legs and started the water. Neither one of us said anything while we showered and washed each other off. He helped me towel off, got a shirt on, and tucked me back into bed. I watched as he pulled his boxers back on and climbed into bed next to me. He pulled me into him, and he was asleep within minutes. I lay there, silent tears rolling down my face as I realized I wasted so many years running away from him. As much as I was hurt, I hurt him too by denying him the truth. Never again. I promised myself then that I would never run again. No matter how many pieces of my heart I had to pick up, I wouldn't let myself do it alone anymore.

"Thank you." I muttered.

"For what?" I turned over so I was on my side facing him. He brushed my hair out of my face, looking at me with so many questions in his eyes.

"For everything." I wiped my nose. "For being my safe place when we were kids. And now."

"God, Holly, if I knew what was going on, I would have taken you so far from that house." His eyes softened and he relaxed into the pillow as he stared into me.

"I'm sorry I never told you." I inched closer to him, letting his body heat be my anchor.

"I never really told you everything about my dad either, so I can't really blame you." He wrapped his arm around me, pulling me even closer to him. His chin rested on the top of my head, and he gently played with the loose strands of my hair.

"What happened with your dad?" As I asked, he stilled around me. "I told you mine, you tell me yours." I prodded.

"He hit me sometimes. He was always pretty rough when he was drunk." He sighed, letting himself fall back into the memories. "I would always hide his keys so he wouldn't try to drive. Sometimes, I second-guessed myself and thought maybe he'd die behind the wheel. As much as he hurt me, I never did stop hiding his keys. I couldn't bear the thought of him dying or hurting someone else." I listened carefully as he told me what we were too scared to talk about as kids.

"Well, I guess we are just two peas in a pod, huh?" I tried to lighten the mood, but he just hugged me tight, wrapping me up in his arms. Silence filled the room after we spilled all our secrets, and we slept wrapped up in each other like the lifelines we had always been for each other.

Chapter 25

Isaac

"Where are you taking me?" Holly looked nervous next to me in my passenger seat. I pulled a few strings to get this surprise to happen and I really hoped it didn't backfire. The past few days have been a whirlwind, and I know Holly is emotionally drained. With everything I found out about her dad, my mind had been spinning out of control. I wanted to be there for Holly and help her heal from this, but I felt like a fish out of water. All the years growing up, I had no clue how bad it truly was for her. It made me sick, and angrier than I ever had been. I was angry at myself for not pushing to find out earlier. I was angry at Holly for not trusting me enough with this years ago. I was angry at Jenn for keeping this to herself. I was angry at her dad for dying. I wanted to turn back time, bust through the doors and beat his skull in. Every opportunity I should have had to make this right was taken from me. Now, all I could do was focus on moving forward and helping Holly do the same.

"You'll see." I looked over and smiled at her. I got the art room we first met in set up for her today with the help of the new art teacher. I took the painting from her bedroom and got it ready on an easel. She would have all the material she needed to let loose. I wasn't sure if she wanted to finish the painting, so I brought back up canvases just in case. She watched out the window as the trees and town flew by. When we rounded the corner to get to the school, her face squished up like she was trying to figure out a puzzle. I pulled in and parked, jumping out of my seat. She climbed out and followed behind me. I buzzed the door, and it unlocked for us. Holding it open, my eyes followed the woman who held my heart in her hands as she made her way inside the doors.

"This way." I grabbed her hand, and we walked the old familiar hallways. She laughed at the kids' drawings, and we pointed out things we remembered, and things that were new.

"It looks so small now." She mused.

"I know. It is weird being here as adults. This place seemed like a maze when we were here."

"Right?" She laughed. We paused in front of the art room, and I dropped her hand so I could usher her inside. Her stare bore into me as she walked by, and my heart felt like it was going to explode. I filed in after her, and she halted as the canvas in the middle of the room stared back at us. Her hands flew to her mouth, and I waited, and watched her eyes wander over the unfinished piece.

"Isaac. Did you?"

"I went back and got it before we left. I didn't feel right leaving it." I shrugged, watching her move around the room. Her hands glided over all the materials laid out for her. "We have the room all day, if you want it."

"Really?" She gasped.

"Yep. I talked to the principal and the art teacher. They were excited to have you come work in here." I pulled a stool out from one of the tables and placed it in front of the canvas. She sat down gently, raking over the painting and running her hands over it gently.

"I started this the night I left." It was barely a whisper. "Ben, from the arcade, gave me a comic book of the Invisible Woman. He told me that she reminded him of me." She smiled, sniffed, and wiped at her eyes. She looked down at her wrist, pulling off an elastic band. Piling her hair on top of her head, she tied the elastic around it. She moved like the ocean, gentle yet powerful. She was in her element, and I took in every detail. "Will you stay with me?" She asked over her shoulder.

"I'll do whatever you need me to do." She smiled a wide, genuine smile at me that I had missed so much. My soul would forever be tied to hers, and I wanted to savor every moment. She motioned for me to move on the other side of the canvas, so I couldn't see what she was doing. Sporting my best pout, I moved and sat on one of the high table tops. She sat up straight and got to work on the Invisible Woman. I watched as she worried her lip while she concentrated. She looked from the paints to the canvas and brushed each stroke one after the other. She was a goddess in her domain, creating her own world. I loved her paintings because it gave me a glimpse into her mind and how she saw her own world. It was beautifully chaotic.

Hours went by and I couldn't get enough of her. I itched to touch her, to brush the stray hair behind her ear that fell out of her elastic. It was killing me not to look at what she was creating. I wasn't dumb enough to peek, though. Every once in a while, she would peek up at me and smirk. The only sound in the room was the brushes against the canvas. It was a symphony and Holly was the conductor. Her arms moved across the work and her peace washed over me. If I could give her little pieces of her life back, in one way or another, I would. I'd gladly die trying to bring her this peace every minute of every day. In a twisted way, I think seeing her come apart was the push I needed to make sure it never happened again. I would claim every smile, every tear, every laugh. She had always owned my heart, but now together, we can put hers back together.

"I think I'm done." She sighed, standing in front of the canvas. She crossed her arms, and bit her thumb nail nervously. "Ready to see it?" I hopped off the table so fast, I barely caught myself. I made my way over behind her and stared at the work she had done, which took my breath away. It was truly exquisite. I was right, it was her. Her red curls flowed over the canvas. It was a close up of her, her eyes being the main focus. In the background were the stars and mountains. They spanned across the canvas in an array of stunning blues, purples and pinks. The mountains were silhouetted and snow capped with trees covering their faces. Her eyes were painted a soft blue, and in their reflection was her dream house.

"This house, the one in my dreams, was where I would go inside my head when he would come into my room."

I wrapped my arms around her, leaning down on her shoulder. "It was my safe place. It protected me when no one else could." She wiped her eyes on her sleeve. I turned her around, pressing my lips softly to the trails the tears left on her cheeks.

"I see you, Holly. I see your pain, your heartache, the innocence you lost. I see it all in this painting." She smiled and leaned into me. "You know what else I see?"

"What?"

"I see healing. I see a new life, one you get to create yourself. I see you for who you are underneath all the layers of hurt."

"I'm glad I didn't finish it that night. I think it would have turned out differently."

"Maybe." We stood there, in each other's arms lost in her art. When her stomach growled and cut through the silence, I laughed and let her go.

"We can leave this to dry overnight. I can come get it tomorrow." She nodded, picking up the material and cleaning up her space. I helped her put the canvas in the back of the room and locked the door as we left.

"I know you're hungry, so let's grab a snack on the way."

"On the way to where?" She raised an eyebrow.

"You'll see." I winked and pulled her out of the school, waving to the secretary on the way out.

Chapter 26

H*olly*

Spending the day in the art room was exactly what I needed. I was able to flow with artistic intuition more than I had in years. It took my mind off dealing with the house, my dad, and even my blooming relationship with Isaac. It helped clear my head of all the unwanted chatter and noise. Isaac, yet again, gave me another reason to love him even more. Would it ever end? It had to at some point, right? Now as we drove to the drive-in theater, yes, I pretend to have no idea, we sang along to the radio and danced in our seats. We pulled in, and Isaac paid the cashier in the little building. I had no idea what was playing tonight, and honestly, I didn't really care. I watched Isaac as he looked for a place to park. The appeal of drive-ins had definitely faded, but there were still a few people there. It was a little sad that it wasn't as popular as it used to be, but I let myself get lost in the charm of it anyway. We got out once he parked and he got to work throwing out blankets and pillows, and even lights that twinkled. Memories of our last night together before I ran from this place flooded my mind. It was such a bittersweet memory. While neither of us knew it was going to be our goodbye, I think deep down we knew it would be.

"Want to go grab some snacks?" Isaac asked, pulling me back from the past. He handed me some cash and I headed to the concession stand, getting our regular favorites. Once I got back, the bed of the truck looked like something out of a fairy tale. My mouth fell open as Isaac was stretched out, leaning on the back of the cab. He patted his lap with a sparkle in his eye.

"Are you real?" I asked, taking in the way the twinkle lights reflected off the gleam in his eyes.

"As real as it gets, little girl. Now get your ass up here and sit on the best seat in the house." Again, he patted his lap, and I tugged myself up into the truck, settling in against him. We opened our candy and sodas and watched as the cartoon advertisements danced across the screen.

"Hey," I asked, pulling his attention back to me. "I've been meaning to ask you something."

"Ask away, baby." He leaned over me, his eyes patient and curious.

"How are things with your dad?" I had been so wrapped up in my own shit, that I completely forgot Isaac's dad was still alive and something he had to face.

"We mostly just talk business at this point. After graduation, we had this huge conversation. I think he meant well, but it was hard to hear. He talked about my mom for the first time, maybe ever." His jaw tightened and his gaze lifted back to the screen.

"But you have the garage now, right?" I leaned back against him, curling into his comforting lap. He nodded.

"It isn't all mine. He didn't want to give it up completely, so he still has a decent share of it. I run day-to-day though. I've honestly hit a wall there. Like, I am just going through the motions. It doesn't feel like mine, and I don't know if it will ever be. I feel like I am just a placeholder, you know?" I nodded in understanding.

"Have you told him that? Maybe he is holding back on giving it to you until he thinks it is something you are truly going to be proud of." He looked at me and frowned like he never considered it.

"I don't even think he knows what he's doing with it. It's just something else he can hold over my head."

"Is he still drinking?"

"Not like he used to, and he has gotten some help. But it still drives a pretty big wedge between us. I don't think I'll ever really trust him or expect him to be the dad he should have been."

"Look at us and our daddy issues." I laughed. He sighed, leaning his head back against the cab.

"The most honest that man has ever been with me was the day of graduation. You know what he told me?"

"What?"

"He told me that I was the reason he started drinking. After mom died, he 'had no idea what to do with me.'" He loosened his grip around me. "He gave up on me before we even had a chance at a real relationship. Now that I am an adult, I think he respects me more. I've done really well at the garage, but the most I get from him is a pat on the back once a quarter when we go over the finances together."

"I'm sorry." I whispered, leaning into him.

"There's nothing for you to be sorry for, Holl."

"I'm sorry I wasn't there." He looked down at me with nothing but a deep understanding that I didn't deserve. My stomach did somersaults as I reached up and ran my hand over the stubble on his chin. "What did I do to deserve you, Isaac?" I muttered.

"Someone, somewhere knew what our lives would be like and decided we needed each other." He kissed the top of my head. "You deserve the whole world, Holly. And I'll spend each day of my life doing everything I can to give it to you."

"What about you? You deserve it too." His smile widened and the lines around his eyes crinkled. A spark of an idea ignited in my head, and I made a mental note to come back to it later. He had always supported me so much, it was time I returned the favor.

"I'm holding everything I need in my arms." I let myself sink into him as his words washed over me. The movie started to play on the screen in front of us, but all I could focus on was his touches and the trail of goosebumps they left behind. I looked up at him, and his focus was all on me, not the movie. He cupped my chin, looking over my face delicately, like he wanted to memorize every detail. Slowly, his lips came down on mine and my skin felt like it was on fire. The kiss was gentle, soft and his hand stayed on my chin, opening my lips for him to invade. I leaned into his kiss, giving him everything I had. Our tongues brushed against each other while his hands buried themselves into my hair. I gripped his legs, grounding myself so I didn't float away on the high he was giving me. Every touch, every caress, every kiss was like the lightning I needed to reawaken the dead parts of me I had ignored all that time.

His hands roamed down my neck, splayed across my stomach, and played with the hem of my shirt. He carefully reached up into it and toyed with my bra, bringing a soft moan out of me.

"Shh, Holly." His finger pressed against my lips. "Don't want to get caught." He kissed down my neck, still playing with my hardened nipples through the thin fabric of my sports bra. His other hand gripped my hair, pulling my head to the side to give him better access to more of me. His kisses trailed down my cheek, to my collarbone.

"Isaac," I groaned.

"Yes, baby?" He asked, toying with me, coiling me so tight I felt like I would combust.

"You're torturing me!" I nearly screamed. His hand left my shirt and cupped my mouth.

"Now, now. We have to be quiet. I'll give you what you want if you promise not to get us caught." I nodded, nearly begging for him to touch me. "Good girl. Grab that blanket and pull it over your legs. No one gets to see you come on my fingers but me." I jumped off his lap and grabbed at the thick blanket, scrambling to get back to him. My body hummed with need. I squeezed my thighs together to ease the throbbing that threatened to consume me. Once he was confident, I was covered, his kisses returned to the soft spot behind my ear. The lights on the bed of the truck went fuzzy as pleasure coursed through me. His hands trailed down my chest and stomach, slipping under the band of my leggings.

"Fuck me, baby." He growled in my ear. "You're already drenched." I rocked my hips against his hand that was touching me everywhere but where I needed him most. Finally, he plunged his middle finger inside of me, gently curling upward. I arched my back, stifling every sound that I desperately wanted to let out. His thumb circled my clit, making stars dance across my vision. Without warning, he added another finger thrusting inside of me, hitting that sweet spot that made my toes curl in my shoes.

"That's it, Holly." He muttered into me. "Chase that high, baby." That is exactly what I did, bucking my hips and riding his hand desperately. My legs shook and I could feel myself squeezing his fingers. My whole body trembled as my orgasm started in my belly and quickly took over my entire body. As soon as I started to moan, his hand covered my mouth again, stifling my scream.

"Your pleasure is mine, Holly. No one else's." My eyes rolled back as wave after wave of pleasure rolled through me. Once the lights became clear again and my soul came back to my body, I looked up at Isaac. His eyes were full of desire, and I reached to touch him through his jeans. He gripped my wrist, stopping me before I got to feel him.

"If you touch me right now, I will absolutely fuck you. I don't think the other people here will appreciate that." His voice was full of gravel and desire, and it lit me up like a firework.

"Then let's get out of here. Because I need to feel you. Like right now." I looked up at him with heavy eyes. In a split second, he ripped the blanket off of us and threw himself out of the back of the truck.

"Let's go." He held out his hand to help me down the tailgate. Heading around to the passenger side of the truck, he stopped, pinned me to the cab while is lips crashed down to mine, hungry, and desperate. To think that I did this to him was mind blowing. I loved this side of Isaac. He was always carefree, but to see him completely unhinged and out of control with desire was my new favorite thing. Tearing himself away from me, he helped me up into the truck giving my ass a smack on the way. He sped out of the drive-in and the tension in the cab was thick. The muscles in his forearms tensed as he squeezed the steering wheel. His eyes stayed glued to the road.

"Are you OK?" I asked, breathlessly. He nodded.

"I'm pretty sure if I look at you right now, I'll come in my pants." I chuckled, glad to know that I affected him just as much as he did me.

"Well, in that case," I unbuckled my seat belt. "I'll help ease that for you." He looked over and raised an eyebrow.

"What are you doing?"

"Making sure you come down my throat and not your pants." I leaned down into his lap, unzipping his pants and freeing his hard, leaking length.

"Christ." He muttered, squeezing the steering wheel so tight I heard the leather creak under his grip. Without warning, I wrapped my lips around him, hollowing out my cheeks. I wasn't slow and I wasn't gentle. The sounds of his breathing and the sloppy, needy sucking coming from me was the only thing I could hear. He bucked his hips into me, groaning.

"Fuck, Holly. I'm going to explode." I quickened my pace, tears stinging my eyes as he hit the back of my throat. I licked his tip, only to swallow him again. He slammed up into me, his come shooting down my throat. I slowed my pace, dragging out his orgasm as long as I could. Finally, I let him go with a pop and sat back in my seat, licking my lips. He stared at me, eyes wide and dark.

"God, you're perfect." He shook his head and returned his focus to the road while he zipped his pants back up. My smile was wide and made my cheeks hurt. I watched the trees go by in the night as we drove back to his house. When we got there, he hauled open my door and threw me over his shoulder only letting me go once he flopped me down onto the bed.

Chapter 27

Isaac

Walking into my office at work while Holly slept in my bed was excruciating. It took all my effort to drag myself to the garage. As much as I wanted the distraction Holly was providing, I couldn't neglect my responsibilities. I had a mountain of financial paperwork to go through and it was always good to show my face to the people that work for me. I always made it a point to make their lives easier and make myself more approachable than my father ever was. I liked to think I did a pretty good job. I hadn't had any complaints yet, so that's always a win. I opened the front door to the shop, the big bay doors were already open. The sounds of tools and lifts echoed through them. I waved to the girls at the front desk, and they smiled back as I headed back to my office.

With a heavy sigh, I plopped down on my chair and set my coffee down on my desk. I went into autopilot opening my email, checking for any fires I needed to put out. They were few and far between now, thankfully. I did a quick look at the mail that had been put on my desk and added it to the pile of paperwork I had been avoiding. Satisfied with that, I headed out to the floor to check on the mechanics. They were really the ones that ran this place. I was just a name for the company that did the boring shit. Their attention to detail and love for the customers are what kept people coming back year after year. I smiled, as I opened the door to the garage.

"Hey! Isaac!" One of the guys shouted over the noises.

"Hey, buddy. How's it going this morning?"

"Smooth as butter. Good to see your sexy face."

"I know, it's a pleasure I like to bestow on you guys every now and then." I winked at him and continued in, checking the equipment logs as I went. I made it a point to talk to everyone, made sure everything was in working order, and took note of the things I needed to look into further. By the time I was done, it was already late morning, and I needed to head over to the bank to go over the financial paperwork. Making my way back to my office, I stopped at the coffee pot for a top off and then to let the girls know I was going to head to the bank. I grabbed what I needed and headed out. What should have taken fifteen minutes took closer to an hour. I was a little more behind than I thought. By the time I got back to the garage, it was well after one o'clock. I headed back through the door to the lobby. Stopping and talking to the girls for a minute, I noticed they were exceptionally giddy. They side-eyed each other after every sentence.

"Ok, what's going on?" I raised an eyebrow.

"Nothing!" One of them said as the other pretended to zip their lips closed. I crossed my arms over my chest and glared at them. We were like a family here, and pranks weren't uncommon. I was definitely skeptical and a little scared.

"We're good here. Why don't you just head into your office. I'll call if we need anything." Her smile was evil, and I questioned everything that was going on, but I reluctantly headed back into my office. I opened the door carefully, expecting anything but I froze as I saw Holly sitting on my desk, one beautiful leg over the other. Her grin was wild, and her eyes were beaming at me. I slowly made my way into my office, taking in every detail of her. Her hair was down, loose and wild. She was wearing a flowery summer dress that hugged her gorgeous tits and flowed loose past her hips. She was a goddess, everything that was perfect in this world. Her smile was radiant, and it made my chest ache with longing. My fingers itched to touch her. As I made my way to her, she uncrossed her legs and held out her hands to me. She pulled me in, wrapping herself around me and burying her face into my shoulder.

"Hey, little girl." I whispered into her hair.

"Hey." She smiled up at me. "I brought you some lunch." She let her arms down and reached behind her. She handed me a paper bag with the diner logo on it. I smelled the fries before I even looked in the bag. I smiled, looking behind her at the single shake in a large Styrofoam cup with two straws poking out of it.

"This is the best surprise." I beamed at her. She hopped down and snagged the chair across my desk, bringing it around so we could sit next to each other and eat our lunch. We sat down, my knees brushing against hers. If I wasn't touching her, I was pretty sure I would spontaneously combust.

"I brought you a burger too, just in case you wanted something other than fries." She slid another smaller bag towards me.

"I might take you up on that. Those burgers are almost harder to resist than you." She blushed, putting a few fries in her mouth. We ate and talked and laughed. These moments, where she was so carefree and happy were the ones, I longed for. I wanted to see every smile, every laugh, and every blush. I wanted to claim them all as mine. I watched her reverently, the crinkle in her eyes made my stomach drop and her laugh made my spine tingle.

"I have another surprise for you." She broke my trance, smirking at me through heavy eyes.

"Oh?" I asked, wiping my mouth with a napkin. I leaned back in my chair, drinking in her perfection. She nodded, standing up from her chair. She headed over to the door, locking it and slowly turned towards me. Her eyes were dark with desire and her movements seductive. She danced slowly towards me, swaying her hips and taking my breath away with each movement. I couldn't take my eyes off of her as she leaned down over me. I ran my hands through her hair, over her cheeks and her neck. She closed her eyes, leaning into my touch and sinking into me. I leaned forward, closing the distance between us, crashing my mouth to hers.

Her soft moans made all the blood in my body go straight to my dick. I pulled her tightly to me, gripping her hair with one hand and tugging her onto my lap with another. She straddled me, arching into my touch. My hands roamed over her chest and around to her ass. Lifting up the skirt of her dress, my eyes locked onto hers.

"You naughty girl." Her smile was wicked and teasing. "You really came to my office in this dress with no panties on?"

"That's your other surprise." Her breathy voice made my cock strain against the zipper of my jeans. With one swoop, I picked her up and put her on the edge of my desk. I brushed kisses along her jawline, down her neck leaving a trail of goosebumps behind every soft touch. A whimper escaped her lips. I brushed my finger over her bottom lip and watched as she squirmed around me.

"I want to see these perfect lips around my cock, Holl." Her head fell back, and her thighs tried to clench, but mine stopped her from getting the friction she needed. I lifted up her dress and pressed my middle finger along her pussy.

"You're dripping already, baby."

"You have that effect on me." Her small smile made me feral. I drove my finger inside of her making her arch back against me. I cupped my hand over her mouth, stifling the scream that would have the whole building trying to break the door down.

"Shh. No one gets to hear you but me." I released her mouth, teasing her dripping cunt even more while I kissed her, swallowing her moans. She moved with me, her inner walls clenching around my finger. I teased her closer and closer to the edge, watching every move, every twitch of her face. Right before she came undone, I pulled my finger out, earning a soft cry.

"Isaac." She whined. I just winked at her, sat back down on my chair and eased her closer to the edge of the desk. She leaned back on her hands as I lifted up the skirt of her dress.

"You're so fucking perfect." I muttered. "All mine." I ran my tongue along her, barely touching her. Her thighs shook and tried to close around me, but I held her open. With one hand, I pushed two fingers inside her, curling upward to hit that sweet spot that made her squirm for me.

"Oh my God." Her head fell back as she let herself move with me, pleasure taking over her. Pumping my fingers in and out, I twirled my tongue around her clit. Sucking, and licking, I moved until she crashed around me. She squeezed my fingers and squirmed against the flat of my tongue. Once I knew she was coming down off her orgasm, I stood up and looked at her. Her fair skin was flushed, and her breathing made her tits strain against her dress.

"Unzip my jeans, baby." She leaned forward, her heavy eyes meeting mine and did what she was told. The sound of my zipper and our breaths filled the room with electricity. "Take my cock out." I ordered. She looked down, breaking eye contact and slowly took my painfully hard length out, pulling down my boxers. Without being told, her lips circled around the tip making my whole body come alive. I gripped her hair and slowly eased her mouth onto me.

"Fuck, Holly." My head fell back as I let her have control. When I hit the back of her throat, she hollowed out her cheeks, sucking me in harder.

"I want to come down your throat." I buried my hand in her hair and pulled her off of me with a pop. She looked up at me, beautiful on her knees. Once again, I committed this sight to memory. I sat back in my chair, legs wide. She inched closer to me, eyes dark and full of need. I gripped her hair, tight enough for her to roll her eyes back and lean down closer to me.

"Reach down and play with your clit. I'm not going to be easy on you and I want you to come on with me. But not until I say so." Her eyes widened as she turned back around and reached between her legs. "Just like that, baby." I picked up the pace, watching her every move, feeling every twitch, every swallow. "Come with me, Holly. Now." Her head fell forward, and her legs shook as she came undone around me yet again. I slammed into her mouth, while she dragged out her orgasm as long as she could.

"Fuck." She muttered, barely holding on.

"That's it," I growled, my own orgasm beginning to take over me. I thrusted in and out her mouth, fast and hard until my spine began to tingle, my balls tightening. With one final thrust, I exploded into her. Her warm mouth took in every inch, and she pulled every bit of pleasure from me. Spit and come ran out of her mouth and tears stained her face. I ran my fingers over her lips, and into her mouth. "Every last bit, Holly." She swallowed as my fingers twirled in her mouth, moaning and vibrating around me.

Our heavy breaths filled the air, and I collapsed against her. We didn't move for what seemed like an eternity, and eventually I slipped out of her.

"I want the taste of me on you as you walk out of my office." I growled in her hair. She shivered and slowly stood up. Seeing Holly in the afterglow of a good orgasm is something I never grew tired of. I made it my mission to make her come apart like this every chance I got. We ate the rest of our fries and melted shake, basking in the afterglow. When it was time to walk her out, I took her hand and unlocked my door. Swinging it open, we were met with the knowing grins of the girls in the lobby. I smirked, shook my head and kissed Holly goodbye.

"I'll see you tonight," she said as she waved goodbye and winked at the girls. There is no way I will ever hear the end of this, but I honestly couldn't give a shit. Headed back to my office, I stopped at the sight of a truck pulling into the parking lot.

"Great. There went my mood." I leaned against the counter listening to the girls talk back and forth while I waited for Dad to make his way in.

"Hey, Isaac." He smiled and waved his way through the door. "Do you have some time this afternoon?"

"Depends on what for." I uncrossed my arms and pushed off the counter leading him to my office.

"Nice to see you too, I suppose," he mumbled as he followed closely behind. We made our way in and settled across from each other, the desk giving us a little breathing room. "I wanted to talk to you about the shares."

"The shares?" I questioned, tension stiffening my back in my chair.

"Yeah," he sighed. His face was worn and his eyes heavy. While he had cut back on drinking, the years of abuse aged him tremendously. "I think it's time I start handing sole ownership to you."

"Really?" I was shocked that he brought this up himself. I never thought the day would come. But, like Holly had mentioned, I never truly asked for it either.

"It might be a long process, but I wanted to see how you felt about it before I did anything." I considered for a moment how hard this conversation was for him. This was the last piece of Mom he had left, and to give it up was a big deal.

"I think you know I can handle it. The business is good, the team practically runs itself. I'd be happy to fully take over. But, I know what that means and I want you to be sure." I leaned over and rested my elbows on the desk between us. His eyes were soft, but unsure. He looked conflicted.

"I know you can handle it. You've done so much to make this place better, what it should have been all along. You've earned it." His mouth curved up in the smallest smile and I wanted nothing more than to tell him yes. But, I could tell he had his own doubts. I didn't want to take over fully because he felt guilty or that he owed me. I wanted him to want it for himself.

"I think you should take some time and really think about this. Of course I want to take over fully, but as much I am ready for that, I'm not sure you are. Why don't you sleep on it, really think about it and let me know when you are ready. I'm not going anywhere." He leaned back in the chair and exhaled so heavily I almost felt it.

"Are you sure?" He asked.

"Retirement is a big deal. Let me know what you plan to do with it and then we can talk." The sadness in his eyes glistened, but he knew he needed to think long and hard about this decision. If I didn't think he would drink himself to death out of boredom, I would have agreed the minute he asked. He nodded silently, and stood up. I followed suit and headed around the desk to walk him out.

"I'm going to say hello to everyone before I duck out of here. You don't need to walk me out." I nodded, shook his hand and watched him disappear through the garage door. I leaned heavy against the door to the office and let out an exhale. As much as I wanted sole ownership, I knew he wasn't ready. The fact that he is starting to consider it is a huge deal, but I can't risk his own life for my selfish wants. It will come in time, but as much as this was about me proving myself, it is just as much about him proving he can handle it to me.

Chapter 28

Holly

This temporary life was starting to feel easy for the first time. The heavy fog that lingered in my head, the one that I had become very well acquainted with, started to lift little by little. I wasn't sure if Isaac had been doing it on purpose, knowing him, he probably was. He had taken the time to remind me of all the good I did have growing up here. The places we went, the things we loved and cared about in our teens, he took each one and wrapped it up in a perfect package for my slowly healing heart. Then, like Isaac always did, gifted them back to me. Maybe it was because I was slowly opening my mind and heart to the good, I deserved, or maybe it was just him being the Isaac I always knew and loved. I had a feeling it was more him than me. Despite all the things we've done together and the way this trip home has healed a part of me, I still felt a little lost and broken. I was slowly picking up the pieces of me I lost along the way, following the trail of breadcrumbs Isaac left for me. In my heart, I knew I could fall, and he would catch me, but my brain had other ideas, and they were at war with each other. I couldn't stay in this fairy tale forever.

Signing the papers to the house was something I knew I had to do on my own. I didn't want anything to do with the ghosts of my past that haunted the walls. I also didn't want anyone else to have to deal with the mess that my family had created. The house was officially mine, and while it felt good to get it done and out of the way, I still had no clue what to do with it. Isaac's adventures he planned, now almost daily, were a welcomed distraction. He never did really tell me what we were doing, but I learned to go with it. Some nights I spent at his house, others I spent in my hotel room. Last night, I laid awake staring at the hotel ceiling thinking about everything. I couldn't shut my brain off. I thought about Boulder and the life I would go back to there, and the one I would be leaving behind here. Staying was never the plan, but every minute I spent with Isaac made the idea of leaving him *again* hurt more and more.

Looking at my phone to check the time, I realized it was a lot later than I thought. Isaac would be picking me up in less than an hour and I needed to shower. I piled my hair up on my head and jumped in to wash away the sleepless night. As I finished getting ready, Isaac's knock on the hotel door echoed through the room. I answered it, grabbed my phone and wallet, and pulled on my shoes as we walked out of the hotel.

"Where are you taking me today?" I asked as we got into his truck. He looked over at me with a wicked smile. "I know, I know. I'll see when we get there." I mocked in my best attempt to imitate him. He laughed and shook his head.

"Am I that predictable?"

"Yes. Always have been." I couldn't help but grin at all the memories we shared over the years.

"I'll work on that, then I guess." He shrugged.

"I didn't say it was a bad thing." I punched his shoulder, making him squirm away from me. "Hey! Eyes on the road, man." His eyes went wide as he gave me his best innocent look. I watched as the familiar places went by as we drove. It still amazed me how much had stayed the same after all this time. It was like stepping back into another time, but with a new set of eyes to see it from.

"The arcade is still here?" I shouted as we pulled into the tucked away parking lot.

"Sure is. Most of the original games are still there, even. Are you going to kick my ass in Pac man like you used to?"

"I may be a little rusty, but I'm sure I can still take you. I wonder if our names are still on there for the high scores."

"I doubt it. This place isn't as popular as it used to be, but we probably got beat by some kids." He looked out his window at the arcade, sadness flashing across his face.

"What's wrong?" I squeezed his knee gently.

"Ben isn't here anymore." He looked at where my hand laid on his leg, and then up at me. "I know you were close, and I didn't want you to go in there thinking he would be behind the counter." I nodded, listening and taking in his words.

"Did he move?" Isaac's face fell, telling me what words couldn't. I looked back at the building in front of us. A mixture of nostalgia and grief tugged at my heartstrings.

"What happened?"

"Heart attack, about three years ago." A breath whooshed from my lungs.

"I had no idea." What else had I missed out on? Would I have come back for his funeral had I known? Was his family there? I had so many questions, none I had answers for. "Thanks for the heads up. I definitely would have looked for him." My chest ached at the thought of walking in those doors and not being greeted by Ben's warm smile. Working at the arcade was amazing and he was the closest thing to a father figure I had. Regret gnawed at me once again for leaving people I cared about behind. Ben didn't deserve that, and I lost the opportunity to tell him what he did for me when I needed it most.

"I know." Isaac's sad smile didn't reach his eyes. He took a deep breath. "Ready?"

"Ready." Was I? Could I walk back in there and relive happy memories knowing the person who made it what it was wasn't going to be there? I had to be. It was one more bridge to cross.

Much like everywhere else Isaac had taken me to, the arcade was like a real-life time machine. It looked almost identical to how I remembered it. It even smelled the same. A small group of kids were gathered around one of the games. I took it all in, remembering the sound of laughter and friendly competition. The hours we spent here were some of the bests I had. It wasn't just the games, but it was the group of people we spent time with. It was Isaac and his warmth and Ben's care and devotion to us kids. It was a safe haven, just like the skate park. When we walked through the doors, life's problems went away. We were allowed to be kids. I swallowed the lump in my throat at the overwhelming sense of peace that hit me. I looked at Isaac, who was watching me with a sparkle in his eye. I don't know how he managed to be exactly what I needed, but I was more thankful than ever that he was.

"I have more quarters than we probably know what to do with, so take your pick, Holl." He nodded towards the games strewn about the building. "I'll follow you." I smiled, looking over the options. When I found the game I wanted, I jogged over to it, giddy with childhood excitement. I ran my fingers over the panel and all the controls looking at all the details. Pac Man's yellow form danced across the screen waiting for me to play. I felt Isaac come up behind me and place the quarters in the slot. He didn't back away, just enveloped me in his warmth. My eyes flashed back to the screen and the world around me disappeared. My hands moved over the controls and my tongue stuck out between my teeth. It was me versus the dots. When the game ended, my eyes tracked the names on the score list. Gasping, I grabbed onto Isaac's arms that were still surrounding me. I looked up at him, his smile lighting up my world.

"My name is still on there."

"It sure is, baby." I closed my eyes as his fingers twirled in my hair and down the side of my cheek. "As much as you want to put this place behind you, to forget this part of you, your life here will never be forgotten." He wrapped his arms around me, kissing the top of my head gently. "What's next? The night is young, and the quarters are flowing." I chuckled, shaking my head. I headed over to the Skee Ball and looked over my shoulder at Isaac. I shot him a wink and held out my hand for him to load me up with quarters.

We played every game in the building, some twice. The sky grew dark and the kids that were there had long gone. Isaac and I stayed until the kid working there let us know the arcade was closing. We thanked him and headed out to the truck laughing at the day's adventure.

"Where to now? The hotel?" Isaac asked, starting the truck. My stomach growled, and I looked up at him with a grin.

"How about the diner? I could use a milkshake."

"Your wish is my command!" We backed out of the arcade parking lot and headed back.

"Isaac?"

"Yeah, baby?"

"Can we share one this time?" He looked at me with the biggest smile I have seen, and I just stared at him, committing every detail to memory.

Chapter 29

Isaac

The hot cocoa warmed my body as I took sip after sip. It was a clear night with a chill in the air. I had set out a blanket and pillows in the backyard for Holly when she was done painting. The view from my porch wasn't magazine worthy, but we could still see the stars and appreciate the Colorado air. I headed back inside and made her a cup of hot chocolate. After I made it just how she liked it, I grabbed the mug and headed to the spare room where she was painting. She was absolutely stunning. Her hair was a mess on top of her head and her face was smudged with different colors. Her tongue was sticking out ever so slightly in concentration. I moved into the room and when her eyes met mine, my heart leapt out of my chest. Those smiles were few and far between, and I had been getting more and more of them every day. I cherished every single one.

"I made you some hot chocolate." I offered her the mug.

"Aww! Thank you." She took the mug, blowing softly onto it and taking a careful sip. A moan escaped her lips, and I had to will my dick to stand down. "This is so good."

"Good, I'm glad. I actually have a surprise for you." I held out my hand and she eyed it skeptically. "I promise you'll like it." I rolled my eyes and nodded toward the door. She took my hand, and I led her out to the kitchen.

"You need to close your eyes. Hold onto your mug and I'll cover them for you and guide you outside."

"Outside? Ooh. Interesting." She giggled. I put my mug down on the counter and put my hands over her eyes, gently guiding her outside. The sun had just set and the lights I put out made the blankets twinkle in the dark. We walked down the porch steps, and I stopped her right before the blanket.

"OK, you can look now." I moved my hands from her eyes, and she gasped as she saw the decorations.

"It's beautiful!" She made her way to the blanket and carefully sat down with her hot chocolate. I made my way down as well and grabbed the other oversized blanket I brought out. She helped me wrap it around us and we tucked ourselves in. I watched her take in the lights, the sounds of the life around us, the stars starting to peak out. It was like she was seeing these things for the first time. It was breathtaking, and this view was mine. I smiled as I remembered one of the other things I brought out here. I reached behind me and grabbed the Polaroid camera that was hidden beneath the pillows. She turned and looked at me, curiosity gleaming in her eyes. I held it out to her, and she let out the most childlike squeal I have ever heard come out of her. I laughed as she grabbed it and looked it over carefully.

"Is this?" She gasped

"Yep." I winked. "Same one."

"You kept it?" She gawked at me.

"Of course I did. How else are we going to capture our life together?" I elbowed her in the side and got a poke in the ribs for it. Then she snapped a photo of me. When the film spit out of the camera, she grabbed it and laid down on her back watching it develop.

"Where will we live?" She asked me.

"Wherever you want to. I'll build us a house." I laid back next to her, looking up at the stars.

"Remember the house I painted when I was a kid?" I looked over at her. Her eyes were distant.

"The A-frame?" My eyebrows pulled together trying to remember what it looked like.

"Yeah. I think that is my dream home. In the woods, but not too far from town. Rustic, open floor plan. I want a big dining room table."

"Really? Why?" She blushed and looked over at me warily.

"I think I want lots of kids. I didn't always, but if I do have kids, I don't want just one. If you weren't around when we were kids, I would have been really lonely."

"That makes sense. So, house in the woods, lots of kids, what else?" I wanted to hear all her hopes and dreams. I was mentally stamping them into my brain so I would never forget them.

"A dog, I think."

"Girl or boy?"

"Girl for sure. I would name her Sadie."

"Why Sadie?"

"I don't really know. I think it's a cute name for a dog. She would be a golden retriever. And we would have a cat named Ginger."

"An orange cat?" I groaned. She just beamed at me. "You know my favorite thing out of all of the things you just said?"

"What?" She hummed, still daydreaming.

"The word 'we.'" She turned to lay on her side facing me. She looked so peaceful and happy. She traced my lips gently with her fingers and kissed me ever so softly.

"I don't think I have a future without you in it." The side of her mouth tipped up and I had to swallow the lump in my throat.

"I want to be wherever you are. I'll build us a house on the top of a Goddamn mountain if that's what you want." I closed my eyes and leaned into her. She curled up and I wanted to savor every feeling, every word. I wanted to memorize these times and hold them close.

"I don't need a mountain." She twisted the hem of my shirt absently.

"No?"

"No. I just need to feel whole but I don't know how. Avoidance has been my go-to but it doesn't seem to be getting me anywhere." I couldn't help the sadness that washed over me. Knowing she viewed herself as a broken version of who she was meant to be made me want to reclaim every one of those pieces. What would it take to get her there? She had to do the work, I knew that but what push would she need to do it?

"I wish you could see what I see." I kissed her hair gently. "I don't see broken when I look at you."

"What do you see?" It was barely a whisper, but it was all I needed.

"I saw the girl I met in the art room when we were six. The beautiful, creative, sparkling girl that showed me what it felt like to be worth something. To be cherished, to be loved. I see the girl who had her childhood ripped away from her but didn't let it ruin her heart. I see the strongest, most incredible woman I have ever met. I see my person. You taught me what it was to truly love and be loved. My world was always wrapped around your finger, Holl." I wiped the tears from her cheeks as she looked up at me with those crystal blue eyes. "The only time I want to see you cry is when your lips are around my dick."

"Isaac!" She squealed and jabbed me in the gut.

"Ow! Hey!" I grabbed her by the waist and tickled her up her ribs. Squirming in my arms, she fought hard and eventually I let her go. She turned and looked at me with wide eyes.

"I have an idea." She worried her bottom look as she watched me try to decipher what she was planning.

"What is your idea?" I laid back down on my elbow, facing her in all her beautiful wildness.

"Would you want to go camping?" She looked at me like she was scared of my answer, and I smiled softly at her. I grabbed her arms and pulled her down next to me, her back to my front. I brushed my fingertips gently over her hair, the freckles on her nose, the sides of her slender neck. Kissing her cheek, I wrapped my arms around her completely.

"I want whatever you want." I whisper into her hair.

"What did I ever do to deserve you?"

"I don't think it has anything to do with what we deserve. Someone out there knew we needed each other. Loving you has made this life worth living every second." She hummed and sank into me even more. We stayed like that until we drifted off to sleep in my backyard.

Chapter 30

Holly

A visit to my mom was overdue. I hadn't reached out to her or even seen her since the lawyer's office. In my mind, she was just as guilty as my dad was for all the trauma I had to endure as a kid. We were never really that close since she traveled for work, and when she did try to be a doting mother, it always seemed halfhearted and empty. She was never mean or violent like dad was, but she was just absent. It was like she always had one foot out the door, ready to escape just like I was. Maybe we had more in common than I thought. Isaac had been hinting at me that I should go see her. As much as I knew it needed to happen, it meant stepping out of the bubble I had created around myself since I had gotten back. I didn't want my happiness to pop, not yet.

Since I had come back to town, I had successfully avoided all my responsibilities. I threw myself into Isaac as a welcomed distraction. It felt like we were making up time for the last decade between us. I think I always loved him in one way or another but loving him like this was something I never thought I would let myself have. I had convinced myself that he would turn his back on me, leaving me to the wolves of my own self-loathing. I should have known better. As I sat watching him make our breakfast, I took in every detail, the way his muscles contracted, and his mouth curved in concentration. His sweats hung low on his hips and his golden skin gleamed in the morning sun through the window. God, he was beautiful.

"Have you called your mom yet?" He asked over the brewing pot of coffee, ruining my moment. I scrunched up my nose and gave him a pout.

"No, not yet." I sighed, leaning back on the counter. I hoisted myself up to sit and watch him better, my legs dangling over the edge. He eyed me over the sizzling bacon, waving the tongs at me.

"You can't fully move on if you don't work on every part of you. Whether you like it or not, you and your mom need to have a conversation. You can't heal without it." Why does he have to be so damn smart?

"I'll call her after we eat. Promise." I held out my pinkie finger. He linked his with mine and pulled me closer.

"Good. As much as I want to spend the rest of my life with you in my bed, there are things we need to do."

"Like what?" I rolled my eyes. "And you act like it has been months. I've only been back a week."

"I still have a garage to run." He winked, flipping the bacon. "And you, Miss Holly, have to figure out what you are going to do with the house, and your mom and, well your life." He looked back at the bacon, a frown forming. "Have you decided if you're going back to Boulder?" I sunk off the countertop and stepped behind him, hugging him close. He smelled like sex and bacon, and I loved him like this. It felt so natural and easy. The thought of not having him around hurt more than I could bear.

"No, I texted my boss to let her know I needed some more time here to sort things out." He nodded and finished up our breakfast.

As promised, I called my mom to meet and talk. We decided to meet at the coffee shop later that afternoon. It reminded me of the one time she came to visit Boulder to see where I worked and how I was getting along. Throughout the years, she would check in every now and then over email, of course. Our relationship was never the ideal, but I appreciated the small efforts she made. It was more than I ever did.

My nerves were shaky, and my heart was beating faster than what was probably healthy. To say that a relationship with my mom was something I wanted would be a stretch. I survived my adult life so far without it, but I can't deny the need to clear the air between us. I got there first, so I settled into a table in the back with my coffee from Audrey. She had just baked a fresh batch of cookies, so I grabbed one and let the hot, sweet treat melt away some of my nerves.

The bell chimed as the door opened, Audrey welcoming her guest. I looked up and saw my mom, our eyes meeting. She ordered her own coffee and made her way over to where I sat. She smiled warmly at me, and I did my best to match it.

"I'm glad you called to meet." She smiled, sipping her coffee. I nodded, looking down into my lap where my hands fidgeted with the hem of my shirt. "Isaac told me you were still in town, so I was hoping to be able to catch you before you left."

"Yeah," I exhaled. "I'm sorry I didn't reach out sooner. I've been a little preoccupied."

"Isaac mentioned that as well." She smirked behind her cup. My cheeks heated, not ready to share that part of myself with her. She didn't deserve it. I cleared my throat and gripped my mug for comfort. What do I even say to her?

"Do you talk to Isaac a lot?" I asked. I knew they shut him out after I ran, but he never mentioned talking to her since.

"I do, now. I asked him to help you while you were in town. I thought you'd feel lost. I didn't want you to be alone."

"You did what?" I stared at her, anger and hurt bubbling through me. "You asked Isaac to babysit me?" Was everything fake? Was Isaac playing nice while I was here because my mother asked him too? No. No way. And why wouldn't she want to step up and be there for me?

"I did." Her face fell. "I didn't tell him anything other than you had a lot to work through."

"Why didn't you come around then?" I glared at her, knowing she didn't have a good answer. "What happened after I left that night?" I asked, watching her expression fall, haunted with memories of a trauma we both fought to forget.

"A lot of things happened. After I saw what I saw, I made up my mind that I couldn't stay with him. When I realized you were running away, I didn't have the heart to stop you. How could I?" She took a deep breath. "I confronted him, and it didn't end well. He didn't even bother denying anything. He just told me to get over it." She rolled her eyes, her words laced both with hate and hurt. "Once he realized you were gone, he was dead set on going after you. He hammered me with questions and tried to beat the answers out of me." She looked up at the ceiling, trying to will away the tears that threatened to fall.

"Did he?" I stared at her, unfeeling. "Go after me?"

"No, but he tried. I told him I was leaving and that he could expect to hear from a lawyer soon. I packed up in a hurry, trying to tune him out as he threw his tantrum, and then I left." Her shoulders sank. "I served him with divorce papers three days after that." She looked out the window, sadness in her eyes. "He didn't even fight it. He signed, and that was that. I never spoke to him again."

"So, he died without anyone knowing what a piece of shit he was?" I tried to hide the bite in my tone, but it was useless. Her apathy made me sick. She looked at me, apologetically but it wasn't enough. It would never be enough. A humorless laugh escaped me as I stared at the woman across the table from me. I knew this was a mistake. I thought we could get some closure, but the itch to run away clawed its way through me.

"Holly," she said, reaching for my hand. I jerked it away, shaking. Sadness and longing took over her features and I didn't have the heart to return the sentiment. "I tried to do the right thing. I know I made mistakes. I wish I could take it all back, but I can't."

"No, you can't. I was really hoping we could move past what happened, but I don't know if I have it in me." I stared at her. "Isaac told me that in order to heal, I have to work on every part of me. That includes our relationship." I crossed my arms in front of me.

"I want to have a relationship with you, Holly. Now more than ever."

"I'm not sure I can do that." She lurched back as if I had thrown a dagger in her heart. Good. "Not yet anyway." She nodded, looking nothing but defeated.

"We burned the house down." Her eyes shot up to mine.

"What?" Her brow furrowed.

"Isaac and I burned the house to the ground. I couldn't bear to be inside it. Hopefully you didn't want anything out of it, because it's all gone." I stood up, grabbing my mug and plate. "I don't know how much longer I'll be in town. Here's my phone number." I wrote it on her napkin. "I don't want to lose you, but I don't know how to forgive you, yet." I looked her over, relaxing my shoulders. "Be patient with me?"

"Of course, Holly. I know it doesn't mean much now, but I am so sorry for what you had to go through. If I'd have known-"

"Stop." I put my hand out. "It's in the past, I'm working on moving on and forward. You should too." She hung her head and sighed a heavy sigh. I turned, walked my mug to the bin, and headed out the door.

My head was spinning, and my breaths were caught in my chest. First, Isaac needed to be asked to even be around me. That hurt a lot, especially since I had given so much of myself to him. It felt fabricated and forced even knowing Mom intervened. Second, she will never fully understand how guilty she is. She ignored my abuse for years and all of a sudden wanted to apologize. No. I knew my fairy tale bubble would pop. I needed to sit alone with all of this and dig deeper. I had let myself get thrown into a whirlwind romance with Isaac, I lost sight of what I needed to be doing. I needed to heal. Ten years ago, running away from this place was what I thought I needed to do just that. Now, I wasn't so sure.

I took my time walking back to Isaac's office where he greeted me with a soft kiss and a knowing hug.

"How'd it go?" He asked as he released me. I sighed. How did I even tell him where my mind was? Where did I start?

"Did mom ask you to help me while I was here?" Right to the point. He froze, looking at me with a sadness in his eyes.

"Yeah. She came by after the funeral and asked me to keep an eye on you. She was worried."

"Right. So worried that she couldn't do it herself?" Tears welled in my eyes. Anger boiled under my skin.

"Would you have let her?" He cocked his head to the side, his eyes piercing into me.

"I don't know."

"Yes you do." He wrapped his arms around me. "I can't imagine dealing with what you did on your own, Holly. Put yourself in her shoes. What would you have done?"

"She gave me her ring." I whispered. "I sold it in Boulder to get my apartment." I looked up at him, shame and sadness coursing through me.

"It was probably the only thing she knew to do." Silence settled between us for a beat.

"Would you have done so much for me if she hadn't asked you to?" I really didn't want to know the answer, but I had to. I needed to know if this was real or just another band-aid I would eventually have to rip off.

"Yes, Holly. I don't think I could have stayed away from you if I tried." He brushed a stray hair away from my face as a grin grew on his face. "I have an idea."

"Oh? What's that?"

"Let's go camping. You've had a whirlwind couple of days, and it might do you some good to have a distraction for a night." It didn't take long for me to say yes to that idea. I needed a breath of fresh air when everything around me seemed to suffocate me.

Chapter 31

H*olly*

I ran through my mental checklist while I stood in front of the shelves in the garage. We weren't planning on going in the house at all, so I wanted to make sure we had everything. I couldn't take being in that house. It was mine, but I wanted nothing to do with it. The idea of just selling it was becoming more and more alluring. The idea of having to go through it and all that was left behind was terrifying. The itch to run, again, was so strong. I couldn't shake the suffocating feeling this town gave me. So far, the only escape I had was Isaac. But it was just that – an escape. It wasn't fair to either of us to rely on him for my own sanity's sake. I felt a little better now that Isaac knew everything, but I still hated him seeing me like that. I felt weak, used, and vulnerable. That house was a place where I had less control of my mind and my memories. It was like a cancer to my newfound happiness. I couldn't let it destroy what Isaac was working so hard to give back to me.

"Got everything?" He asked, coming up behind me, wrapping me in his arms. He felt like home. I think he always had.

"I think so. If not, we can just come back. It isn't too far." I turned and faced him, wrapping my arms around his waist. "Besides, we don't need much do we?"

"Hmm. No, baby. You're it. And maybe some toothpaste. I have fallen victim to your morning breath more times than I would like to remember at this point." He winked down at me, and I poked a finger in his side while I tried to get away. He just tightened his grip around me, fisting my hair at the back of my head, forcing me to look up at him. "But I would burn down the world to wake up to your morning breath every fucking day." Releasing me, I let out a sharp breath trying hard to hide how undeniably turned on I was by him. He was giving me glimpses of a different side of him, one I have never seen before. He was always careful with me, especially now. He knows I'm broken, fragile. I hate that he has to tiptoe around me. He has helped me so much already, I want to give him everything, but I don't know how yet.

Isaac changed pleasure for me. He taught me to accept it from him and take what I want without pushing my own boundaries. That was something I had never had before. My father destroyed that part of me. When he said he would reclaim every inch of me, he wasn't exaggerating. There is not a part of me that has been left untouched by Isaac. He had worshiped my body and made me fall in love with him in the process. He's growing braver and braver by the day, too. His touch, his intensity, it takes my breath away. He takes my breath away. Those emerald eyes have stripped down my walls one by one and laid me bare in front of him. I never thought this would be my reality. I never thought I could be this happy, this whole.

"Get whatever else you need, Holly. Let's get out of here." He smacked me on the ass as he turned towards his truck to shut the tailgate. We really weren't taking much. I had found my old hammock and made that priority number one. I could spend the entire weekend in that thing and be perfectly content. I brought a sketchpad because I had been secretly trying to sketch Isaac without his knowing. The bastard pays attention to everything I do. While I like the attention, it makes my plotting difficult.

The roads to the house – my house – were windy and beautiful. The fall colors mixed in with the Colorado pines made a perfect backdrop to this weekend. We passed Isaac's old house and the skate park, and literally drove down memory lane. I was less nervous this time because I knew we didn't have to go inside and face the demons that were locked away inside. I could enjoy this drive today. Progress.

"I will never forget your mom's brownies. Think she would make them again for me?" He asked, grabbing my hand off my lap and kissing my knuckles softly. My heart felt like it was going to burst at any minute. Driving down these old roads, I realized I had always loved Isaac. It has taken me longer to realize it than him, but we had always been it for each other. I was too locked away inside my own head to see it, though.

"Probably. It may cost you an oil change though." I winked over at him as he smiled, showing off his perfect boyish dimples. Even in our thirties, he still looks like the boy I skateboarded with. I ran my fingers through his hair, twirling the strands around, cementing this vision in my head. I didn't want to ever forget this. I don't need to escape my reality anymore. My reality finally is my escape.

"I'll pull around the back and we can walk up the trail a bit to a good spot. Sound OK?" He eyed me, warily and my heart sank knowing my father has hurt him almost as much as he hurt me.

"Sure. I can grab the bags if you want to get the tent. We shouldn't have to make more than one trip."

"Nah, we got this. This is why we packed light, babe." He got out of the truck, coming around to open my door for me and helping me out. I glanced back at the house, letting myself feel the past for a second and then forcing the demons away. I put up that mental wall I was so well acquainted with, and Isaac must have sensed it. He wrapped his arms tight around me, burying his face in my hair. I could feel his heartbeat and his warmth. He grounded me, reeling me back in. I pulled away, smiling up at him.

"I'm OK, babe." I ran my fingers over his chin, feeling the rough stubble, I loved so much. "I'm ready." Together we started the small hike up to the little clearing in the trees. While Isaac started on the tent, I looked for the perfect place for the hammock. No matter how many times I come into these woods, I still feel like I hardly knew them. It's like nature has so much more power over us, that we can never fully understand it. I love how it seemed new each time I came here. I set up my hammock, then made my way back to Isaac to help finish up the tent. We got ice in the cooler, and food organized in the bins we brought. It was perfect.

Not quite as perfect as watching Isaac chop wood, though. I laid in my hammock, unashamedly drooling over him. While there was a chill in the air, he worked up a sweat and shed his hoodie and shirt. He was a sight to behold. His perfect, lean, swimmer body moved with ease as he chopped log after log. Occasionally, he would look over and catch me eye fucking him. His smirk made my cheeks flush, and I quickly pretended to go back to reading. Eventually, I must have fallen asleep, because next thing I knew, the shadows were long across the ground and the air was colder. Isaac had brought over a blanket at one point and tucked me into the hammock. I looked over to the now roaring fire and watched him read his own book and sip the mug of coffee he made.

As graceful as a slinky wobbling down a flight of stairs, I attempted to get out of my hammock, only I landed on my ass on the ground with a hollow *thump*. He turned towards me, laughing, and shaking his head. I glared over at him.

"Oh no, don't get up or anything! I'm fine! No worries." I punched him in the shoulder as I walked by, taking the seat next to him.

"I had no doubt, baby girl. You had it all handled perfectly." He winked and my visions of his working body from earlier instantly made me clench my thighs together. "Do you want some coffee? It's still hot. I just made it."

"Sure." My eyes trailed after him, watching his every move. He made me a cup of coffee, just the way I liked it and kissed me softly on the forehead as he took his own seat back. I inhaled the rich smell deeply and let this feeling wash over me. "This is perfect."

"I know. I made it." He quipped, not looking up from his book.

"Not just the coffee, asshole. All of it. The trees, the weather, you, everything." He leaned down and put his book on the ground. Leaning his forearms on his knees, coffee in hand, he looked at me. It was the kind of look that made me feel like he could see into my brain. He knew every ache and pain, every joy, every dream, and every nightmare.

"This, Holly, is what it feels like to live in the moment. You don't need to escape somewhere else in your head. You don't need to run. This, babe, is what happiness is." Tears stung my eyes as I wiped them away with my sleeve. I only just started to allow this feeling to be real for me. I didn't know what to do with it. So, we sat, and we drank our coffee. We read our books; we held each other's hands gently. We watched the sun start to go down and listened to the crackle of the fire. Isaac got up to load it again and I followed him over to the pile to help carry some wood over closer.

"Are you getting hungry, baby?" He asked.

"No, not really. Do you want to take a walk before it gets darker?"

"Absolutely, I do." He smiled wickedly at me as he pulled me into him. We walked around the trail that headed deeper into the woods and the air smelled cool and crisp. The breeze whipped my hair around my face. Other than the wind, the only other sounds were our footsteps against the fallen leaves.

"Do you remember when we used to play out here as kids?" He asked, not taking his eyes off the trail ahead of us.

"I do. We used to run through these woods all the time." I laughed and imagined us running through these same trees in what seemed like a lifetime ago. I never would have thought we would still be right here. Then again, maybe I did. Maybe I always knew.

"I sure hope you are a better runner than you used to be." I stopped, and he turned to face me, his eyes full of heat.

"And why would you hope that?" I asked, a tremor in my voice. Excitement buzzed through me and electrified my entire body. Adrenaline pumped through me.

"Because I am only going to give you a ten second head start. And you better hope I don't catch you." I was shaking already, and my panties were already fucked. It's these moments that I remember we weren't the same kids anymore. We are full of pent-up desire, primal energy that tried to claw its way out.

"Baby?" He growled, pulling me closer, running his finger along my jawline, forcing me to look up into his eyes. "Run."

I shoved myself out of his arms, taking off into the woods as fast as my shaking legs could carry me. I could hear my heartbeat in my temples, pounding so loud it drowned out every other sound around me. I weaved in and out of the trees trying to get ahead of him. I had no awareness of where he was or even where I was. I looked behind me every few seconds, but my vision was blurry because of the cold breeze stinging my eyes. There was a clearing, up ahead with a large enough tree to hide behind. I pushed myself faster, sprinting towards it.

I ducked behind it, landing between two roots that helped hide me even more, although I doubted it would be enough. I covered my mouth with my sleeves to stifle my heavy breaths. It was quiet around me. For what seemed like hours, I listened around my pounding heartbeat. Finally, I heard his steps behind the tree. He had to only be a few feet away. My heart raced, the thrill making my skin itch. I slowly turned around to look around one side of the tree. My heart sank when he was nowhere in sight.

It was starting to get even darker, and my eyes strained to adjust to the dark woods. I turned back around and looked ahead of me. He was nowhere. Real, tangible fear started to take hold of me, and my breaths were heavy and strained.

"You're about as good at hiding as you are running, little girl." He growled into my ear as he nipped at my ear lobe. I screamed, ducked away and took off, running straight ahead of me, not daring to turn around and look. Seconds later, I felt him pull at my arm and whip me around to face him.

He wrapped his strong hands around the sides of my neck and a pathetic whimper escaped my lips. He had me, body, and soul. He had always had me; I had just always run. Somehow, I always ended up back in his arms. This game was over before it even started. The moonlight danced in his eyes as he drank me in. My core clenched and I ached for him. I needed him to touch me, to claim me. I licked my lips, and his eyes followed the motion, hunger in his eyes.

"Please," I cried.

"Please, what, baby girl?" His voice was like gasoline on the fire that smoldered in my heart.

"I need you, Isaac." I didn't even recognize this desperation. I didn't know I could crave someone so intensely, or how I had ignored this longing for so long. He was just as desperate as I was. He fisted my hair, pulling my head to one side. His mouth delicately moved over my neck so carefully, I could barely feel it. He was driving me wild, and he knew exactly what he was doing to me.

"And what do you *need* me to do? Hmm?" His mouth and his fingers brushed over my skin as I cried out for him.

"More! I need more of you, all of you. Please." Tears stung my eyes and rolled down my cheeks as he looked back at me, devouring me with his eyes.

"I've gone slow with you, Holly. I've been gentle, and easy. I will not be tonight. You have tested my patience. I have waited *years*. I will break you, that's a fucking promise. Do you hear me?"

"Yes," I gasped. 'Please." Something in him snapped as he dragged me back to the tree that I was hiding behind. He let me go and caged me in, one arm on each side of my head against the tree. I looked up at him with hooded eyes, desperate for something, anything. I was pretty sure he could breathe on my skin, and I would explode. His lips crashed down onto mine, his hand cupping my chin and forcing himself deeper. His kiss was rough and primal, like he needed me to breathe, to survive. I let him in and met his kiss with everything I had in me. He drove his other hand up my hoodie and I gasped at the cold touch. My nipple strained against my sports bra, aching against the fabric. He pulled away from me, leaving cold emptiness between us. I groaned in frustration, as the corner of his mouth hitched up in a cocky smirk.

Without warning, he ripped my hoodie and shirt off over my head. The bark of the tree was rough against my skin, the pain only made the sensations more intense as anticipation ripped through me. I felt everything. The cold, the pain, the aching desire it all created within me. He ripped off my sports bra and then my leggings, leaving me naked and vulnerable in front of him. His eyes trailed down my body as he closed the distance between us. He got down on his knees, pushing me further up the tree. I squealed as he lifted one of my legs over his shoulder, kissing the crease right inside my thigh. I screamed in pleasure and my voice echoed through the night.

"That's right, baby girl. Let it all out. It's just you and me out here." He nipped the entrance to my core, and I yelped as he smoothed the pain over with his tongue. "But, if you are going to scream, it better be my name coming out of your mouth."

Before I could even react to the words, his tongue was crashing into me. Pleasure exploded through my entire body. He swirled his tongue in and around me, making my legs tremble with ecstasy. My vision blurred as he tongue fucked me into oblivion.

"Goddamn, baby. We didn't even need to bring food out here. I could survive on you for the rest of my life." He worked me over, euphoria consuming me from head to toe. My head rolled back against the tree, my moans filling the night. "Come for me, little girl. I know you want to." His words pushed me over the edge and my body felt weightless against the tree.

"God, Isaac! Fuck me, please." He stood up, his beautiful face inches from mine, his eyes full of desire.

"Your wish is my command. But first, baby, get on your knees." My eyes widened at his words. I never imagined him like this, but it made me ache for more. I would do anything for him right now. I know now how hard it must have been for him to keep this part of him subdued for so long. How long had he fought his desire, this primal man that lurked beneath the surface? I slowly got down on my knees, the rough ground digging into my skin. I looked up at him with heavy eyelids, still coming down from my own orgasm.

He took off his hoodie and shirt with one arm as I undid his belt buckle. I couldn't get his clothes off fast enough. Shivering with desire, I pulled his pants and boxers down in one sweep. His cock sprang up in front of me, a bead of precum already leaking for me. I looked up at him hungrily, taking him all into my mouth. His hand wrapped around my hair, and I could feel him vibrate as he moaned into the night. Working him in my mouth, I swirled my tongue around him, tasting every bit. Drool pooled at the corners of my mouth and tears rolled down my cheeks as I strained to take him all in. I gagged as he hit the back of my throat, but I didn't care. I kept going as he moved my head, bucking against me.

"Fuck, baby. You are incredible. So, fucking perfect. Beautiful." I looked up and met his eyes, continuing to suck him in. He gripped my hair tighter, stopping my movement. He pulled out of my mouth, with a *pop*. "Get up, turn around, hands on the tree." I obeyed, legs shaking with anticipation. I looked over my shoulder and watched him stroke himself, consuming me with his eyes. "Bend forward more. Let me see all of you." Again, I obeyed. "God, you're a vision. So pretty and wet for me."

With his body pressed behind mine, his fingers traced my soaking entrance. I shivered with need as he circled my clit with his middle finger and pressed his thumb inside me. Working me gently, I dropped my head between my arms and bit my lip to keep from moaning. He worked me over until I was clenching his thumb, my fluttering walls aching.

"That's right. Come for me, baby." He groaned. "Mine. You are mine. We are all that exist now. Say it, baby. Who do you belong to?"

"Yours. Fuck, I'm yours. I have been since the day we met." I came undone, again, falling into pieces around him. I barely had time to recover before he was reaching around me and pulling me up towards him. My back to his front, skin to skin. There was nothing between us and the energy pulsed around us. He brushed my hair from my neck, kissing it softly. Up my jaw, and down to my collarbone. His other hand wrapped around my front, circling gently over my swollen clit. I shuddered in his arms, letting him move over me and around me.

"Get down on your hands and knees." He whispered into my ear. Goosebumps erupted over me as I lowered myself down onto the ground. The leaves crunched beneath me, and the earthy scent surrounded me. He was on his knees behind me, one hand splayed across my back, one hand wrapped around the base of his length. He pushed into me, groaning, and stiffening as he pushed further and further. Feeling this intrusion for the first time made me feral. My head sank between my arms as my elbows fell to the ground, leaving me wide open for him. He thrust hard into me, and I cried out. We had danced around penetrative sex, but feeling Isaac unleash on me was the most cathartic thing I ever experienced. My nightmares had no hold over me, my pleasure or my life. Not anymore.

"Isaac! Fuck, I need you to move. Please, God, fuck me." With no warning, he pulled out, leaving me aching and empty only to crash back into me, hard. His thrusts were rough and hard and made flashes dance across my eyes. I could feel his sweat dripping onto my back, and his cock stiffening inside of me as I came again, drooling all over myself.

"Your body is mine, Holly. You are mine. Your hurt, your past, your pain, it's all mine now. Don't you ever fucking forget that." I melted into the ground, tears and snot running down my face as he exploded inside of me. His thrusts slowed, as he leaned over me, gripping my hips and slowly pulling out of me, leaving me shaking and euphoric.

We collapsed into each other, naked, sweaty, and filthy on the forest floor. We laid there for minutes, in silence looking up at the stars. After a while, he moved out from under me.

"What are you doing?" I pleaded. He smiled back at me pulling a knife out of his pants pockets. He nodded towards the tree.

"Commemorating this moment. This tree will never recover from what it just had to witness." He laughed and set to work carving out our names in the bark.

"Whatever. That was the hottest thing that tree will ever get to see."

"Oh, really now? Is that a challenge, little girl?" He raised an eyebrow at me as he lunged forward and tickled me. I squealed and, in my head, I remembered thinking *I never want to leave this place.*

Chapter 32

Isaac

I woke up curled around a soundly sleeping Holly. The light was dull outside, so I knew it was still early. I could see the shadows of the smoke against the canvas tent, so I carefully got up and headed outside to put some more wood on the fire. The air was cool and there was frost on the ground. Grabbing my hoodie off the camp chair, I slid it on and started grabbing wood. The flames picked back up in no time, so I made a pot of fresh coffee and sat down, watching the flames dance around.

I had to convince myself that last night was real. There was something so powerful in the way she looked at me. I know how hard it was for her to let go and let me take control. Just thinking about what she went through made my skin hot. I can't believe I went to that disgusting bastard's funeral. I wish I could do more for her, take away even a fraction of her trauma. She was taking baby steps towards happiness, but it seemed like she was always just out of reach. Last night we took a huge step, and I was terrified that I did more damage than good. I could have sent her headfirst back into her trauma. The way she pleaded and melded to me gave me a glimmer of hope that she took one big leap out of the darkness. I clung to that hope like my own life depended on it.

Holly stirred inside the tent, and my heart rate picked up a notch or two. I wasn't sure why I was nervous, but I couldn't help but feel on edge. I heard her get up and watched her carefully as she stumbled out of the tent. I chuckled to myself. Everything about her is perfect, even her imperfections.

"Morning." She mumbled. "Is that coffee I smell?" She wiped her eyes and stretched. She was more relaxed than I had seen her in years. I stared at her, in awe.

"Sure is, little girl. Do you want me to make you a cup?" She blushed and shyly nodded her head.

"Yes, please. I have to pee." She laughed and pulled her converse on. While she disappeared into the trees, I went to work getting her coffee. I caught a glimpse of those beautiful blue eyes on her way back. It could have been the morning sun, but I thought, maybe for a second, I saw that spark of life come back. As I watched her, I knew at that moment that I needed, now more than ever, to get *my* Holly back. I meant what I said all those years ago about staying kids forever. Somewhere along the way, a monster stole that from her. Now, piece by piece I would reclaim that for her. I had to.

I handed her the mug of steaming coffee and sat back down. Without hesitation, she curled up on my lap and leaned into me. I set my mug down and wrapped my arms around her, pressing a gentle kiss on the top of her head.

"Isaac?" She whispered.

"Yes, baby?" She looked up at me, hesitation in her eyes.

"Where did you learn to fuck like that?" I stared at her in disbelief for a second, and then shook with laughter.

"Well, I guess I watch a lot of porn." She smacked me in the chest which only made me laugh harder. "Honestly, I don't really know. I have this connection with you, Holly that just drives me fucking crazy. You make me crazy in all the best ways. I just don't want to push you too far."

"You make me feel safe, Isaac. I don't think there is anything you could do that would push me away. I feel like I let go of so much last night. I feel like I can breathe again." A tear streaked down her cheek, and I gently brushed it away with my thumb, cupping her face in my hands.

"Holly, I can't make you whole again. That's something you have to do yourself. But I will make damn sure you don't have to do it alone. I promise." She curled back into me, and we sat in silence listening to the birds and the breeze through the trees. I thought about her darkness, her demons she had to fight and how to put them to rest for good. I stared at the fire, getting lost in my thoughts, in her.

"Holly?" Pins and needles rippled through me as an idea interrupted my thoughts.

"Hmm?" She mumbled, half asleep.

"I have an idea, but it may be a crazy one." She sat straight up, her wide eyes focused on me.

"I'm listening."

I FILLED THE LAST OF the three gas cans I had stored in my garage. Holly waited in the truck, bouncing with nerves and adrenaline. I had to give away my idea to her when we got a permit to burn the property. I wanted to do this for her, but I didn't want to cause her any more trouble than necessary. Adding arson to her list of problems would not be helpful at this point. Once we got that taken care of, I loaded plastic gas cans into the bed of my truck, shutting the tailgate. Bounding back up into the truck, I started the engine and headed back towards the house.

"Are you sure we should do this?" Her voice was shaking, and I could see the hesitation all over her face.

"Baby, I have never been so sure of anything in my entire life." I smiled confidently at her and took her hand in mind, kissing her knuckles softly. "We aren't going to just do this and run though. We are watching the whole thing turn into ashes. Got it?"

"Got it. No running." She sighed and stared out the window. I wished I could read her mind, see what was going on inside of her. I wanted her to have her life back. Last night was another step. This would be a leap. I just hoped it would work. My mind was spinning with ideas and plans, but we had to take this one step at a time. I can't rush this for her. I was in it for the long game. We pulled into the driveway and faced the front of the house. I squeezed her hand and leapt out of the truck. I walked over to the other side and opened her door. Her breaths were heavy, and her eyes wide. She looked terrified.

"Baby. I am right here. Your dad is dead. It's just you and me. I will be with you every step of the way." I reached out my hand and she grabbed onto it like a life raft. I pulled her around the back of the truck and handed her a gas can. She just stared at it, and then looked back up at me.

"It's not a snake, Holl. It won't bite you. Just make sure you don't get any on you." She reluctantly took it, and I chuckled and grabbed the other two. We headed towards the front door, and I opened it slowly. She pulled back and shook her head, eyes glued to the porch. I turned to face her, pulling her into me.

"This house holds so much power over you. He still has power over you. It's time to let that shit go, baby. It's time to live. Right here, right now. I am here for you, but I can't do this for you. You have to be the one to see this through."

"What if I can't do it?" She sniffed.

"You can and you will because you don't have any other choice. It's now or never, baby. Kill these demons of yours. Take all that power back." She looked up at me with tears falling down her flushed cheeks. Pulling her even closer, I kissed the top of her head and held her tight. She wrapped her arms around me, sobbing into my chest. After a few minutes, she started to let go and her sobs slowed.

"Are you ready, little girl?" She nodded and picked up the gas can. I left one on the porch, took the other in one hand, and held her hand in the other. We walked into the living room. It was exactly the way it was when we left it last time we were here. Dust coated the furniture and cobwebs clung to the walls. It smelled stale and lifeless. She walked into the middle of the living room and looked all around her.

"Is there anything you want to keep?" I asked.

"No." She looked at me over her shoulder, eyes blazing. "Burn it all."

We started in the living room, dousing everything in sight with the gas. We moved on to the kitchen and then the dining room. Her can was empty, so I handed her the one I had. We made our way up the stairs and covered the bathroom, and the guest room, then the master bedroom. She stopped in front of the closed door of her bedroom. She stood so still, I thought she would pass out again. I put my hand on her shoulder, reassuring her I was there. I leaned forward in front of her and slowly opened the door.

Her sobs started slowly, but her breaths picked up and she buried her face in her hands. She started shaking and trembling.

"I can't do this, Isaac! I can't do it." Tears, snot, and drool ran down her face. Her cries were deep, guttural and terrifying. I stood there, watching her fall apart in front of me for the second time and I questioned all of it. Was this right? Is this what she needed?

"Yes. You can and you will. Listen to me, Holly." I turned her around to face me, holding her tight. "Your dad was a monster.

What he did to you destroyed your life. This house, this room, is a mausoleum of pain, betrayal, and fear. Burn. It. Down." She collapsed into me, hitting me, and flailing so violently, I was almost scared of her. Almost. I moved behind her, scooping her up by her armpits. Like a puppet master, I held onto her hand and guided her towards the gas can. I curled our fingers around the handle and drenched the entire contents into the room. Her screams were deafening.

"The monster is dead, little girl. It's time to live again. Let's go." I dropped the can in the middle of the room, picked her up wedding style, and carried her out, down the stairs, and back through the front door. I set her down by my truck.

"Wait here. Don't you move from this spot. Do you hear me?" She nodded, looking up with jaded eyes. I ran back up to the porch, taking the stairs two at a time. I used the last gas can and soaked the outside of the house, front and back. I moved quickly to get back to Holly as soon as I physically could. She was still there, hugging herself, panting and looking at the house. Anger lashed across her face, and she screamed the most heart wrenching scream I have ever heard. My heart cracked in two and I knew I would never ever get that sound out of my head. I watched as she fell to her knees, doubled over by my truck. I ran over, bent down, and cupped her chin, forcing her eyes up to mine.

"It's time, Holly. End this." She nodded and I held out my hand to help her up. I handed her the box of matches. Her hands trembled around it, but she managed to get the match lit. She walked up the porch and threw the match as hard as she could, without blowing it out. She turned, ran back towards me and I caught her in my arms. We both stumbled back as the flames burst to life. I turned her around so she could watch them destroy her fears.

"Don't take your eyes off those flames, little girl," I whispered in her ear. She nodded, wiping her nose on her sleeve. Slowly, I pulled her hair to one side, exposing her neck to me. I kissed her as carefully as I could, feeling her tremble under my touch. I ran my fingers along her neck, down to the collar of her shirt. She swayed in my arms, and I could feel her legs weaken at the sight of her nightmares being wholly consumed by the flames.

"What have we done?" She whispered into me.

"Starting over. You deserve this." I ran my fingers through her hair, watching every muscle in her face twitch and move. Her eyes stayed locked onto the house. "Tell me three things you want in this life, Holly." She looked back at me, the lines in her forehead creased together as she did.

"What?" She asked breathlessly.

"Three things you want to do while you're alive. What do you see in your future?" She turned back around and slumped against me. The heat roaring off the house was intense, but I wanted her to see this through until the very end. No matter what her past looked like, this was the fresh start she needed and getting her to think about her own future in this moment seemed like the perfect time.

"I want to have my dream house. The one I painted." I nodded against her, holding her close to me. "And I want my art in a gallery."

"The one in Boulder?" She nodded. "One more thing."

"I want to be able to love you like you deserve." She turned around and those glossy eyes met mine, boring into me. There was so much emotion swirling around in her features I couldn't pick just one to focus on. All the sadness, the fear, and the pain all meshed into one giant conglomerate of unbridled feelings. It was uncharted territory. My fingers brushed over her face.

"I don't think I will ever deserve you, Holl." I smirked. "You are so perfect. I wish you could see yourself the way I do. Your talent, your heart, and your very being are so beautifully crafted, I feel like getting this time with you – however long you let that be – is the most precious gift I could ever have." I kissed the top of her head gently and wrapped my arms around her. Everything in me told me to hold onto her and never let go. I wanted to protect my heart, but I knew holding her down could make her hate me. So, I cherished the moment in front of us, a new beginning for her.

"Thank you," she sniffed into my chest. We stayed there in comfortable silence until the house was all but smoldering embers. I took her hand in mine and helped her back into my truck. We drove back to my house in silence, but there was a heaviness to it. When we pulled into the driveway, I opened my door and dashed around to get hers, but she was already climbing out. Like a zombie, she walked to the front door with me trailing behind her.

"Hey," I stopped her, grabbing a hold of her elbow. She turned towards me, her eyes distant. "Talk to me." She sighed and dropped her eyes to the floor.

"It's over." She said, barely a whisper. "But I don't feel any different."

"Holly, baby," I tugged her to me. "The kind of healing you are doing takes time. The house is gone. It needed to go. But you need to clean house in here." I pointed to her heart, her eyes following my finger. She gently took my hand and held it to her.

"I know." Her eyes drifted close and my heart sank. I was losing her. "I think I need to go back to Boulder."

"I'm not going to pretend that it won't hurt like hell to watch you leave again. But I know you need to do what is best for your heart, and your life moving forward." I wiped a tear off her cheek. Her wide eyes were stuck on mine. "I love you, Holly. So much. I won't ever stop. I'd follow to the ends of the earth if I could."

Chapter 33

Isaac

I already knew before I fully woke up that Holly was gone. Something in my heart prepared me for it. I stretched out on the bed, feeling the cold she left behind. A small part of me had hoped that she would be in the kitchen making coffee, but my house was empty. I opened my eyes, rolling over on my back to stare at the ceiling. I wasn't upset, not yet anyway. My ignorant heart was longing for a sign that she didn't leave me again. I ran my hands over my face and sat up. Swinging my legs over the bed, I slowly made my way through the house. She hadn't just left. All signs of her were gone. Her clothes were gone, her shampoo was gone, her travel coffee mug was gone. I walked into the living room and froze when I saw the painting staring back at me from the chair. It was the only thing that was left to remind me that these past few weeks were real.

The painting wasn't one that I had ever seen before. It was a painting of me. I'm not sure if it was from a specific time or place, but there is only one thing in this world that would have made me smile like I was in this painting. Somehow, she had captured everything she meant to me in one painting. It was incredible. She paid so much attention to the details of my face and my emotions. I don't know how she did it. A folded up piece of paper caught my eye in front of the canvas. I leaned down, already knowing what it was going to say. I almost didn't read it, but I guess I liked to torture myself.

Isaac,

I'm sorry I didn't have this conversation with you in person, but I don't know how to have it. Over the past few weeks, you have taught me how to live again. You showed me how to move on. I couldn't have gotten this far without you, and for that I will always love you. The truth is, I don't think I am cut out to be happy in this life. I'm angry, Isaac. I'm angry with my mom for abandoning me. I'm angry at her for betraying my trust and breaking my heart - again. I'm angry with myself for not knowing how to live in this town without feeling imprisoned in my own memories.

I'm not leaving forever. I promise. But I am leaving to try and fight the rest of my demons. I can't finish this here. I need space to think, to figure out what the rest of my life is going to look like now. I know you probably hate me, and you have every right to. I hope you will be patient with me. It's a big ask, I know. I promise I'll call, and text you. I still need you. I just need room to breathe. Please don't give up on me.

Yours Forever,

Holly

I probably read that note a hundred times. Each time, a new emotion bubbled over the surface. Could I give up on her? Never in a million years. Could I hate her? Absolutely. Did I? I don't know. I think a part of me did hate her for giving up on us, and her life here. Another small part of me knew this was inevitable. I was always on borrowed time with Holly. Heading back to the bedroom, I tucked her note into my top drawer of my dresser. I wanted to burn it and ignore its existence, but I didn't have it in me. I had one option at that point, and it was to make sure Holly had no reason but to see her future here.

I couldn't stay in this house and it's emptiness, so I got in my car and drove. I didn't know where, yet. I wanted to go get her, but I knew I couldn't do it. Not yet. She said she needed room to breathe, so I would give it to her. I found myself driving the roads back to her old house. It was a pile of ashes, but it was still hers. I slowed when I pulled up to the corner store. Parking, I rested my head on the steering wheel.

"Fuck!" I yelled, clenching my hands into fists. I punched the steering wheel, hard and recklessly. Anger, frustration, hurt, and desperation all descended onto me like a feral pack of wolves. They closed in on me, and I rubbed my chest trying to make the pain go away. I shook my head, kicked the door open and went inside the corner store. I wandered the aisles, waiting for wild red curls and baggy overalls to come bouncing around the corner. But they never did. I went to the cooler section and grabbed a forty of Coors Light. The candy aisle pulled at my heart. My feet felt like lead on the tile walkway. I stood in front of the licorice and stared, mindlessly, at it.

"I don't even like licorice." I laughed, humorlessly and turned away from it heading towards the counter. I paid, got back in my car and headed down the road. I stopped at the skatepark, pulling in the parking lot and staring at the kids there. I knew this park like the back of my hand. Still do, really. I grabbed my forty, opened the door and walked over to the benches facing the park. Cracking open the beer with a hiss, I took a long sip and watched the kids skate. I couldn't help but smile at the memories we had here. They were perfect.

"Isaac? Isaac McKnight?" A man's voice called me out of my day dream, and I looked around for anyone I would know. A guy, probably a little younger than me, came walking over, hands in his pockets.

"Hey, man. Sorry, do I know you?" I asked.

"Nah, you probably wouldn't. I mean, maybe. You did punch me pretty good once." He laughed and took a seat on the other end of the bench. Realization hit me and I shook my head, laughing at the memory.

"Jesus, that seems like a lifetime ago. I'm sorry, man." I said through a chuckle.

"Please, don't even be sorry. I definitely deserved it. I was an asshole kid. Still kind of an asshole adult." We both laughed and watched the kids skate around. "I bet these kids could skate circles around us now. I know mine sure does." I glanced over at him, pride glowing from him.

"Your kid is here skating?" I asked, trying to see if I could pinpoint which one it could be.

"Sure is. Green helmet. I'd say I taught him all he knows, but I'd be lying." He smiled, and pointed at a kid, probably about 6 years old. "Where's yours?" He asked. I dropped my gaze and my heart sank.

"I don't have any kids. I just stopped by for nostalgia." God, I sounded depressed.

"Cool, I gotcha. I feel like it hasn't changed at all here." I nodded in agreement, unable to tell him just how much everything has changed. I finished my beer, crushing the can as I stood up.

"See you around, Isaac." He called after me. I waved and tossed the can in the trash bin. Again, I sat in my car, numb and restless. I didn't know where to go or who to talk to. Would anyone even really understand what the hell I was feeling? I doubted it. I was alone, again, living in the wake of Holly's pain. I started my car and headed to the pile of ashes that was soon beginning to resemble my fragile heart. I didn't know how to put up walls like Holly did. I never had it in me. I guess, living in the ashes is what I get for hoping Holly could move on with me. She'd rather move on from me, though and I had to start living in that reality.

I pulled up to the open space of charred land. The space was beautiful, surrounded by trees and life. Burning the house down was the best thing for this place. I got out of my car and walked around it, so I was in the same place I was that day. I remember watching her fall apart in front of me. She was magnificent, letting go of all her bullshit as I fucked her demons away. I honestly thought it would be enough, that I would be enough. For the millionth time that day, my heart shattered into pieces over her. I lost track of how many days I would come up to the door as a kid and her dad would tell me she was sick.

"She can't come to school today, Isaac. She's a bit under the weather." He looked at me, with empathy in his eyes. He must have seen the worry flash across my face.

"Fuck!" I screamed into the trees. "Why?!" I yelled so loud I could feel the veins in my neck popping. My head surged and my pulse skyrocketed. I fell to my knees, my head rolling backward letting out another visceral scream. I always thought Holly had demons. It turned out, I had some of my own too. Maybe that's why she ran. She saw in me what I couldn't. She saw how much I needed to heal her to avoid my own damaged past. I could never in a million years say that my hurt was as bad as hers, or that my childhood was even that bad. But, for the first time in years, I wanted to talk to my mom, to cry on her shoulder, or see her smile. My dad always did what he could, but he had his own hurt to bear. I guess, in life, we all do.

I sat there on the ground for what felt like hours. I replayed all of Holly's plans for her life. She told me about her house, and how she would build it. She told me about the art gallery in Boulder.

"I can just see it now." She said, gazing into the stars. *"My art is going to be on display, and people will pay to see my work. Can you*

imagine?" She asks, rolling over on her side to look at me. My eyes never left her, I could see the spark in her eyes, glinting in the starlight. I swore her eyes alone could give me life. Who needs air?

I wanted nothing more than to make that dream come true. I'd give anything to see that spark come back to her for good. Watching it disappear over the years before she left was the most painful thing I had ever endured. Then, watching it slowly come back to life, I knew I had to do everything I could to fight for it, for her. My mind started flying a mile a minute as ideas came flashing in front of me. There was so much I could do for her here, to get her to see her own future. I just needed a place to start.

I jumped off the ground and jogged to my car. Getting in, I called the only other person I knew I could rely on right now.

"Hello?" She answered.

"Hey, meet me at the diner in like 20 minutes."

"Umm, OK. Is everything OK?" I laughed a humorless laugh, shaking my head.

"No, absolutely not." I hung up and pulled out of the driveway heading towards the diner.

The diner was full of regulars, and the noise was both comforting and nerve racking. I wasn't sure if Jenn knew Holly had left, but I doubted it. The way Holly left it with her mom, she didn't seem like she wanted anything to do with her. I could see why Holly was upset by what her mom did, but I also know how hard this has to be for Jenn. He hurt both of them in different ways, and neither one of them handled it in healthy ways.

By the time I ordered a burger and a milkshake, Jenn walked in and sat down across from me in the booth. The waitress brought me my shake and took Jenn's order as well.

"Are you going to tell me what's going on? Where's Holly?" She looked nervous, and I couldn't blame her. I was too.

"She's probably been back in Boulder for a few hours by now. But I'm not sure what time she snuck out in the middle of the night, so who knows how long she's been home." I took a drink of my milkshake. I wasn't playing games, or dancing around the truth. Not anymore.

"Jesus, Isaac. I'm so sorry." She placed her hand over mine, sympathy in her eyes.

"Me too, Jenn." I wrapped my hand around hers, stroking her hand gently with my thumb. "Did you know she was leaving?"

"I had my suspicions. Especially when this was in my door this morning." She held out an envelope and placed it on the table in front of her. Sliding it my way, she eyed me warily.

"What is it?" I asked. She sighed heavily.

"It's a power of attorney for the land." She looked at the envelope, and then back at me. "It's yours, Isaac. The deed is still in her name, but you can do whatever you want with it." Her gaze drifted out the window. I leaned back in my seat as the waitress put my plate in front of me.

"Huh. Well, I guess that makes my plan a hell of a lot easier." I smiled, tossing a French fry in my mouth.

"What plan?" She smirked.

"I'm going to build a house."

"Really?" She whispered.

"Yes. I'm going to build *her* house."

Chapter 34

Holly
One month later

The familiar smell of baked goods and fresh coffee surrounded me, barely easing the ache in my chest that has been haunting me since I left home. I knew if I stayed any longer, I would never make it out and I needed to clear my head. Loving Isaac was easy, but everything that came with it was what made it impossible. He helped me heal from my past in a way I would be forever grateful, but I needed to make sure I wasn't cutting my dreams short by staying. I had slipped back into a routine in my apartment, and at the bakery. My painting, however, was another story. I hadn't touched a brush or a canvas since I left Isaac's painting in his living room. I had tried, sure but every time I sat in front of a blank canvas, my mind and inspiration mirrored it.

Nights were the worst. I barely slept without the safe haven Isaac created for me. In the little time we allowed our relationship to bloom, he quickly became the center of my universe. That's what scared me. I didn't want to live my life dependent on someone else. I wanted to be able to finish healing and be comfortable in my own head without the distraction Isaac created. I needed to finish this process on my own. The last look I took at Isaac sleeping soundly before I disappeared would haunt me forever. My heart had shattered, and every mile on the bus back to Boulder made it worse.

With every day that passed, the pain turned into an ache. It felt like a weight that wouldn't ease up no matter what I did or tried. When I left home the first time, the feeling I had was completely different. It was freeing and allowed me the time I needed to make a life on my own.

Lynn was so generous when I returned. She had every right to turn me away when I showed up at the bakery, but instead she hugged me and told me I always had a place with her. Her kindness eased the pain in my soul enough to get me through the days. She asked about the funeral, my mom and all the things I was able to do while I was home. I gave her the PG details about Isaac, and she giggled like a little school girl. We laughed together, I blushed, and she winked at me, knowingly

"You've got it bad, baby girl," she laughed over bread dough. I shook my head, trying to mask my smile.

"Am I that obvious?" I rolled my eyes.

"Oh, yes. You are exactly that obvious." Her face fell, and she looked like she was thinking hard about something. "Tell me," she quipped.

"Ask me anything."

"You went home, buried your demons, literally, rekindled a relationship with Mr. Perfect, and then came back here?" I nodded. "Why?"

"For a lot of reasons, I think." I sighed, working the dough between my fingers.

"It can't be my old ass."

"Partly, yes. I missed you." I chuckled. Silence fell over us for a beat, and when I looked up from the dough, she was staring at me.

"What?"

"What are the real reasons, Holly?" My shoulders fell. How do I explain everything whirring through my mind on repeat? It was like an endless loop that never failed to break my spirit. I felt like I was being ripped open over and over again.

"I want to be OK on my own." I settled on the simplest answer.

"What do you mean?" She leaned on the counter, crossing her arms over her apron.

"I don't want to rely on a distraction rather than really get over everything."

"That's what Isaac is? A distraction?"

"Yes and no." I shrugged.

"You do realize that none of us truly heal on our own, right?" She raised an eyebrow at me. "We all need someone to grab our hand on the way out of the hole we dig ourselves out of." Her eyes softened while mine threatened me with more tears. I was so tired of crying. When would it end? This ugly version of me that holds on to the one that is fighting to be free was ruthless, unforgiving. I ached to reach that final step, the one that would let me live the life I wanted without fear, without regret.

"Holly?" Her gentle touch on my shoulder centered me, bringing me back from my thoughts. "Isaac may seem like a distraction, but it seems to me that he is the push you need to be whole again. You need to let yourself be loved as a whole." She dropped her hand, smiled at me softly and went back to her work. I let her words take center stage in my mind. I had convinced myself that Isaac was impeding my progress, that he was a blip in my healing. The truth was, leaving him behind hurt more than anything I had ever had to do. He helped me let go of so much, and I felt more whole around him than I ever had. I think that is what scared me the most. I didn't want to put all of my trust in him because eventually, that trust would snap. I let myself get close, expose all my darkness, and he loved me through it. What happens when the darkness gets to be too much? Would he get tired of picking up the pieces of my heart I leave trailing behind me everywhere I go? No. I couldn't bear to lose him like that. Leaving things the way I did, the memories we will always have of that time would have to be enough. For now, anyway.

The rest of the day in the bakery went by quickly. When it came time to lock up, she caught my attention again.

"I know you have a lot on your mind right now, and I am only going to bring this up once."

"OK?" I asked hesitantly.

"You will always have a place with me here. I know the bakery isn't your dream, but I like having you here."

"Thanks, Lynn." I smiled at her kind words.

"I'm not done." She put a hand out to stop me. "You want to heal from your past, move on and be free of the things that hold you back. You won't be able to do that until you accept that you can't do it alone." Her eyes shone in the low lights around us. "As much as I view you as a daughter, I am not your mother, Holly. You have one that loves you and wants to see you become everything you deserve and more. You have to talk to her. I know your relationship is strained but have the hard conversations. Dig deep and bridge that gap. You deserve it, and so does she." I blinked back my own tears, her words hitting me like a punch to the gut. Dealing with my mommy issues was the last thing I wanted to do. I had survived a lot, and I will continue to survive. But facing that gaping wound head on would be my undoing. Would it be worth it in the end? I nodded to Lynn and finished up closing duties and walked back to my empty, lifeless apartment.

Chapter 35

Isaac
 6 months later

The incredible amount of help and support I got from the town to build this house was overwhelming. I had poured over design ideas and blueprints taking every little detail into careful consideration. Holly's dreams were in the forefront of my mind every single step of the way. It made her absence that much more evident and excruciating. The thought of her coming home to see this house, this home, was everything I needed to keep going through. Jenn was there every day, helping where she could. Everyone from the shop came by in their time off to help as well. I never really realized just how much love I had in my life until this house. The people around me came through when I needed it the most. It gave me an overwhelming sense of humility. I didn't ask for these people to care about this house, and some of them didn't even really know Holly.

I looked at the progress we had made while I ate the sandwich Jenn brought me. The outside was almost complete, and the walls on the inside were all up, taped and mudded. Jenn and Audrey volunteered to paint, and I wasn't about to turn that down. Give me a hammer or a drill, and I'm good. A paint brush though, not so much. I very willingly let that task get delegated.

"Hey, Isaac." A soft voice called, pulling my attention away from the house that sat in front of me.

"Hey, Aud." I scooted over on the log I was sitting on to give her room to sit next to me.

"This house really is amazing. You should be proud of the work you've done." Her soft smile eased the constant ache in my heart.

"Thanks," I said between bites of the sandwich.

"Have you heard from Holly at all?" I choked on the bite in my mouth, forcing it down my now dry throat.

"Not really. I text her and call her every day, but I don't get much more than a sign of life. Sometimes, it's just a read receipt." I ran my fingers through my hair trying not to let the stab of hurt show too much on my face.

"I text her, too." The side of her mouth quirked up.

"Really?" She nodded.

"We exchanged numbers while she was here. She once asked me if I would want some help at the shop." I turned to her, my eyes widening. I had to suppress the hope in my voice.

"And?"

"I told her she would always have a place if she wanted it. You know I could use the help, and with her experience, I wouldn't have to teach her much, if anything at all." I nodded, taking in her words carefully. "You know, I don't know all the details of her past, but I know it wasn't an easy one." Her shoulders sank and her eyes were glued to the soft grass in front of us. "I wish that getting over trauma was easy, and we could just snap our fingers to make it all go away."

"Me too." I sighed. "I wish more than anything that what I did for her, what I am doing would be enough for her to forget it all and come home."

"I know you do, Isaac. And one day it will be. She has to come to that on her own though."

"Were you able to?" I could hear the heaviness in her voice. It was from someone who knew firsthand how hard it was to heal.. A sad smile formed as she looked up at me.

"I'm working on it." She patted the space between my shoulder blades. "Don't give up on her, OK?" She stood and walked back over to the house where Jenn was toting cans of paint.

"I could never give up on you, Holly." I whispered into the wind.

THE SUN STARTED TO set behind the trees surrounding the property. Most of the people that had been there for the day were gone. Jenn, Audrey and I were still there. They were finishing up painting and I was working on some small details throughout the house. I was incredibly proud of this place. It was exactly how Holly described, and I hoped more than anything that it would bring her a sense of peace. Her restless spirit deserved it and needed it. I poked my head into the room the girls were painting.

"Do you need anything in here," I asked. Music played softly in the background as they worked. Jenn tiptoed down the ladder she was on and set her paint roller down.

"I think we are just about done in here, and probably ready to call it a day." She wiped sweat from her forehead with her shirt sleeve. "Sounds good. Want me to order pizza?"

"Sure." Jenn said, Audrey agreeing.

"Cool. I'm on it!" I pulled out my phone and placed an online order for delivery. The girls cleaned up and rinsed out their brushes, and I picked up trash and tools from the day's work. We chatted comfortably and talked about what all needed to be done. Believe it or not, we were getting really close to being finished. I wouldn't have been able to pull it off without everyone who stepped up to help. Half an hour later, there was a soft knock on the door.

"Pizza is here." I called over my shoulder as I opened the front door. The smell of pizza wafted over me, but rather than the pizza delivery guy was the last person I expected to see here.

"Dad?" I froze, my hand still on the door.

"Hi." He held the pizza in front of him. "I was heading up when the driver was here, so I went ahead and tipped him and thought I'd bring it in for you." I blinked. My brain had short circuited, and words weren't forming. "Can I come in?" He asked. It sounded like he expected the answer to be no, without me even answering. I nodded, moving aside so he could make his way in. I followed him through the house as he took in all the details.

"This place looks amazing," he said with an air of awe to his voice.

"Thanks. It's everything Holly wanted in her dream home." He smiled and waved at Jenn and Audrey as they came out of the room they were painting.

"The pizza smells amazing." Audrey chirped.

"It does. Thanks, Isaac." Jenn raised her eyebrow at me, questioning the presence of our new guest.

"Help yourselves. Dad, you too." I waved a hand over the boxes. We all ate in stifled silence. Jenn and Audrey clearly picked up on the tension between my dad and me. Once they ate and finished cleaning up, they left with a quick farewell leaving me alone with my father.

"So," I offered. "What are you doing here?" He tensed across the kitchen.

"I wanted to see the work you had done. You should be really proud of this place, son."

"I am proud of it." I crossed my arms over my chest. He breathed a heavy sigh and looked at me with heavy eyes.

"I'm sorry." He shook his head.

"For what?" I quipped.

"Everything. My shitty parenting, abandoning you, all of it."

"Sorry is just a word, Dad." I pushed off from the counter, gathering the pizza boxes. "You are going to have to prove it to me."

"I know. Tell me how and I will."

"You could start by helping out with the house. There is still work to do here." He nodded, a small smile forming and a shine in his eye I don't think I had ever seen before. Did I want him to share this part of me? Not really. After everything I learned about Holly's dad and what she went through, I saw my own dad in a different light. Did I forgive him? Not exactly. He still needed to earn that. Did I understand him a little more? Possibly. I wasn't going to shut him out anymore. He came here wanting to start building a bridge between us, so I could at least meet him halfway and do my part. I was reluctant to say the least, but willing to give him this chance. I was curious what he would do with it.

"What time will you be out here tomorrow?" He asked.

"Probably around eight or so."

"I'll be here. Can I bring anything?"

"Just a set of hands. I have everything covered."

"Sounds good." He nodded and followed me out of the front door. I turned and locked it after us. "Isaac?" He muttered. I raised an eyebrow at him. "I know what I want to do in my retirement.." He shoved his hands in his jeans pockets and sniffed as he looked at me. A lump formed in my throat as I realized that was the first time I had seen him cry since mom died.

"Really?" I raised my eyebrows, genuine curiosity taking over me.

"One of the places your mom always wanted to visit was Paris. I think I want to take a long vacation and visit." A sheepish grin flashed across his features.

"Paris would be amazing. I didn't know she wanted to go there." I never felt like I really knew her to begin with.

"She wanted to do a lot, but it wasn't in the cards. Now, I'm done wasting away. She'd be so angry with how I spent my life without her. I can't bear to think about it." I took a step closer towards him, watching the tears fall down his wrinkled cheeks. "I know she would be proud of you. I don't know where you learned how to be such a good man, but I am damned proud of how far you've come."

"Dad," I sighed, pulling him into me. I wrapped my arms around the sobbing man that caused me so much torment over the years. After a beat, he pulled away, digging back into his pocket.

"I have something I want to give you."

"You don't have to do that." I waved him off.

"No, son. I do." He opened his hands to me and nodded for me to take a small coin. I took it, looking it over and flipping it over in my hand. There was a big number six on it and underneath was the word "month."

"Is this?" I asked, a tidal wave of emotions hitting me so hard it nearly knocked the breath out of me.

"It is. I've been sober for 6 months, and I wanted to prove to you that I'm ready. I'm ready to move forward with my life and stop standing in the way of yours." I hugged him again, hard, and the feeling of his arms wrapped around me was overwhelming.

"Retirement is going to look good on you, Dad." I laughed as we let each other go and headed back to our trucks. "Proud of you!" I yelled over the hood. A complete sense of peace washed over me. I felt like I could breathe for the first time in years. It faded as soon as I remembered the first person I wanted to tell wasn't here.

Chapter 36

Holly
3 months later

Despite my best efforts, I couldn't get Lynn's words out of my head. She had become such a mother figure to me since I moved to Boulder. For her to tell me flat out that she wasn't my mom and that I had one, waiting to love me, cut deep. So deep, that the bleeding felt like it would never end no matter how many band-aids I tried to cover it with. I tried so many ways. Everything pointed me back to myself and the real work I had avoided for so long. Lynn stuck to her word and never brought up my relationship with my mom again, but she had given me information on a support group she knew about. The brochure gathered dust on my kitchen counter. She gave me sad smiles here and there like she wanted to ask, but she never did. For the most part, we carried on like we were used to and enjoyed each other's company while we worked.

On my walk back to my apartment, I thought about mom and what I needed from her to forgive her. If I could just tell her what I wanted her to say, or do to make it better, I would. The truth was that I didn't know anymore. I had lost sight of what was at the core of my hesitance towards her. I didn't know what I was even mad about or why I was so hellbent on staying away from her. Did she hurt me, absolutely. Was it irrevocable? I wasn't sure anymore. Putting distance between me and what I knew to be home was what I needed ten years ago. It forced me to grow up, find out who I was and what I wanted. As I looked around at the city I made my home, it looked so distant, so cold. There was no warmth there, aside from the glimpses I got from Lynn. Even that is fleeting now. I couldn't stand the silence that enveloped me in my apartment that I once considered my safe haven. I couldn't stand the constant unanswered text messages from Isaac, my mom and even Audrey. I had a home. I had a place. I had people who loved me. They weren't here. Everything I once ran away from without a second thought is now what beckoned me to come home. *Home.*

I turned the key into the lock, opened the door to my apartment, and looked around. Its lifeless, barren existence took hold of my heart and yanked. I was never meant to stay here. This was never truly where I belonged. I collapsed onto the couch, hugging my knees to my chest. I let the overwhelming realizations wash over me. Tears didn't fall. Sadness didn't take over. A resolute, positive assurance took over. I looked at my phone, scrolling through all the attempts to get a hold of me. I paused on my mom's text thread, tapped it and hovered over the call button. Letting my pride go, exhaling a deep breath, I tapped the button and let the sounds of the ringing fill the air around me.

"Holly?" She picked up on the second ring.

"Hey, Mom."

"Is everything OK?" Her words were muffled and there was a lot of background noise.

"Yeah, I'm good." I heard her shuffle and a door close. Then, silence.

"I can't tell you how happy I am to hear from you." I could hear her smile through the phone.

"I'm sorry it has taken me a while. I needed to sort my shit out." I chuckled.

"Don't apologize, honey. Everything is just...a lot. It's heavy and I don't know how to say sorry without it sounding cheap, or shallow."

"You know what I forget sometimes?" I swallow looking at the ceiling.

"What's that?" She asks.

"He was my dad. He hurt, abused, and traumatized me and I will never be able to forget it. But you? He was your husband. He was supposed to be the one you felt safe with too. He broke your trust just as much as he did mine. He ripped your heart out just like he did to me. I got so wrapped up in my own head that I never once stopped to think about how it *actually* affected you."

"Holly." She sniffed.

"Instead of focusing on how we could help each other, I made you the villain in my head because it was easy."

"It's OK." She whispered.

"I want to forgive you, I really do. I want to make things better and I want to be a daughter to you. I just. I don't know how."

"We both have a lot to learn, honey. We'll take this one step at a time. I'm here, ready for you. I'm ready to work on us. I want to earn your forgiveness."

"And I want to give it to you." Both of our sobs filled the line. We breathed, sniffed, and cried to each other.

"Do you think you will ever come back?" She asked me with a hope in her voice I had ever heard before.

"I think so. Boulder doesn't feel the same as it did ten years ago."

"We will all be ready for you when you do, baby." I knew in my heart she was right, but I couldn't bring myself to tell her, or even make plans to leave Boulder. The little shred of doubt was all I needed to stay put, stay safe.

"Holly?"

"Yeah, I'm still here."

"Take the time you need. I love you. Please don't ever forget that." Snot bubbled out of my nose and a sob ripped through me. With those words, she was able to crack me open and see inside my soul. She stayed quiet on the phone while I let myself cry and sob and scream. It was cathartic. It was so incredibly freeing to be vulnerable not in front of her, but *with* her for the first time. She was never the villain I made her out to be. She took the role I needed her to at the time and welcomed me with open arms as I ran back to her. She wasn't perfect by any means, and I was far from it. We pushed each other away for so long. This homecoming felt more like breathing again after spending a lifetime of drowning. We said our goodbyes over the phone, and for the first time in a long time, I slept like the dead without any nightmares to haunt me.

The next morning, I answered all my texts that had been left untouched for months. I opened the text thread that Audrey and I shared and tapped out a quick message.

Holly: Hey, Audrey. I hope everything is going well! I was curious. Were you serious when you said I could work for you?

Audrey: Dead serious. I could use it, and I would love to work with you! Just let me know :)

Holly: Will do. Thank you!

I walked out into the kitchen, glancing at the brochure Lynn had given me. I picked it up, took a deep breath, and opened the website listed to find a schedule for the meetings they held. It was time to put in the real work and I finally realized I couldn't drag myself to the finish line. I needed a push and swallowing my pride was the first step.

Chapter 37

I *saac*
   One Week Later

I walked around the finished house. It was absolutely perfect. The a-frame structure, rustic and rugged, glowed from the inside out. It was everything she ever wanted. It was our future. I smiled and closed my eyes, envisioning the life we could have here.

The kitchen would be full of delicious smells while Holly painted with our kids at the dining room table. Laughs would fill the air, and happiness would radiate around us.

Perfection. Now I just needed Holly to be here with me. She was so stubborn, holding onto her pain like it would save her. I wished I understood it. I wished I could crawl inside her brain and rewire whatever her piece-of-shit father destroyed. But that's not how it worked. I could only push and prod until she was forced to come out of her shell. I wished I knew what it would take to get us there. I wished I could be more for her, enough to break through to her.

I walked into the house to make sure everything was shut down before I left. It was so peaceful and quiet here. The trees surrounding the place blocked out all the noise coming from the road. Thoughts of ways we would fill the silence had the corner of my mouth twitching and my dick stiffening against my jeans.

"Fuck," I whispered. It only felt like yesterday that I was chasing her down in these same woods. The desire I felt for her was delicious, powerful. I remembered the sight of me burying myself inside her as we burned her childhood castle of nightmares to the ground. I growled and rolled my head back.

"I can't do this here." Nearly running, I went back to my car and pulled out of the driveway, heading back to my house. The drive wasn't long, but it seemed like it took forever. Thoughts of Holly's mouth around my cock flooded my brain and it took everything I had to focus on the drive.

"God damn it, Holly!" I yelled to the empty air around me. "Why did you fucking leave me?" I screamed into the night. A lump formed in the back of my throat, and I breathed heavily, trying to steady my thoughts. My mind was spiraling down a dark place I fought to stay far away from. I never realized how angry I was at her for leaving. I was devastated when she left after graduation, but I was angry when she left almost ten months ago.

"Ten fucking months." The tears fell, and my heart broke all over again as I thought about what we could have and the life we could create together, if she would just let us. I rubbed my hand over my face as I pulled into my driveway. Turning off the car, I sat in silence for what felt like an eternity. I felt numb. Emotional walls started building themselves up around my heart. This anger, frustration, scared the hell out of me. I always loved Holly, and always would. But, she has shattered my heart more than once and I was beginning to be more protective of it, even if I didn't see it before. I wouldn't dream of giving up on her, but I had to prepare myself for the fact that she may not come back here.

With a heavy sigh, I kicked open the car door. I had to keep these doubts reigned in. I couldn't let my frustration with her choices taint my thoughts about her, no matter how much they confused me. I'd fallen for her the day we met, and nothing will ever change that. She had always been it for me no matter how hard I've had to fight for her to see it. I needed a hot shower to get my shit together and hopefully even get some rest. My bed was too cold without her, and I couldn't sleep right, not like I could when she was curled up in my arms. I stripped out of my work clothes, throwing them against the wall next to the hamper. I smirked, she always complained about picking up my clothes.

"Sorry baby," I smirked.

In the shower, thoughts of Holly came flooding back to me again as they often did. The sound of her heavy breaths beneath me, her small gasps as I nipped at her ear, the sight of her wild red curls splayed out across my pillows. I closed my eyes, imagining her wrapped around me. I wanted so badly to have her here with me, pinning her against the wall. Water would run down her perfect face, her hooded beautiful eyes looking up at me. Her mouth parted, she would moan my name as I trailed my fingertips down her body. I leaned my forehead against the shower, straining to keep the fantasy alive in my head. I gripped my straining length and chased the orgasm desperately. Images of her flipped through my head as my heart pounded in my chest. Finally, ropes of cum ripped out of me and I braced myself against the wall. With both arms holding me up under the hot water, I steadied myself, breathing deep. The hot water trailed down my spine leaving goosebumps behind it.

I needed her like a drug addict needed their next fix. She had become my obsession and the longer she was gone, the harder it became to keep my soul intact. I was coming apart at the seams. She took a part of my heart with her when she left me after graduation. This time, I didn't have it in me to let her go. I was holding on to whatever thread we had left between us. I turned the water off, and I wrapped myself up in my towel. I walked across my room to my phone, still in the pocket of my pants I threw. She hadn't called or texted me at all today. Now that her house was done, it was harder to keep it a secret from her or use it as a way to get her here.

"If only she knew what was waiting for her on the other side." I stared at my phone screen. I didn't care how desperate I sounded anymore.

Isaac: Holly, you need to stop running. I know you are hurt. I can't imagine dealing with what you have. But you're doing it alone and you don't have to.

I looked at the words, our text thread was mostly my unanswered texts. My heart sank and my head spun. I let myself fall on the bed behind me and stared up at the ceiling..

WHEN I WOKE UP, I WAS still wrapped up in my towel, splayed out on top of the bed. I blinked, looking around the room. It was still dark, but I could hear birds starting to chirp outside the window. I sat up, checking my phone for a reply, but when I saw my blank screen, I fell back onto the bed. It was about 4:30 in the morning, and there really wasn't much use trying to go back to sleep. I got dressed, made coffee and opened my laptop to check my emails. There were a few from the general contractor from the house, mostly just following up on the last minute details. The last one he sent was a congratulatory one for finishing the project. I should be excited, but doubts of Holly ever seeing it crept into my mind. I shut the laptop, and flopped down on the couch, trying to find something to focus on. I flipped on the TV, and mindlessly watched the news until it was late enough in the morning to head to the garage.

Business there was uneventful, and now that I owned it fully, I didn't have to spend as much time there as I had before. It still felt like home though, and I was greeted with smiles and warmth from everyone there. It was a strange comfort being there. While my dad was not a warm and fuzzy kind of man, the memories I had there as a kid were always good ones. I smiled to myself as I headed to the office to check on the books and the schedules.

"Hey, Isaac!" Trent called after me.

"Hey, Trent. What's up?" I turned to face him, his smile big, showing off his deep dimples.

"Want me to give your truck a once over? It's been a while. It could use some new brakes." He gestured to my car in the lot behind him.

"Nah, I will look at it later this week. It'll give me something to do." I winked at him as he shook his head and laughed. I chuckled to myself as I added that to my mental to do list. I checked my phone again for any sign of life from Holly. I typed out another text to her, hope becoming harder and harder to feel.

Isaac: Come home, baby. Please.

I spent the day there, and as the afternoon shadows lingered in the open bay doors of the garage, I decided to take dinner to Jenn on my way home. We had learned to lean on each other over the past few months. She was as much a connection to Holly for me as I was for her. Her warmth and familiarity made the hardest days easier. I ordered takeout online as I headed out of the garage.

I surprised Jenn, and she welcomed me with open arms. We talked and laughed over our Chinese takeout. She even made brownies. I was pretty sure she kept them regularly just for me. I loved her for it.

"Do you want the last egg roll?" She asked through a mouthful of fried rice. I laughed and shook my head. She grabbed it from the Styrofoam box, and took a bite out of it, rolling her eyes dramatically. I chuckled to myself, seeing so much of Holly in her. Holly definitely got her features from both her mom and her dad, but her personality was so much like Jenn. Life had dealt Jenn a rough hand too though, so she hid a lot of that away. I was glad to see it come through at times like that.

"This really hit the spot. Thanks for this, Isaac." She gave me a warm smile leaning back in her chair. The sun was starting to set outside. "Want me to make some tea? We can sit on the porch. It's nice out tonight."

"That sounds good to me. I'll clean up all this." I set to work getting leftovers put away as she plated brownies and put the water to boil over the stove. Jenn had always felt like family, and I needed her more than I ever had. She picked up my broken pieces when I couldn't. I headed out to the porch and sat on the swing, watching the breeze roll through the trees. The street was quiet, but I couldn't help but count the yellow cars that drove by. After a few minutes, Jenn came out and handed me my tea and the plate of brownies. I set them down on the table next to me and took out my phone, glancing hopefully at the screen. Nothing. Again, I wrote a text to Holly.

Isaac: I love you, Holly. We can have all the things we want. You just have to trust me.

Jenn eyed me warily. Catching her eye, I sighed and grabbed my tea. The scent was warm, and I closed my eyes, letting it roll over me.

"Why did she leave, Jenn?" I asked, almost in a whisper. I heard her sigh next to me. She looked out over the street, lost in a daze.

"I wish I knew Isaac. I really wish I knew. I know she is angry at me, and that is probably a big factor for it. But." She cut off, and I moved closer to her, wrapping my hand around hers. She looked at me with watery eyes.

"I wasn't there for her when she needed me. I let my own selfishness get in the way. When I tried to do right by her, it backfired on me. I wanted you to know what happened so you could help her through it. If anyone could do it, it would be you. I didn't think of it as a betrayal. I was trying to help her."

"It wasn't, Jenn. Talking to me wasn't a betrayal. No one was innocent in any of this, though. I watched her deteriorate all through high school and never once questioned it. No one did. We all failed her. She isn't gone for good though. She isn't lost. I will get her back." She leaned her head against my shoulder, quiet sobs rolling through her. We sat there for minutes in silence, watching the cars go by.

"When she comes back, you two need to talk about it." I said and I kissed her lightly on the top of her head. She sat up slowly, wiping her eyes.

"I know," she said. "I'm afraid she won't listen though. I want more than anything to tell her my side of the story. The hurt and pain that he caused me as well as her." I nodded, smiling at her softly. "We aren't that different, after all." Again, we sat, silence enveloping us. My anger from last night started to creep up again. Seeing the damage that was dealt in these two amazing women's lives has ruined me. I was angry at him for abusing them both the way he did. I was angry at Jenn for letting Holly go. I was angry at Holly for being so damn stubborn. I was angry at myself for standing by and watching it all fall apart around me.

My skin flushed with heat and my heart pounded. I stared out into the street, seeing everything but nothing all at once. My breaths were heavy, and I noticed Jenn was staring at me, concern flashing across her face.

"Isaac?" She looked at me, putting her hand on top of mine. "Talk to me." I looked at her, and then back out of the street, gripping her hand tightly in mine.

"I'm angry, Jenn. I'm angry at her for leaving and giving up. I'm angry at him for doing this to you two. I'm angry at myself for watching it happen and not doing a fucking thing to stop it. I went to his funeral, Jenn. I listened to everyone talk about how wonderful he was while Holly sat next to me silently being ripped apart again by him." I caught my breath, fighting the stubborn tears that threatened to fall.

"I let that fucker ruin her and all she could have been. I don't know how to fix it, Jenn. I don't know what to do to get her back. I can't lose her again." I turned and looked at her. Tears ran down her face as she covered her mouth, sobbing. She didn't say anything, and neither did I. For so long we had pretended we were OK, that life could go on and she would come back on her own. We both knew the reality.

The heavy realization that Holly had left us again, probably for good, hung over us like a fog in the air. Rain drops started to fall on the porch roof above us. The sky was dark, and it was getting late. The rain would probably last all night. I brought her hand to my lips, kissing it gently. Then, I let her go, standing up and grabbing my mug and the untouched plate of brownies. I took them inside, setting them on the counter. Back outside, Jenn stood up, pulling me close to her and wrapping her arms around me. I hugged her tight, holding on like my life depended on it.

"I'll get her back, Jenn. I promise." I pulled away from her and cupped her head in my hands. I gently rubbed the streaks away with my thumbs. I kissed her on the cheek and walked down the porch steps to my car.

The rain beat down on my windshield on the drive home. My thoughts spiraled and my emotions ran high.

"Fuck!" I yelled, hitting my steering wheel. I couldn't do this anymore. With the house done, it was time for us all to move on, to live for the future. I was done living in the past. I was done watching Holly run away from her fears and her demons. I stopped my truck on the side of the road, turned around and headed the other direction. I dialed Holly's mom, and she picked up on the second ring.

"Isaac?" She asked, surprised.

"I can't do this anymore, Jenn." I was nearly yelling.

"Do what anymore? Where are you?" She sounded worried, frantic even.

"I'm driving. I am going to get her ass and bring her back here. I will drag her kicking and screaming if I have to. I'll even pay her fucking rent, if that's what it takes. I'm not waiting around for her to dig herself out of her own head. She'll never do it on her own." I was panting, heart beating in my chest. I waited for her to answer, but we sat there in silence. The sound of the rain beating on the windshield echoed around me.

"Isaac, I don't know. She may hate you for it." I smirked.

"Wouldn't be the first time she got mad at me for doing something stupid. It won't be the last. She isn't doing herself any favors hiding from you, this town, or from me. I made her face her demons before, she'll do it again." My grip on the steering wheel tightened as I took the sharp turns. It was hard to see because of the rain, but nothing was going to stop me at this point.

"Isaac," She nearly whispered. "Thank you. Thank you for always doing what I couldn't do for her." I heard her sniff on the other end, and I knew that she needed this to happen just as much as I did.

Headlights streamed in through my window, and I turned to see where they were coming from. My eyes widened as a truck came at me at full speed. I reacted and slammed on the breaks, skidding on the wet pavement. It wasn't enough. I couldn't stop.

"Jenn, I gotta -" The sound of metal crashing echoed in my ears. My skin crawled and stomach bile burned my throat. And then, nothing.

"Isaac? What was that?"
"Damn it, Isaac, what happened?"

Chapter 38

Holly

Isaac: Holly, you need to stop running. I know you are hurt. I can't imagine dealing with what you have. But you're doing it alone and you don't have to.

Isaac: Come home, baby. Please.

Isaac: I love you, Holly. We can have all the things we want. You just have to trust me.

I stared at my phone, fighting the part of me that was stubbornly holding onto all the hurt, the pain, the scars. I wanted so desperately to hate her. I needed her to blame for not being able to move on from this. If I picked up my phone to call her back, I knew I would slowly start loosening my grip on that angry part of me that hid in the shadows. If I reached out to her, I would put yet another shovel full of dirt over the bitterness I buried with the monster who gave it to me. My phone buzzed again, and I sat there, staring at it.

As much as I wanted to hate her, I also wanted so desperately to have a relationship with her. If I went home to be with Isaac, it would be easier. I could start over with her. He always made things so much easier, and I didn't think I would have gotten that far without him. Tears threatened at the brim as I faced, yet again, the demons that raged inside of me. I was in constant war within myself. I reached out, picked out my phone, and looked at the text messages and the phone calls. Isaac had been texting me more and more lately, and while I admit I hadn't always responded, I felt comfort in knowing he was still there. His last text message ripped my heart open. He loved me. I knew he did, he told me all the time. Every time he did, a piece of the shell around my heart chipped off and fell away. His love was visceral. It was imprinted in my soul.

Holly: I love you too, Isaac. I'm coming home. I promise.

I pulled up my mom's text thread and decided to call her. My fingers trembled, and my heart raced. "I can do this," I told myself. It rang twice before she answered.

"Holly?" She asked. My mouth went dry, and I struggled to find words to say back to her.

"Yeah, mom. It's me." I took a deep breath, doing my best to calm my nerves.

"Are you at home?" She asked. It sounded like she was driving.

"Yeah, I'm at my apartment. Why?"

"Well, I am about ten minutes away. Stay there, please. We need to talk." She sounded rushed, and maybe even scared. I stood up off the bed, pacing around my room.

"OK. I will leave the door unlocked. Is everything OK?" I asked, uneasy.

"No, sweetheart. I don't think it is." She hung up, and I looked at my phone, shocked at the exchange. I went to unlock my door so she could come in when she got here. I knew we had to have this conversation, but something about the rushed exchange didn't fit. I paced my entire apartment in the eight-and-a-half minutes it took my mom to get there. I ran through everything I had learned from the other women in the group I had joined. I controlled my breathing and went through everything I wanted to say over and over in my head. It was time to move us forward.

"Holly?" She called out from the door. I went to meet her, tears streaming down her face.

"Mom? What is it? Why are you crying?" I stood feet in front of her, scared to get closer. She dried her face with her sleeve and sniffed, avoiding eye contact.

"Holly, you need to pack a bag. You need to come home." She sniffed.

"I was planning on it, but I need to get things wrapped up here first. I can't just leave this place. I was calling you to tell you that. I texted Isaac, too." She looked pained when I mentioned him, and I froze. Something happened. I felt it bone deep.

"Mom. Tell me, what is going on?"

"Isaac. He was on his way here to get you. He had been fighting himself on how much space to give you. It was raining. Holly. I had been on the phone with him. I heard the crash, I heard everything." I stared at her, frozen in shock. I heard the words she said, but my brain just couldn't comprehend the meaning behind them.

"No." I shook my head, eyes stinging, legs shaking. I gripped the table behind me. "What are you saying? Where is he?" I stared at her, my grip on reality loosening every second she stood in front of me.

"Holly, I'm so sorry." She buried her face in her hands, violent sobs shaking her slender frame. "There wasn't anything they could do." My throat ached, and my knees buckled. I caved in on myself, every last bit of me unraveling. She moved around me and wrapped her arms around me from behind. Grabbing her arms, I melted. I screamed, I sobbed, I wailed.

"Why, mom?! Why him?" I shook in her arms, anger tightening its hold on me. "It should have been me, mom. I can't live without him. I can't."

She caressed me, held me, while she stroked my hair. She didn't say anything else; she was just there. As my sobs quieted and my body stopped shaking, I curled up in her arms. Sniffling, I held her close, letting her presence be a grounding force in the chaos that consumed my heart.

"Holly?" She whispered to me. "Can I pack you a bag?" I nodded my head, letting her get up from underneath me. Once she got up, I curled up on the floor. Wrapping my arms around my middle, I tried my best to breathe through the nausea that washed over me. Within seconds, I realized I couldn't fight it. I forced myself up and to the bathroom just in time. Mom must have heard me move, since she was right behind me, holding my hair out of the way as I emptied the contents of my stomach into the toilet violently. Once I was calm again, she brought me a glass of water and continued packing my bag.

She got me into the car. I pulled my oversize hoodie over my head and curled up in the passenger seat. The drive was a few hours, but it seemed like days. As we got closer to home, I started to shake uncontrollably, my mind flooded with memories.

Isaac's cocky smile after he wiped out at the skatepark. Brownies on the porch. Kissing for the first time under the stars.

Chasing me through the woods. His love. His arms. His words.

"Mine. You are mine."

It all came to me like a tidal wave. Mom looked over at me, worry and sadness in her eyes. My body shook as I cried ugly, loud, desperate tears. I cried so hard I couldn't catch my breath. Mom reached over and gently touched my leg. I grabbed her hand and squeezed, hanging onto her for dear life.

"Mom, I don't know if I can survive this." I whispered, looking out the window. She looked at me, compassion in her eyes.

"I know, Holly. I know." She never once told it would be alright or that everything was going to be OK. I think we both knew that it wouldn't be, not for a long time. She understood what this was going to do to me. I started to appreciate her more at that moment than I ever had before. I saw who she was for me now despite what she wasn't for me in the past. It took another loss, another life, for healing to become a reality. I knew I wanted to fix things with her, but not at the cost of Isaac's life. It was going to be hard to reconcile the fact that it took losing Isaac for mom and me to understand each other fully. I both loved and hated her for it.

It took me longer than it should have to realize we weren't going to her house. We were going to the pile of ashes that lay where our home used to be. I looked out at the familiar stretch of woods and then back at mom.

"Where are we going?" I asked.

"You need to see something." She answered, not taking her eyes off the road. We pulled up and where I was expecting the empty place where my memories burned to the ground, there was a house. It wasn't just a house, though. It was one I felt like I had seen before. I slowly got out of the car and took it all in. It was the house I had painted a picture of. It was our dream house. The beautiful wood a-frame stood like a beacon in front of me. A knot formed in my throat as more tears threatened to break free.

Mom walked over to me, putting her arm around the small of my back. She guided me up the stairs onto the perfect wraparound porch. The wood was golden and shiny and beautiful. I ran my fingers along it, trying to convince myself it was real. I looked back at mom who was standing in front of the door.

"Was this his project?" I asked.

"Yes. It was. He was so proud of this house, Holly. He asked me over and over how to get you here." She looked at me, with so much emotion in her eyes. I could tell she was reliving those conversations in her head. "I never-"

"Shh, mom, don't. Don't do that to yourself." I wiped at my eyes, snot running down my face. No matter what I did, the tears kept coming in waves. "I don't know if I can go in there, mom. All of this.

It's too much." I looked around me at the stunning work Isaac had done. It was exactly what we imagined together.

"You have to, Holly. He did this for you. He did this to give you a future I never knew how to give you. This house, this place, is the last thing he knew you needed to *really* heal, to start fresh. He knew you better than I ever did, and for that I will never forgive myself. But this is a fresh start for me too. While you were gone, he helped me understand you better. I always thought I knew you, what you needed, but I was so wrong, Holly. He never gave up on me, and he sure as hell never gave up on you. Don't let it all go to waste, now." She paused, looking up, searching for words.

"I always imagined your future with him in it, and I know you did too. This is how you keep that future alive, even though he isn't. Keep him close, Holly. Don't ever let what he did for you go."

I stared at her, tears and sobs pouring from me as her words ripped my heart to shreds. She stepped closer to me, wrapping her arms around me as we stood and cried together. We were each healing in our own way. I knew then that just as much as she had hurt me, she was hurting too. As much as I hated this, and what my life was going to be like without Isaac in it, I embraced her, and all this meant for us.

"Will you show me the house?" I asked, breaking the piercing silence.

"Of course," she sniffed. She took my hand in hers, wrapping her fingers around mine, and walked me through the door into the house. We stopped in the huge, open living room. Large bay windows lined the room overlooking the woods just outside. Wood beams lined the ceiling giving it the perfect rustic look. A spiral staircase to the right led up to a loft above the kitchen. The kitchen and dining room were at the back of the house, big and open, facing the trees that surrounded the area. The table in the dining room was long and rugged. The kitchen was the perfect balance of modern and rustic. Butcher Block countertops lined the walls with beautiful mahogany cupboards. Large windows lined the entire back wall, and a patio door led out to a huge deck.

"I want a deck with a swing and a fire pit to lay on and watch the stars."

"Yeah? What about a hot tub?" He asked, turning to me. I wrinkled my nose at the thought.

"And turn it into human soup? No, thank you. I would rather feel the heat of a fire than a hot tub. I never really understood why people love them so much." He laughed at me and turned his eyes back on the stars above us.

I never realized he was storing everything I had said away into plans for this house. They were dreams, dreams I never thought I would see become reality. Even with him alive, I couldn't picture this. Now that he was gone, I clung to it with everything I had. Those hours we spent sharing our dreams together are what helped me move forward then, and now they would be what kept me alive without him. I hadn't noticed mom go back outside to get my bag and bring it in. I turned and looked at her as she set it down on the overstuffed sectional in the living room.

"I think you should stay here tonight. There isn't much here, but everything you would really need is here. He made sure of that. I can stay with you if you want." She looked at me hesitantly, unsure of herself. I looked around, taking in the smell, the feel, the sights around me. I nodded.

"Please stay with me, mom."

Chapter 39

H*olly*

I stare at my reflection in the mirror as I put the last bit of mascara on. I'm not sure why I even bothered to put it on in the first place. It'll just be running down my cheeks by the end of today. Deep breaths. In and out. In and out. I straighten in front of the mirror looking over my features. Sleepless nights have taken a toll on me.

"That's as good as it is going to get today." I took a big deep breath again and checked my phone for the time. Mom would be here any minute. Walking out of the bathroom, I kick some unpacked boxes out of the way. I still don't really feel like I live here. It seems like a dream, one that I desperately want to wake up from. The doorbell reminds me that I am very much awake and have to face this day whether I am ready to or not. I opened the door to see my mother's wary face. She doesn't look much better off than I do. I let her in, and she hugged me tight for several seconds. Welcoming her embrace, I wrap my arms around her.

"I would ask if you are ready, but I don't think any of us really are." She lets me go, twisting one of my curls between her fingers. I shake my head, willing the tears to hold off for now.

"I am as ready as I can be. Do I look presentable?" Mom smiles warmly at me as she takes me in. My simple black dress with my white converse and wild hair is exactly how Isaac would have wanted to see me. "I thought about heels, but they got stuck in the grass at da-"

"Shh. You are perfect, Holly. He loved you so much. Don't make this day about the man who broke you when it is all about the man who healed you." Her eyes shined with unshed tears and apologies. Nothing can take back the years of abuse I endured, but nothing can stop the healing either. I can't take my mom's own guilt away for lending a blind eye to the monster she knew existed, but I can love her and grow with her. I can forgive her. I have to. Taking in a deep breath, I grab my purse and mother's hand, and we walk out the door together.

Isaac's funeral was packed. There was standing room only in the funeral home. It shocked me to see how many people he had made an impression on. I guess I had always been selfish in thinking I had him to myself. In a way I did, but his love for life, big heart and enchanting smile impacted everyone he came across. The whole town showed up for him. The last time I was in this building, we buried my monster of a father. Now, we have to bury the man that saved me from the monster. I was never truly convinced that I would get a happily ever after, but I see now that Isaac already gave that to me. He helped me love myself again and showed me I deserved to be loved. He built me the very home that protected me in my darkest of times, the home I dreamed about. Isaac gave me my life back, and he was taken in return. He taught me to heal, and from this I will heal too. Eventually

I shook hands and cried with everyone who showed up for Isaac. It was overwhelming how much love was in the room with all of us. I gazed over the crowd, people comforting each other and laughing at memories. My breath hitched as I locked eyes with Isaac's father. He stared at me with so much intensity it made me shiver. I excused myself from the group I was in and walked over to him. He was getting older, gray and white peppered through his hair. His hands trembled and he looked weak.

"Hi," I whispered. "I'm so sorry."

"No," he stopped me, putting a hand up between us. "It's you I should be apologizing to. You were there for him more than I ever was." Tears ran down his face and he sniffled, rubbing his nose with the back of his hand. I led him to a chair in the foyer and sat down next to him, keeping his hands wrapped in mine.

"He loved you, you know." I squeezed his hands.

"To a fault, I think." He muttered. "No matter how much of a mess I made, he was always there to make sure I was OK. You know he used to hide my keys from me? Even as a little kid." He chuckled and snorted through a sob. I got up and grabbed a box of tissues and sat them on his other side. He grabbed one, drying his eyes and trying to breathe evenly.

"I have something for you." He leaned over and pulled an envelope that was folded in half out of his pocket. "He asked me for this not too long ago, but I didn't get the chance to give it to him yet." He handed me the folded envelope and I took it, looking at him questioningly. "Open it, go on." He nudged.

I carefully peeled the top back and peered inside. My heart hammered in my chest and my breaths came ragged and short. I didn't even try to hold back the tears that now ran down my face. It was an ugly, grief filled cry, and it took everything not to scream in the middle of the funeral home. I felt an arm wrap around my shoulders, and I met his grief filled gaze. He took the envelope, dumped the ring into his hand and slid it on my finger. It was stunning and perfect in every way possible. I clutched my hand to my chest and tried to even out my breaths.

"It was his mother's." Another sniff and another tissue. "He asked me to give it to him so he could give it to you. At first, I was hesitant. But he showed me the house he built for you. He told me what the house meant to you and why it was so important he make it a reality. He said it was his responsibility to make sure you have the life you deserve. I knew then, maybe I always did, that you two were made for each other. I was just to blind and drunk to care."

We sat in silence watching the people remember Isaac and all he meant, all he did. When it was time for the service to start, I helped his dad up to the front row where mom was already sitting and waiting for us. The service was beautiful and heart wrenching. Just when I thought I had cried all my tears, new ones fell. Everyone had something beautiful to say about him and it made my heart so grateful. We eventually made it through, not a dry eye in attendance and filed out to the cars to go to the cemetery. Mom and I were first, and Isaac's dad rode with us. We were silent the whole drive there, a thick blanket of grief covering all of us. We pulled into where we were directed to park and slowly got out of the car. A breeze blew through the trees and the fresh dirt smell surrounded us. Isaac's casket, covered in flowers, sat front and center. We filed in the first row of seats. It seemed like the steady stream of people never ended. Eventually, the man's voice broke the silence, and the final eulogy was delivered. One by one, people walked by saying their final goodbyes. Isaac's father squeezed my shoulder and left my mom and I alone. I stood up, walked to the casket that held everything good and perfect in this world, and placed my hand on it. No longer holding anything back, I screamed into the air. Every emotion, anger, fear, grief, sadness, love, it all came through as I fell to my knees next to Isaac. I needed this. To let go. To let it out and be free. There was no more room for shame or guilt.

I felt mom kneel next to me and wrap her arms around my shoulders. I could feel her shaking with silent cries. I don't know how long we stayed like that, but she let me have the time I needed. Finally, I stood up and helped her up with me as they lowered the casket. I took the dirt, letting it shift and move in my hand, and slowly let it fall onto the love of my life.

"I need to make one stop before we go." I wiped my cheeks and headed towards the grave of my father. Mom stayed behind in the car, giving me space to feel and experience everything. I found his grave and stopped my feet in front of it.

"Dad?" I called out. "I will never stop hating you for what you did to me. I will never forget what happened and how you ripped my innocence away." Peace washed over me as I stood in front of the man that was supposed to love and guide me in my life. "But I will forgive you. Not because you deserve it, but because I deserve to be free of you. You no longer have a hold of me or my life. I will not forget, but I will create the life I deserve despite you." Taking one last look at his cold stone, I turned and walked away for good.

Chapter 40

To say that life moving forward was easy, would be the biggest lie I ever told. Having a new life to start without the one person that built the foundation of it was devastating. My therapist told me that grief never goes away, but it ebbs and flows and those waves get easier to maneuver as time went on. I wanted to believe her, I really did. The only thing that kept me going in the weeks after his funeral was his voice in my head telling me to get up and keep living. Isaac gave me the most precious gift of healing. He reclaimed me after I felt lost, used and soulless. He helped me feel whole again and taught me to take my own power back. To him, my pain was not invisible. He saw it all for what it was, took my hand, and led me through the battlefield. He didn't leave me with pieces to pick up. He left me with a fresh start and a new path to discover. His death wasn't fair, and my anger may subside in time, but my grief over losing him will never truly fade away. This town, the house he built for me, and everywhere I go is filled with memories of him.

It took me weeks to be semi-functioning, but eventually I got there. I had made a goal to unpack one box at a time in my new house, and eventually the empty house became more like a home. Mom came and helped me most days. Sometimes we worked in silence, sometimes we danced to music and laughed together. There were days when I couldn't get myself out of bed and she laid next to me, and we cried together. The relationship we grew during that time was another gift Isaac left me. I don't know if we would have come together like we did without the bond grief created between us. I never realized I was mourning the loss of our own relationship for years until I knew what it could have been all along.

"Holly?" Mom asked from the kitchen.

"Hmm? Sorry. I was lost in my head." She walked around the table, hugging me from behind. Planting a gentle kiss on top of my head, she just held me. I leaned into her embracing her comfort. "I'm OK." I promised.

"I love you, Holly." She squeezed gently and then made her way back to the kitchen, eyeing my fancy coffee machine. "Now, I know I have asked this a hundred times, but how the hell do I make a cup of coffee with this thing?" We laughed as I helped her make a perfect latte, and then made one for myself.

We settled into the overstuffed couch with our coffee and let the comfortable silence infiltrate the room. The coffee worked its magic and warmed up my body and my soul. I let the space around us breathe as I took in the house that was built just for me. It wouldn't have been possible without Mom here to help me through the process, and I was exceptionally grateful to have her.

"Hey," she nudged me.

"Yeah?" I said through a sip of latte.

"You still have all those Polaroid pictures?" I set my mug down and thought for a second. They were still in the envelope Isaac had them in, but where was it?

"I do. They are around here somewhere. Let me go check my room." I got up and went digging through some of the stuff strewn about the space. I found it pretty quick. I brought it to my nose and sniffed the paper. It still smelled like his house, and it made my heart ache. I opened it just enough to peer inside and smiled at the goofy faces staring back at me. Hugging it to my chest, I brought it out and sat it on the couch between us. Mom leaned forward, setting her coffee down. Her lips twitched in a small smile.

"Can I look through them?"

"Of course." I nodded, carefully dumping out the pictures onto the couch cushion. We turned them all over, flooding the place with memories of another life.

"Oh, my goodness," she laughed, picking one of them up. She held it up and looked at it for a minute. "I remember this. You guys loved that arcade." She handed me the picture, Isaac's smile beaming back up at me. His arm was wrapped around me, my hair all over the place. We beamed at the camera with cheesy over-the-top grins. I stared and stared at it until my eyes started to water. I put it back into the pile, glancing at all the other memories. There was one from the drive-in. The sun was just starting to set. All you could see was our feet over the blankets and the radio between us.

"I still have those shoes." I smiled and I picked up another one. My breath caught and my eyes stung at the image. We were at the skatepark on that concrete bench. I was making a silly face in the camera, but Isaac's attention was all on me. The adoration in his eyes was so clear. He looked at me like I was his whole world. He loved me so much; it ached to see now. I knew I hurt him when I left before graduation, but I had no idea how much damage I actually caused. I didn't deserve the love he had for me, but that was one of the lessons he taught me. Love isn't about deserving it, or not deserving it. It was always unconditional with him. He was always there. I wiped away the tears and put the picture back onto the pile. I sniffed, wiping my nose on my sleeve.

"He always loved you; you know?" Mom picked up another picture. "I never realized how much until you left."

"What do you mean?"

"He tried to talk to us, to find out anything he could about where you went or what happened." She paused, lost in memory. "I think he assumed we were shutting him out, but that wasn't what I was doing.

Not intentionally, anyway. I had to plan my own escape, and I knew your story wasn't mine to share."

"I bet he was relentless." I laughed.

"He was. He was so hurt, and I wanted to explain everything to him, but I wasn't ready, and neither were you. I knew he would be there with open arms when you came back."

"I was so selfish." I muttered, picking up another picture.

"No, don't do that to yourself. You did what you needed to do to survive." She sighed, leaning back into the couch. "I blamed myself for years for what you went through. I grieved for the childhood you lost. I never thought I would see you again, and I thought I deserved that too." She sniffed, looking at the ceiling. I gently folded my hand into hers, watching her. "I'm so sorry, Holly." I reached over and wrapped my arms around her, hugging her tight. Her shoulders shook with sobs and my own tears ran freely.

"It's OK, Mom." Her fingers ran through my curls, gently. "I don't know why things happened the way they did. If it weren't for Isaac, I don't think I would have survived what Dad did to me. Now, I don't think I could have survived losing him without you."

"I wish I could make it easier." She leaned back away from me, drying her eyes.

"That's just it," I smiled. "You do make it easier. It took me a long time to figure that out. I don't think I would change a thing. I don't understand it all, and I am still so angry that I don't get to share this life with Isaac. But one of the things he gave me back was the relationship with you that I had lost over the years."

A soft knock on the door echoed through the house. I got up, squeezed mom's shoulder as I walked by her and opened the door.

"Hey," I answered. Isaac's dad stood in the doorway, pizza boxes in his hands and a sheepish smile on his face.

"Hey. I hope I'm not intruding, but I wanted to come by and check on you."

"Not at all," I moved aside, holding the door open for him.

"Hey, Jenn." He waved as he made his way to the table, setting the boxes down.

"Hey, Dennis." She smiled and gave him a warm hug. "How are you holding up?"

"I'm hanging in there." His eyes wandered to the pictures scattered across the couch.

"Mom and I were just looking through all these. Want to look at them?" His soft smile met mine and I moved to pick them up. Mom got paper plates from the kitchen and some drinks, and we all sat down to eat. The pictures were passed around and covered the table. We talked and laughed and cried over all the memories and the love we shared for Isaac.

Our lives were never perfect. They were full of broken hearts and regret, but what mattered most is that we had each other. The three of us clung to each other, holding onto what Isaac meant to each of us and living our lives as fully as possible. Not a day went by when he wasn't missed. His legacy was the rest of our lives and the transformation all our relationships went through. I wondered if Isaac knew this would be our happily ever after all along. It was broken, unconventional, but it was ours. It was all of ours. And that was enough.

Epilogue

1 Year Later

The morning sun danced across the trees as I sat and looked at all he had built for us. I swung lazily on the porch swing with Ginger curled up, purring on my lap. The chill in the crisp air made goosebumps pop up all over me. It was still, and quiet, with a beautiful blue sky. I could smell the tall pines that surrounded the house. It was perfect. I can tell you that right then, in that moment, everything felt OK. I don't know if it was the first time since Isaac died, but it was at least the first time I consciously thought about it. I felt OK. The constant ache in my chest was finally starting to fade. I don't think it ever went away, it just transformed into something different all together. I realized I could be OK without him. I could survive it. The raging fire of anger and hatred I felt towards my life turned into a smoldering one. I started to live despite it. I forced myself to see the beauty around me. Because in those things, I saw him and what he wanted for me. I started living, really living for me and me alone. While I felt guilty for living on without him, I knew that he would be proud of me. I knew he would want me to be content here, in this home he built. It's mine now. It was supposed to be ours, but it will remain mine until the day I die.

The flowers I planted about a month ago were blooming and they added the perfect splash of color against the gray stone along the house. It took me a long time to truly appreciate the beauty of this house, to really claim it as my own. He built everything exactly the way we talked about. It was cruel at first, I couldn't stand to be here. I hated it, in fact I almost burned it down again. Ginger stirred in my lap as I put my coffee down on the table next to me. I saw the golden blur running up towards the house, a stick bobbing up and down in her mouth as she did. As Sadie made it to the porch, Ginger arched her back and glared up at me. While Sadie loved Ginger, my poor cat was still getting used to the idea of sharing my attention with something other than my art. I adopted Sadie about two months ago from the local shelter. I had regularly checked in with them after Isaac died to see if I could find our dream dog. Sure enough, just about the time I started to give up, they called me in to meet a puppy.

She had been found as a puppy, a stray. She was matted and dirty and tiny, but she had the golden fur that matched the flecks in his eyes when the sun would hit them just right. The day I met her, she clung to me like I was the only thing in the world that mattered to her. Now, just like this house, and just like the life we had dreamed up for ourselves, she was mine. Isaac was right. Golden retrievers are fiercely loyal. I didn't know then how much I would need that in my life. She dropped the stick in front of me and plopped her head in my lap, Ginger moving next to me to make room. She looked up at me with longing in her eyes. Petting her on the head, right behind her ears, I leaned down and picked up the slobbery stick.

"Alright, Sadie. One throw, and then I have to go in, girl." I laughed as she barked and wagged her tail so hard, I thought it would fly off. Ginger stretched next to me and curled up, trying hard to ignore Sadie. Sadie licked her between the ears anyway, which earned her a quick swipe to the nose. "Ginger, she loves you. You better get used to it!" I launched the stick as far as I could, Sadie racing after it.

"Holly?" Mom called through the dining room.

"Out here, mom. Coffee is still hot." Mom had made it a regular habit to come and enjoy these mornings with me. I enjoyed her company more than ever. Some days we talk a lot, some days we just sit. Regardless, I am grateful for her. He taught me to forgive, to love, and to move on. He taught me I couldn't heal on my own. Mom and I coped with our losses in our own way, but I don't think we could have without each other. Now, finally I can look at her with love and appreciation without that familiar stabbing pain in my chest and the flashbacks that came from it.

"I see Sadie found a new favorite stick. I don't think I even need to bring her new toys over anymore. She would just rather run around with a tree in her mouth." I laughed as she let Ginger back in the house and sat next to me. "I grabbed your mail for you, I hope that's OK."

"Oh, yeah. Thank you. I forgot to check it yesterday."

"I think you should open this one." Mom handed me an envelope and looked at me with a glimmer in her eye.

"What are you up to, now?" I grabbed the envelope like a bomb would go off if I moved too fast.

"This one wasn't me. This was all you, Holly. With maybe a little push." I looked down at the envelope, running it through my fingers. It was from an art gallery in Boulder. In fact, it was the one I had told Isaac about when we dreamed about our future. Ripping open the envelope, I read it over, tears stinging my eyes.

Miss Valles,

We were pleased to receive and review your piece that was submitted. After much consideration, we have decided to publicly display and sell your art in our gallery.

With this letter, you will find a contract to read over, sign and return by mail or in person. If you have any questions, please feel free to reach out to our submissions department.

Best Regards,

Mr. Barrett Sullivan

Owner & CEO

They wanted to display *my* art. My work would be in a gallery, *the* gallery. I looked up, snot and tears running down my face as I started to shake and sob. I couldn't believe it. Mom wrapped her arms around me, stroking my hair just as she had done so much in my life.

"How did they find my work, mom?" I already knew the answer, but I needed to hear it. I needed to hear his name.

"Isaac sent them pictures of some of the paintings you did. The one that got their attention was this one." She pulled out her phone and scrolled through her pictures. Stopping on one I recognized well. I remember her taking this picture. I had refused to be in it, but Isaac was there, beaming into the camera. The painting was of him. It was my favorite piece I had ever done. It was how I remembered him on the first day we met, all smiles and messy hair. I had captured him perfectly. Of course, this would be the one they wanted. It was perfect.

"He was so proud of you, Holly. *We* were always proud of you. You get to make your dream come true, now."

"I get my happy ever after." I sighed.

"You deserve it. More than anyone." I looked over at her. Her eyes were red and puffy, a mixture of pain, pride, and sadness. That is our life, after all. The good is better than anyone could dream of, but the pain and the loss is just as strong. Neither one of us deserved any of it, but we lived through it all and clung to each other as we continued our lives in the aftermath. If we had learned anything from our years on this planet, it is to live fully in the good and appreciate every moment, because the bad will always come. And we live fully through that too. I feel it all, wholly.

"So do you, Mom. We can be our own happily ever after."

LATER THAT NIGHT, WHEN the sun cast long shadows across the handmade dining room table, I stopped painting and looked around the house. Where there should have been kid's messy drawings and toys, and loud laughter, there were takeout boxes and expensive paints I convinced myself to buy. I promised myself I would cook more, and I made good on it, but sometimes I ordered our favorites and pretended he was here to share it with me. I couldn't let him go completely, and I never planned to. Especially tonight, celebrating my success, I had to feel close to him. I decided to take our favorite walk through the trees, just me, although Sadie protested.

I walked up the path we had traveled so much and stopped to breathe the evening air. The chill was enough to make me wrap my arms around my chest and throw the hood of his old hoodie up. I walked slowly, allowing myself to feel everything. I felt proud of my success, grateful Isaac made it happen, and angry he wasn't alive to see it. When I turned the corner and headed further into the trees, I paused and remembered the last time we were out here together. My body ached at the memory. I remember the feeling of the bark under my nails as he consumed me, body, and soul. I walked over to the tree we carved our names into and leaned my back into it. Memories invaded my vision, and it was like I could feel him here. My breath hitched as the pleasure of it washed over me.

"Isaac," I whispered to the trees. "I need you." The trees swayed in the wind and my hair whipped around me from under my hood. My eyes fluttered shut as I slowly ran my hands over my skin above the waistband of my sweats. My nipples hardened at the sensation and my center ached as the need grew into desperation. With one hand gripping the tree behind me, and one hand tracing down to my dripping core, I let myself go. Tears stung in the cold air and my chest heaved as I breathed hard. Slowly, I circled my throbbing clit with my thumb, crying out into the stars that were starting to appear above me. I worked myself over, picking up speed, dripping and soaking my lace thong. Closing my eyes, I imagined Isaac hovering over me. He taught me to love myself again. He showed me that sex was not selfish. He showed me what pleasure I could experience. I ached for it.

My thumb circled my clit, slowly and delicately as I slid one finger into myself. I groaned loud, and desperate. I needed more but didn't want this fantasy to end. I imagine Isaac's mouth worshiping my body. He left no part of me untouched. He claimed me as his over and over until I finally believed it.

"Mine. You're mine. We are all that exists from now on." He would say. By the time I believed it with my whole heart, I lost the chance to tell him. Sobs took over me as the anger I had let go of made its way back into my head.

"No!" I screamed. "You don't get to take this away from me. Let me have this!" My voice echoed through the trees, and I sank to the ground, arching my back against our tree. I reached under my hoodie, toying with my nipple as I worked my fingers in and out of my soaking cunt faster and faster. I yelled, and I cried, and I screamed as my orgasm crashed over me in endless waves. I rode it out, feeling myself clench around my fingers. Once I recovered enough to sit up, I sat by our tree, curling into myself.

"Your painting is going to be on display in Boulder." I leaned my head against the trunk, trying to control my breath and calm myself down. "We did it, Isaac. We made it."

I don't know how long I stayed out there, but I woke up and it was so dark I could barely see through the trees. I could see the faint lights of the house and pulled out my phone to turn on the flashlight. I slowly got up and brushed my fingers over our roughly carved names in the bark.

"See you later, Isaac. I'm still yours. I always will be. I love you." I kissed the letters, and slowly made my way back home.

Don't miss out!

Visit the website below and you can sign up to receive emails whenever Belle Shaw publishes a new book. There's no charge and no obligation.

https://books2read.com/r/B-A-LHAKC-CEMIF

BOOKS 2 READ

Connecting independent readers to independent writers.

About the Author

Hi! I am Belle Shaw, your friendly neighborhood daydreamer. I live in Ohio with my amazing family, including two spoiled cats. I am working on my degree in Education to teach English. I have always loved to write and am very excited to be on this romance journey. Life is hard, and finding a little bit of joy in books is what we all need sometimes. Hopefully, the stories inside my head bring you a little bit of joy or at least don't scare you off.

Thanks for being here!
-B.S.
Read more at www.belleshaw.net.